Praise for the Noodle Shop mystery series

"Will appeal to fans of Chris Cavender's Pizza Lovers mysteries." —*Booklist*

"Funny, warm, and terrifying at times, *Wonton Terror* adds yet another delicious dish to Vivien Chien's growing menu of enticing, cozy mysteries." —*Suspense* magazine

"Provides plenty of twists and turns and a perky, albeit conflicted, sleuth."
—*Kirkus Reviews* on *Dim Sum of All Fears*

"Vivien Chien serves up a delicious mystery with a side order of soy sauce and sass."
—Kylie Logan, bestselling author of
Gone with the Twins

"Thoroughly entertaining . . . fun and delicious."
—*RT Book Reviews*

"*Death by Dumpling* is a fun and sassy debut with unique flavor, local flair, and heart." —Amanda Flower, Agatha Award–winning author of *Lethal Licorice*

HOT AND SOUR

SUSPECTS

VIVIEN CHIEN

St. Martin's Paperbacks

This is a work of fiction. All of the characters, organizations, and events portrayed in this novel are either products of the author's imagination or are used fictitiously.

First published in the United States by St. Martin's Paperbacks, an imprint of St. Martin's Publishing Group.

HOT AND SOUR SUSPECTS

For information, address St. Martin's Publishing Group, 120 Broadway, New York, NY 10271.

www.stmartins.com

ISBN: 978-1-250-78261-8

Our books may be purchased in bulk for promotional, educational, or business use. Please contact your local bookseller or the Macmillan Corporate and Premium Sales Department at 1-800-221-7945, ext. 5442, or by email at MacmillanSpecialMarkets@macmillan.com.

St. Martin's Paperbacks edition / February 2022

Printed in the United States of America

10 9 8 7 6 5 4 3

For cancer survivors and fighters:
Here's to conquering all challenges that
may come our way, both big and small.

ACKNOWLEDGMENTS

More than ever, I find myself in a sea of gratitude for the many wonderful humans in my life.

I'd first like to thank my agent, Gail Fortune, who has been such an unwavering support. I truly have no idea what I would do without her in my life. When you find an agent who truly shares your dreams and sticks by your side no matter what pitfalls may come, you know you've struck gold.

Next, I'd like to express gratitude to my editor, Nettie Finn, for the continual encouragement and understanding she's shown me through this entire process. Thank you for making this book become a reality even under these trying circumstances.

That gratitude is extended to Kayla Janas, Allison Ziegler, Mary Ann Lasher, and all the outstanding folks at St. Martin's Press.

I would like to thank my oncologist, Dr. Kristine Zanotti. Without her skilled medical expertise, this book wouldn't have made it from my hands to yours. I'd also like to praise the excellent caregivers, nurses, and support staff at University Hospitals of Cleveland and UH Seidman Cancer Center in Westlake. The work that you do and the support and dedication you provide are the stuff heroes are made of. Thank you for fighting the good fight.

Thanks to my father, Paul Corrao, who stayed by me every step of the way, and listened to me while I rambled on about the plotting of this book. Xie xie ni to my sister, Shu-Hui, and my mother, Chin Mei, who made sure that my noodle bowl was always full.

Thank you to my friends, extended family, the writer community, and all my amazing readers. Your support has gotten me through some of the toughest times. It is both an honor and a privilege to be in your company.

AUTHOR'S NOTE

During the late summer of 2020—only a week after the release of *Killer Kung Pao*—I was diagnosed with stage 3 clear cell ovarian cancer. It was pertinent that I have surgery and begin chemotherapy treatment right away. To my oncologist's relief, the surgery was wildly successful and all traces of visible cancer were removed. Chemotherapy followed as a precaution, and while the rest of my life was put on hold—including my writing—I began a journey of unexpected outcomes.

In that time of healing, I was awed at the amount of support I was receiving from you—the reader—and it showed me a kindness in humanity that many are not privileged to see. For that, I am eternally grateful.

In March 2021, I was given a clean bill of health, and I set out to restore some semblance of normalcy to my life. The book you hold in your hands became a sort of therapy for me. At first, it was slow moving, and I struggled to find the words that used to come so easily. But I stuck with it and battled "chemo brain" with everything I had. I began to lose track of time and reality as I delved back into Lana's world. A world without cancer, and a world without Covid-19— something I think we could all do without.

But as I neared the end of the story, my health went in an unexpected direction, and the presence of cancer had returned. It was a devastating blow, but I wasn't about to give up this far into the game. Now, it was more important than ever that I persevere. So I continued to chug along through the testing, the preparation for treatment, and finally the beginning of chemotherapy. As I write this to you now, I am undergoing treatment.

All this to say—this book is a labor of love. It has followed me through "dis-ease," restoration of health, and recurrence. It is one of the things that has kept me grounded through this whole process.

I don't know where this book will find you in your life, but I hope it is filled with happiness and good health. If you find yourself struggling, I am here to tell you to keep going, no matter what the odds and no matter what anyone else tells you. Believe in you. Always. If I can do it, you sure as hell can. After all, I am just a "little gal" from Cleveland who had a really big dream. And though my health has wavered, that dream stands firm in my bones. Nothing will take that away. Not even stupid jerkface cancer.

Take care of you, my friends. You are all some kind of wonderful.

CHAPTER 1

"You young folks and your weird dating concepts," my father, William Lee, said with an amused smirk. "I don't know why the lot of you are opposed to meeting people the good old-fashioned way."

My dad, who could sometimes fall under the category of traditionalist, was currently in the middle of explaining to me and my best friend, Megan Riley, why the youth of today struggled with finding lasting relationships. The three of us were standing in the now empty dining room of Ho-Lee Noodle House, our family restaurant and my current place of employment.

As he went about romanticizing "the good ole days," he looked rather official in his black pinstripe suit, crisp white shirt, and polished dress shoes. Fresh from showing a luxury home in Pepper Pike, he'd stopped by to see what shenanigans I was up to.

And who am I? I'm Lana Lee, his youngest daughter, and manager for this fine Asian establishment. At the moment, you could also add "annoyed" to the list of descriptors.

From time to time, my dad liked to razz me about generational differences. He found it funny—and sometimes I did too—but now was not one of those moments.

"Because *Dad*, people like action and spice in their life," I replied in defense of the speed dating event we were going to host. Granted, it wasn't a conventional setting for something like this, but Megan had "called in a favor."

Over the course of the summer and fall months, the bar where she worked—the Zodiac—had started hosting speed dating events on an almost weekly basis. It brought them a surge of business, and that outcome was something I was highly interested in at the moment. I figured my parents would also be more than happy to cash in on that possibility. Unfortunately, my dad wasn't totally sold on the idea. His main concerns lay with the fact that online dating was now all the rage, and he didn't hold out much hope that people would really shell out the money to come to an event like this.

I—despite my original protests—thought it was an excellent way to drum up extra business and knew the potential that it held. After all, I had witnessed a speed dating event in action.

There was an admission to get in, so it was an automatic moneymaker. Along with the entry cost, we provided a sampling of appetizers and beverages to all of the participants. If they happened to want meals to go, or shimmy off to a private booth with their newfound honey and a full-sized dinner, who was I to stand in their way? I saw dollar signs, and dollar signs were what we needed after the slower months of business we'd experienced.

We were nearing the holiday season, yes, but it never hurt

to end the year on an even greater note than anticipated. Plus, I was thinking that if I could manage it, I'd like to give our small staff of employees a holiday bonus. It probably wouldn't be as much as I'd like to give them, but at least it would be something. Without question, it was well deserved. We'd seen a lot of challenges this year, both on personal and professional levels, and in my book, everyone had earned a little extra padding in their pockets.

"Now I'm no fuddy-duddy"—my dad smoothed his lapel—"but to me this seems like a wackadoo idea. What happened to the days when men picked women up for a proper date and went to dinner . . . for longer than five minutes? What can you really learn about anybody in five minutes anyways?"

Megan's hazel eyes lit up, accepting the challenge my father presented. She opened her mouth to provide a counter argument, but before she could say anything, I held up my index finger. "Allow me to demonstrate."

Clearing my throat dramatically and putting on my best smile, I said, "Hi, my name's Lana Lee. I'm twenty-eight years old—half Taiwanese, half English—live with my best friend, and manage my family's restaurant. I enjoy lots of browsing in the bookstore, I'm a dog person through and through, and I've never met a doughnut I didn't like. And as we can all see; I enjoy dyeing my hair various colors of the rainbow." I pointed to my angled bob that now included a mermaid ombré of color. The teal, blue, and purple dyes exposed themselves beneath the contrast of my naturally black hair. It was my most vibrant hair to date.

My dad pursed his lips, but I saw the amusement hiding in his eyes.

I kept going. "I'm a lover of all music, but I prefer rock. I enjoy going to the movies, but hate the butter they use on the popcorn. My ideal first date would be getting coffee or drinks with a chance of dinner."

My dad crossed his arms over his chest. "Are you finished?"

"Has it been two and a half minutes?" I shot back.

Megan chuckled. "You should have added that we always bring our own snacks to the movies. Guys like a woman that plans ahead."

"This is true . . . I always bring my big purse," I said with a grin.

My dad inhaled deeply, which I registered as him pulling together all his patience. "I still don't think it's a good idea, but your mother is excited about the prospect of the business it will bring in." He sucked in a breath. "I wouldn't want to rain on her parade."

"Exactly, Papa Lee," Megan replied. Her ruby-painted lips turned up in a confident smile. "Trust me when I say that the bar is at full capacity when we host one of these events. And we've covered the Zodiac in flyers about moving the evening here. People were really excited about a change in venue."

"Yeah, and it's been a long time since we've seen this place filled to the brim," I added.

The three of us took a moment to examine the restaurant. I don't know what the other two were thinking, but I was thinking about the crazy things that had happened since I began working for my parents on a full-time basis. There was the whole mess of being held at gunpoint just past booth number six, or the awkward conversations I had with witnesses and suspects at table eight, and meetings with a PI at lucky number seven.

Behind those memories were fonder ones. But they were further in the past and a little harder to grab on to. I'd grown up in this restaurant and it was an enormous piece of my childhood. I'd played in the dining room—much to my mother's dismay—skipping and weaving between tables just to pounce on the swinging kitchen doors and plant myself in the employee lounge. When I say "lounge," I use the term loosely. It's really a small, cluttered back room with enough space for an old couch, an even older TV, and a dinette table for two. How many days had I sat in that back room, watching cartoons on Saturday mornings while my parents worked in the restaurant? Or struggled with my math homework after school? By the way, Asians automatically being good at math is a myth . . . I'm proof of that.

"There she goes off in la-la land again," Megan teased, giving my arm a nudge. "You care to join us?"

I shook my head, loosening the grips of memory lane. "Yeah, sorry, I'm here. Just thinking about all this restaurant has seen in the past thirty-odd years."

My dad nodded. "It's been an adventure, kid, that's for sure.

"Dad, I need you to be okay with this, all right? Trust me a little bit."

"Well, as they say, you're the boss," my dad replied. "I guess it'll be fine, right? I mean, what do I know about modern dating anyways?"

I smiled at him. "It's going to be great. I promise."

CHAPTER 2

Ho-Lee Noodle House is located in an Asian shopping plaza, Asia Village, and sits unexpectedly in Fairview Park, Ohio. In case you're wondering where the heck that is, it's conveniently located roughly fifteen minutes away from downtown Cleveland.

I say "unexpectedly" because even though there is a decent population of Asian Americans living on the west side of greater Cleveland, it's not a huge demographic. All things Asian can predominantly be found on the east side either near Payne or Rockwell Avenues.

But the late Thomas Feng—former property owner and founder—had a vision to expand the offerings of what you could find on the other side of town. Clevelanders tend to have loyalties to their sides of the city and so this provided a solution to that "problem."

Asia Village became a beautiful hidden gem in a suburb that has continued to build upon itself steadily over the years. My dad has been known to say things like, *"I remember in my day, you couldn't take the freeway to this area because it was still being built.*" Then I usually teased him and made a general reference about the time of horse and buggies. On an especially playful day, I'd bring up dinosaurs.

But today was not a day to be playful. No, I had the proverbial manager hat on, and I was getting ready to be hostess of the century. I didn't just want these people to come in, sit down, stuff their faces and flirt. I wanted them to have an experience. I wanted them to tell their friends about the amazing Asian restaurant they had stumbled upon. And then I wanted them to bring those friends here.

The restaurant was closed to the general public for the evening. I'd locked the doors at five o'clock—just as my dad had surprised us with his visit—to give myself and the staff enough time to get organized. The event would start at seven and go until nine, when a majority of the plaza closed.

The square tables in the dining area had been moved to the center of the room and I'd had Peter Huang—best friend and head chef—help me move the excess chairs into the back room. My plan was to have people begin rotating throughout the booths that lined the walls, and then, if we had enough people, they would fill up the tables in the center of the room. Though most of the tables sat four, I cut the seats down to two per table for a little more privacy. I'd gone on a tangent about getting partitions for the tables so people didn't feel like others were eavesdropping on their conversations, but Megan assured me that this wasn't necessary. We had two larger round tables, and Peter shoved those against the far wall near the banquet area. The banquet area would house all the main appetizers, and the round tables nearby would be the drink and dessert stations.

Megan had tried to talk me out of the dessert station, but

hey, for twenty-five bucks, if it were me, I'd want dessert. Plus, if we had leftovers, who did you think would be taking those home?

At around six p.m., as I stood surveying the tables, anticipating when they'd be filled, and as I was running over what else I had to do, my mother and grandmother showed up outside the restaurant. I felt like a high school kid trying to have a sleepover where their parents didn't pop in the room every fifteen minutes to "see how things were going."

My mother unlocked the door, and the two women came shuffling in. My mother's critical eye scanned over the restaurant, assessing the changes I'd made to the setup of the dining area.

"Mom, what are you doing here?" I asked, greeting them near the entrance. I had broken out my stilettos for the evening, so I was exceptionally taller than both her and my grandmother.

None of us is a tall woman, but I was standing at an impressive five foot eight with these shoes on, so to me, they seemed a lot shorter than usual. I'd be lying if I didn't say I took at least a little pleasure from towering over them.

"I came to check on your party. Make sure everything is okay." My mother, who is about five foot two, had to look up at me, and after her eyes met mine, they traveled down to my feet, inspecting my shoes with a discerning eye. "You will break your neck this way, Lana."

My grandmother hardly speaks any English—she's much newer to the U.S., like less-than-a-year new. Aside from a couple of words she's picked up over her time here, she generally speaks through my mother, who translates how she sees fit.

A-ma followed my mother's line of sight and also investigated my shoes. She tilted her head to the side and said, "Jin swee." Which meant "very beautiful" in Hokkien, my family's Taiwanese dialect.

I knew these sparse phrases from growing up around my mother chattering away in her native tongue. I couldn't speak it myself, but I was able to understand quite a bit and could usually cobble enough together in order to keep up with the conversation.

My mother's main objective while my sister and I were growing up was to Americanize us as much as possible, so pushing us to learn multiple languages and go to Chinese school weren't at the top of her list. Of course, later on in life she wanted us to learn Hokkien, Mandarin, and if possible, work our way into Cantonese. But by the time we'd grown, my brain was too Westernized to retain anything new. In high school, I took French, and I swear I left that class knowing less than I knew going in. Figure *that* one out.

Though I understood my mother's perspective in raising us the way she did, it was a little frustrating as an adult to not speak the language of my cultural background. People assumed—by looking at me—that I knew how to communicate in some sort of Asian dialect, but sadly all I could do was roughly follow along with what was being said.

"See, A-ma likes them," I threw back at my mother. "I can't walk around here in boat shoes tonight."

"Boat shoes?" my mother asked.

"Never mind," I said with a shake of my head. "Did you only stop through to give me a hard time?" I had a lot to do, and I was getting nervous the closer we got to start time. My eyes drifted to the clock above the entrance.

"Ahh, no, we only stop by to take a look. Now we are leaving for the casino. Dad is coming too."

This surprised me since my father wasn't a huge fan of gambling. He'd rather be relaxing with the *Wall Street Journal* or some yawn of a history book talking about pivotal wars throughout the ages. My dad was a total guy.

My dad came out from the kitchen and smiled when he saw that my mother had arrived. I love their marriage. Even after all these years, they are still as smitten as they ever were.

"Betty, my love," my dad sang, extending his arms.

The two hugged and my dad kissed her properly—as a gentleman would.

I made gagging noises. "You guys are grossing me out."

My dad chuckled. "I think we should get out of this young lady's way for the night."

"Yes, shoo shoo." I waved my arms, gesturing for them to clear out."

"Call me tonight and let me know what happens," my mother said, digging for her keys. "I cannot wait to hear how much money we made."

We all said our goodbyes, and after they walked out the door, I locked the dead bolt and took a deep breath. Finally! Now with my family out of my way, I could focus on the task at hand.

My heart started to thud as I realized how close we were to the evening beginning. I headed back through the kitchen to my office. Peter was jamming out to his usual heavy metal ballads while he cooked up the appetizers we'd be serving in what was now less than thirty minutes. Peter spared no expense in putting together our spread for this evening. We had teriyaki skewers—both beef and chicken—mini spring rolls, panfried *and* steamed dumplings, lettuce cups with kung pao chicken and cashews, crab rangoon, shrimp toast, and steamed pork buns. If these people didn't meet the person of their dreams tonight, the least they could take away from this experience was a full and happy belly.

Megan had disappeared to make a phone call, so she'd been saved from being reprimanded for her shoes. If they thought mine were bad, they should have seen hers. I think "stilts" would have been an understatement. She was in midconversation when I entered my broom closet of an office, and held up a finger for me to wait while she wrapped it up.

"Oh my God, Seth talks more than a teenage girl," Megan said when she'd hung up the phone. "I don't need to know every single detail going on at the bar right this very minute. He was the one who wanted me to handle this speed dating situation. I can't be two places at once."

"What's going on over there?" I asked. She was sitting at my desk, so I opted for one of the guest chairs. It felt weird sitting on this side of things.

"Oh, nothing worth repeating, really," she waved the idea away. "He's being . . . well . . . a man. He's being a man."

"As men do," I replied.

"Are we ready to go?" she asked, moving on. "What's left on our to-do list?"

"Nothing, really. You missed my mother and grandmother stopping by. I'm glad I got them out of here before everything started."

"You realize this dating event is going to be the talk of the town, right?" Megan stood up from my desk and adjusted her black pencil skirt. "I wouldn't be surprised if people wanted to do even more events here. Think of all the money you guys could make if you became a party place."

"Let's focus on getting through tonight," I said, standing and following her out of the office. "If we can pull this off without a hitch, I'll feel more confident."

"Relax," Megan said, looking at me over her shoulder. "When have I ever steered you wrong?"

CHAPTER 3

If there were any doubts in my mind that this speed dating shenanigan would be a flop, they were quickly squashed by the line of people that had formed outside of the restaurant doors. As Megan and I made our way through the dining area, I got a clear shot of the back of Kimmy Tran's intentionally messy bun and exposed shoulders pressed up against the entrance. The faux-lace halter top that she wore for this evening's event was snug and left little to the imagination.

Her loud voice carried through the door and into the restaurant, and I could hear her telling our newly arrived guests to get in line. Literally. "Okay, everyone! Single file, we're all adults!" Kimmy yelled. "Hey you, crew cut! Get in line, buddy. This is kindergarten stuff!"

Megan's eyes widened in horror. "Ohmigod, Lana! She's going to scare people away!"

I couldn't help but laugh. "Don't blame me, I didn't ask her to do that."

Megan rushed to the door and unlocked the dead bolt.

"Welcome everybody! Please come in, and sign up at the hostess station." She gave a glamourous sweep of her arms that would make any spokesmodel jealous. "And remember, each ticket is twenty-five dollars, cash or charge."

Peter's girlfriend, my childhood friend, and Megan's personal pet peeve, Kimmy was here to help for the night, and clearly taking her duties seriously. She sidestepped the crowd and shuffled over to the hostess area where I was standing, blindly smiling at the man in front of me. It was safe to say that I was a little overwhelmed by the onslaught of people. A quick head count informed me there were already almost fifty people lined up.

"Look lively, Lee," Kimmy said, coming behind the counter and standing next to me. Her apple cheeks were flushed from activity, and her breath appeared labored. Out of the corner of her mouth, she whispered to me, "Anybody home in there?"

I shook myself out of the haze that was beginning to resemble stage fright, and gave her a thumbs-up. "I'm okay." Focusing my attention on the customer in front of me, I turned on my customer-service voice—which is about two octaves higher than my regular voice—and curved my lips in an exaggerated smile. "Hi, thanks for coming out tonight. Did you want to pay with cash or credit?"

And so it went. I handled the money while Kimmy took down the names and gave them name tags. When she was finished with them, Megan showed them to their seats.

I was thoroughly impressed with the people who showed up. There were a variety of ages of both men and women, and everyone was dressed well.

When I looked up from the cash register, I found myself staring at my good friend, and fellow Asia Village shop owner, Rina Su. Her soft curls were swept up in a ponytail and wisps of hair framed her face—a rare hairstyle for her to entertain—and her slinky black dress complete with plunging neckline was also out of character. As my eyes traveled the short length of her outfit, I became concerned that when she bent down, the whole restaurant would see a little more than they should.

"Rina! What are you doing here?" I asked, maybe a little too surprised. When I'd originally mentioned the event to her, she'd been a tad unsupportive, saying that things with this sort of platform put a lot of pressure on people to deliver in a short amount of time. She'd gone on to say how she felt more comfortable with online dating because there was no element of being rushed to impress someone, and you had the safety of hiding behind a screen before you met that person face-to-face. However, as much as she felt that to be true, I knew that she hadn't met anyone that way either.

My friend blushed, tucking her chin inward. "I know, I know. But I thought, why the heck not, right? It's been months since I've moved to Cleveland, and I still haven't met any decent guys. Thought this might be a good way to mingle with people from outside our Asia Village bubble after all."

"Good for you, girlfriend!" Kimmy replied, clapping her hands together. "You get that sassy New York City booty out there and shake your moneymaker."

"Kimmy!" I hissed.

"What?" Kimmy crossed her arms over her chest. "You know I could have said way worse."

Rina and I exchanged a glance and erupted into laughter.

"I suppose that's fair." I said, stifling my outburst. "Well, good luck, Rina. I'm glad you decided to come tonight, and I hope you meet someone. I'll have my fingers crossed for you."

After she paid up and was outfitted with her very own name tag, I felt a sense of guilt. She'd changed her mind about something she'd previously been adamantly against, and it made me think she was lonelier than I realized.

I hadn't spent much time with Rina outside of our weekly get-togethers at the Bamboo Lounge. Maybe she needed more excitement in her life. When she first moved to the city, I tried to invite her almost everywhere I went so she could learn the lay of the land. But over time, our hangouts became less and less frequent. I suppose it had a lot to do with our conflicting schedules at Asia Village and how busy we'd been with our own lives in recent months. Because she owned and solely ran the plaza's cosmetic shop, the Ivory Doll, there wasn't a lot of room for hanging out throughout the week. Most of the time when we met at the Bamboo Lounge for our weekly get-togethers, she was exhausted and anxious to head home. When she *was* available—predominately on Sundays when she closed the shop—I was with my family having our weekly dim sum.

Plus, she wasn't exactly a fan of my "extracurricular activities," so I naturally ended up spending more time with Megan and Kimmy. I made a mental note to start including Rina in more of my escapades or nights out, even if she couldn't make it. At least the offer would be extended. Unless she hit it off with a total hottie tonight, in which case I was sure she'd have enough to keep her busy.

The restaurant was packed to capacity—maybe even more than the legal limit—so I shut the doors and hung my newly created sign that alerted anybody trying to come in that we were conducting a "Private Event." It was time.

I stepped into the dining area, and Kimmy let out an ear-splitting whistle. My voice could carry the length of Asia Village, but I couldn't whistle like that to save my life.

The room quieted and I held up the stopwatch I purchased specifically for this event. Megan had chided me about buying it since my phone was already equipped with a timer, but what can I say? I like to accessorize.

"Thanks again to everyone for coming out tonight. I hope you all meet your match!" I smiled wide and attempted to make eye contact with as many people as I could.

"Each of you will have a total of five minutes with the person in front of you. There will be a 'ding' at the two-and-a-half-minute mark, so each person gets fair usage of the time. However, you're not bound to it. You'll hear a buzzer at the five-minute mark, and that will be your cue to move around the room counterclockwise." I gestured by swinging my arm around so everyone was clear on what I meant. "If you find your match—for the evening or longer!—you can break off from the group and are welcome to sit at one of our specially reserved booths. Have fun chatting!"

I hit the timer and the room burst into a choir of conversation. Putting my hands on my hips, I assessed the room with a sense of pride. We had pulled it off.

Megan and Kimmy joined me where I'd been standing.

"Now what, boss?" Kimmy asked.

"Do you mind keeping track of the time?" I handed her my stopwatch. "It's already programmed to repeat. All you have to do is hit this button right here when the buzzer goes off."

She gave me a salute. "You got it."

"Megan, can you keep an eye on everyone and make sure that everything is running smoothly? I'm going to run into the kitchen and bring out the new appetizers."

With a wink, she headed over to the tables, beginning her unintrusive walk past each of the couples.

Feeling satisfied with myself and my team, I made a beeline for the kitchen, my eyes drifting over to where Rina was meeting with her first man of the night. She seemed to be completely at ease, and it gave me a bit of relief. Maybe this was better for her than me taking her out and being the honorary "wingman."

After all, I already had my guy, the wonderfully handsome Detective Trudeau, and I wanted others to find their happiness as well. Adam was more than I could have asked for after the onslaught of nightmare men I had dated in the past decade. Of course, it wasn't *that* bad, but I can't tell you the amount of tissues that were wasted throughout my early twenties.

Okay, who was I kidding? It *was* that bad. And I had used a lot of tissues in my mid-twenties too. But that's part of the whole dating experience. Or so I have been told countless times.

Aren't we all a little sick of those platitudes?

You have to kiss a lot of frogs to meet your prince.

There are plenty of fish in the sea.

The right guy is going to come along. You have to be patient.

Snore, and yada yada blah. I'd had my fill of the generic, sympathetic conversations that people had with each other in regard to failed relationships, and I'd gathered that so were a lot of the people in this room, Rina included.

My dad didn't agree with this being a good way to meet people, but I was really hoping that I could prove him wrong. After all, isn't *another* one of those sayings, *You'll meet the right person in the most unlikely of places*?

We were a half hour into the event and everything was still going smoothly. Megan, Kimmy, and I worked in a nice rhythm alongside one another in the dining area while Peter kept the grills and woks running at full steam.

I was ecstatic to see the number of people who drifted off to private tables. Since I was busy running the food back and forth, Megan helped with placing orders. The time of the evening had come when I officially regretted my footwear.

On one of my trips back to the kitchen, I caught sight of Rina out the corner of my eye. She was snuggled up in a booth with a thin man dressed all in black. His hair was sandy brown, spiked, and based on the regrowth around his ears, in need of a trim. When he turned in my direction, I noticed he had thick-rimmed glasses that were a little too big for his face. A smirk played on his lips that I'd seen on too many ex-boyfriends of my own, but his blue eyes showed signs of innocence and maybe a bit of amusement at the scenario he found himself in.

Rina's body language spoke volumes. She was positioned toward him and leaned forward with rapt attention. She rested her elbow on the table and coyly twirled a strand of her hair as she talked with animation. Her pouty, full red lips were getting a workout.

When the man replied, his thin lips barely moved, but whatever he'd said, she was completely enthralled by it and bobbed her head in agreement.

Kimmy caught me spying and rushed over. "Do you see these two lovebirds sitting on the same side of the booth? Yack, Lana. I want to yack."

I chuckled, repositioning the empty plates I was carrying back to the kitchen. "It's cute."

"Cute smute," Kimmy replied. "I am going to give that girl so much crap about this, she won't know what to do with herself."

"Do *not*," I said firmly. "She already had issues with the idea of speed dating, and this is the first guy she's really met since she's moved here. Don't make her feel even more weird than she already does."

"Ugh, whatever. You're always robbing me of my fun." Kimmy rolled her eyes. "So anyway, we've got quite a few seats that have opened up. Do you want me to open the doors again? Maybe we'll get some stragglers. I noticed quite a few women spying through the windows about five minutes ago."

"Sure." My eyes scanned the main doors, and I saw a few people loitering out in the plaza. "I'll be back. I have to take these to the sink, and I think Peter has some appetizers waiting for me. Grab Megan and have her get them situated so you don't lose track of time."

"Aye, aye, Captain."

We separated and I headed into the kitchen. Peter was

in the middle of an air-guitar session with a giant stainless-steel spatula standing in as his instrument of choice. Sensing me in his peripheral, he froze mid-strum, lifted his head, and turned. His cheeks blushed bright pink. "Oh hey, Lana. . . . What's up?"

I snorted a laugh. "I came to check on my appetizers."

"Oh right . . . uh . . ." He fumbled around, removing covers off the dishes that were below the heat lamp. "Here ya go."

I placed the dirty dishes next to the industrial sinks and grabbed a fresh tray from the pile of clean serve ware.

Peter turned his back to me to clean the grill—and probably to let his face adjust back to its normal color.

"I'll be going then . . ." I said over my shoulder as I pushed through the double doors. "Your audience awaits."

"Dude . . ."

I didn't hear the rest of what he said because I was too busy snickering on my way out the kitchen.

Re-entering the bustling dining area, I headed straight over to the buffet table to replace the empty spots with fresh food. I was so preoccupied with getting the new plates out that, at first, I didn't notice a rather angry woman hovering over Rina's table. It wasn't until I looked up from what I was doing that I realized there was a short brunette attempting to tower over the sitting couple, pointing and making rude hand gestures that would not be considered "ladylike."

I saw Kimmy catch on to what I was witnessing and then we both made eye contact, Kimmy's eyes bulging out of her head even more than my own. We both made our way to see what the commotion was about. Other people were starting to notice, and I didn't want whoever this woman was to cause a scene.

A moment later, Megan noticed the disturbance and quickly rushed over to join us—she, Kimmy, and I forming a human shield around the woman and the booth.

"Excuse me." I tried my best not to sound annoyed. "Is there a problem that I can help you with?"

The woman's pin-straight, raven hair fanned out around her head as she whipped around to face me. "Not unless you plan to kick out this stupid jerk bag for being a lying piece of—"

"Whoa!" I interjected, holding up a hand. "Let's try and keep it civilized."

She smirked. "Nothing is civilized if Gavin Oliver is involved. Trust me." She turned away from me to glare at the man sitting next to Rina. "You are a lying piece of crap, you know that?"

Gavin didn't say anything, his eyes focused on the glass of whiskey he held in his hand.

"Can't even look me in the eye, can you?" she fumed. "Can't admit you're a liar? Well, that's just fine." She knocked over the glass in his hand, causing the liquid to spill out and splash all over Rina's dress.

Kimmy, Rina, Megan and I all gasped in unison. Rina shifted herself in the booth, grabbing for a cloth napkin on the table. Gavin's face reddened and he pursed his lips, finally regarding the scorned woman with an angry stare.

Kimmy took a step forward and her mouth started to open. I held out my arm to stop her. It was better if I was the one to throw out this woman, because I didn't know what string of obscenities would come out of my friend's mouth if I let her take point.

But before I could manage to say anything at all, Gavin spoke, his tone gravelly and impatient. "That's enough, Brandi. I think you should leave now."

"Oh, I'm going," she said, snarling her lips. "But before I do, let me give you a piece of advice, honey," her eyes flitting over to Rina. "If you have any sense at all, you won't spend another minute with this sorry excuse for a man. Trash . . . that's what he is. A big pile of trash."

My attention slipped over to the next booth and the couple whispering to each other. Both were gawking at the woman standing at the edge of the table.

Megan nudged me with her elbow.

"Okay," I said, re-centering my attention. "Let me get you a refund, Miss . . ."

"Fenton." Brandi said curtly, addressing the table. She spun on her heel and stormed up to the hostess area.

"Kimmy! The time!"

"Oh shoot!" she yelled, glancing down at the stopwatch. "Hey everyone!" she shouted, addressing the room.

When I turned to make my way to the hostess station, I realized that most of the room had been focusing on the drama at Rina's table. Blushing, I shouted a quick apology to everyone and rushed up to the hostess counter, with Megan trailing behind me, to refund the irate woman's money.

At best, Ms. Fenton was indignant. I don't think it even occurred to her that she should be apologetic for her behavior or say something as humbling as "I'm sorry."

I quickly processed the transaction, and she snatched the

money from my hand with a sarcastic "thank you" before storming out the door.

I inhaled deeply through my nose, then let out a calming breath. Megan crossed her arms and stared at the entrance, shaking her head. "Well, it wouldn't be a night with us if there wasn't at least a little drama."

CHAPTER 4

Thankfully the rest of the night went on without any more theatrics. There was a lot of chatter after the debacle at Rina's table and I suspected it ignited a lot of compelling conversation. I've always found it interesting how people bond in the face of drama.

Our guests started to drift out as closing time approached and I was making my way around the room, clearing up empty glasses and plates when Rina came over to say good-bye. The exaggerated smile on her face said it all.

"I want to thank you so much for doing this," she said, glancing over her shoulder. "This is exactly what I needed to get the ball rolling. We've hit it off so well, we're going to keep the night going."

Setting the plate back on the table, I gave Rina my full attention. "Oh?" It was difficult to stifle the surprise in my voice. I couldn't imagine not taking what had gone down with this other woman, Brandi, as a red flag. "Do you think that's a good idea?"

She tilted her head. "Why wouldn't it be?"

"Well, with that woman showing up and calling him out like that."

Rina clucked her tongue in amusement and waved my concern away with a manicured hand. "Oh Lana, come on. You know how some women can be. Gavin explained the whole thing to me."

"Did he?"

"Yes, you big ole worrywart. He told me that they went on a blind date set up by one of their friends. He's in a band and the mutual friend brought Brandi to one of his shows. She expressed interest in him and the friend decided to do a little matchmaking. Gavin ended up not liking her but she seemed overly sensitive, so he let her down gently by telling her that he had reconciled with his ex-girlfriend. I mean clearly he didn't think he'd run into her at a speed dating event." Rina rolled her eyes, insinuating that this should have been obvious to me.

I groaned. This was the problem with dating. People weren't always honest about their intentions. It clearly would have served Gavin well to just be honest with Brandi. Why were men always so worried that women couldn't handle the truth? When it came down to it, that's all we ever wanted. I decided to say as much. After all, Rina was my friend.

"Even if that is what happened, it's still a red flag," I said, as gently as possible. "What story is he going to make up should he decide he doesn't like *you*?"

Rina's face fell flat. "Lana, that is a harsh thing to say."

Kimmy came up from behind me, placing a hand on my shoulder. "No, sweets, that's the reality."

Rina's postured slumped. "Of course you'd take her side."

Kimmy chuckled. "See here, girlfriend, you can spin it however you want. But Lana has a point. You know me, and you know I don't put up with BS. To me, what happened tonight is a loud warning bell."

I didn't take pleasure in this conversation, but I was glad that someone understood where I was coming from. My last intention was to be the bad guy. "We're concerned for you is all."

Rina nodded, her lips curved in a frown. "I'm sorry you guys feel that way, but I'm a grown woman. And I really like Gavin."

Kimmy and I glanced at each other, but made no comment. Rina was right. It really wasn't any of our business.

"Of course. Have a good time and be safe tonight," I said.

The three of us stood there awkwardly for a few moments. I was relieved when I saw Gavin return from the restroom. He sidled up next to Rina, wrapped an assertive arm around her waist, and kissed her cheek. "You ready, doll?" he asked. It came out as a half whisper, and to be honest, it kind of creeped me out. There was definitely something that didn't sit right with me when it came to this guy.

Her face lit up as she leaned her body into his. "Yes, I was saying goodbye."

Gavin turned to me with a cordial smile. "It was a great event. Thanks for having it. I really hit the lottery tonight."

Rina giggled.

We all said goodbye and watched as the new lovebirds made their exit.

Kimmy tsked.

"Did the way he talked to her kinda gross you out?" I asked.

"Um . . . on more than one level," she replied. "I hope our girl is prepared for what she's walking into."

"What do you mean?"

"It's clearly written all over his face what he's out for, and it ain't stimulating conversation."

Adam Trudeau aka Detective Hottie aka my boyfriend leaned against the side of his car with the collar of his black peacoat turned up. His arms were crossed over his broad chest, and his eyes scanned the surrounding area as Megan and I pulled into the parking lot of our quaint two bedroom, one bath apartment.

Since college we'd lived together in this garden-style apartment—mostly because it allowed dogs. It was your standard-issue apartment with boring brown carpeting and eggshell-colored walls. After a rather lengthy debate on whether it was more important to upgrade our living situation or put our extra dollars toward wardrobe aspirations, we both agreed we loved shopping too much. So instead of renovating a space that we didn't actually own, Megan began making small upgrades to the color and décor of our living space.

Megan and I had driven separately since she'd been working earlier that day, and we parked our cars next to each other with such precise timing, synchronized swimmers would have applauded.

Stepping out of the car, I felt my toes throbbing in my stiletto heels. There was nothing worse than walking across an asphalt parking lot with sore feet.

Adam let out a sharp whistle. "Hey there, good lookin'."

Megan came up from behind me and linked an arm

through mine. "Detective, you are in the presence of two master event planners."

He nodded an acknowledgment to my best friend and asked, "Tonight went without a hitch, did it?"

"No, not totally," I admitted. "Can we get inside? I need to take off these horrid shoes."

Adam held up a finger. "Just one second. I brought us pizza and wings."

"Oh good, because all I have is this box of sweets." I held up the plastic bag I'd toted home. "I accidentally ordered too many doughnuts."

Megan rolled her eyes. "Uh-huh. Do you believe that either one of us would fall for that?"

Ignoring them both, I continued on to the door, dragging Megan, who was still holding onto my arm, along with me.

Upon opening the door, I was met by yips and snorts from my black pug, Kikkoman. Kikko pawed desperately at my leg, wiggling her tail and attempting to sniff the bag I was carrying.

I dropped down to give her a pat on the head, but before I could even greet her, she caught wind of the pizza and Adam coming through the door. She immediately abandoned me and redirected her attention to her favorite man in the world. "Traitor," I mumbled, standing back up and flipping off my shoes.

Adam chuckled. "Well, well, who's my new best friend all of a sudden?"

"She doesn't care about you, you know. She wants the pepperoni," I teased.

Megan shut the door behind Adam. "I'm starving." She

whizzed past me and hurried into the kitchen, grabbing plates and napkins. "You guys get your own drinks. I need to eat before my stomach implodes."

"You know, we were just at a restaurant," I reminded her.

"I never eat when I'm working, you know that."

Adam relinquished the pizza box and Styrofoam wing container over to Megan and held his hands up in surrender. "I know better than to stand between a woman and her pizza."

"Damn right," Megan replied, digging into the box.

While Megan went about acting like a scavenger, I pulled out a few bottles of beer from the refrigerator. It was Christmas Ale season in Cleveland, and I made it a point to stock up since I knew it was one of Adam's favorites. The local brewery, Great Lakes, had one of the best Christmas beers around—according to Adam, anyhow. I wasn't a huge beer person, but I was always willing to entertain a bottle or two every once in a while.

We sat around the table, gorging ourselves on pizza and teriyaki wings. Per usual, Kikko danced around our legs, always hoping for a piece of pepperoni to come her way.

"So, tell me what happened tonight," Adam said between bites.

"Rina made herself a new friend." I paused to sip on my beer. "He's an interesting fellow."

"And that means?" he asked.

I told the story of the drama that was this evening. Megan laughed at my impersonation of the very angry Miss Brandi Fenton. I ended the story with "I'll never forget it."

"Me either," Megan said, wiping pizza sauce from her lip. "We'll be telling this story for quite a while."

Adam laughed. "Sounds like Rina is going to have her hands full."

"That's what Kimmy said."

"I've found most women like to learn these types of things the hard way."

Megan and I both stopped chewing and glared at him.

"Tough room," he said with a smirk. "But you know I'm right."

Seeing as I was exactly one of those women—stubborn as all get-out and determined to see things for myself—I really didn't have much of an argument. I hoped for all our sakes that we were wrong about Gavin, and that he and Rina were having the time of their lives right now.

I was in the middle of a really weird dream about stocking the shelves of a Giant Eagle when the ringing of Adam's cell phone stirred me awake. I probably would have fallen right back into dreamland if his rough voice, even filled with the grogginess of sleep, hadn't sounded so sharp and intruding. I felt the weight of his body lift from the bed, Kikko stirred at my feet, and I groaned in frustration. What the heck was going on?

As I opened my eyes, he said to whomever was on the phone, "I'm about fifteen minutes away. I'll be there as soon as possible."

"What happened?" I hoisted myself on my elbows and watched him move through the darkened room.

"I have to turn the light on, I can't find my damn socks."

Light abruptly filled the room, and I squeezed my eyes shut. "Adam. What's the matter? You're freaking me out."

"You're never going to believe the call I just got . . ." He knelt down, found his socks under the bed, and sat down on the edge of the mattress next to me. "That was Higgins . . . calling in about a DOA."

"Yeah . . . ?"

"The name of the DOA . . . Gavin Oliver."

I felt my throat closing. I inhaled deeply through my nose. "Tell me that Rina was not there. . . . I need you to tell me that right now."

Adam put a reassuring hand on my thigh. "Babe, she's okay."

I released the breath I'd been holding. "Oh, thank God she wasn't there."

"Not quite, I'm afraid."

My hand grabbed for his arm, and I clutched so hard my nails were digging into his skin. My heart thudded in my chest at the many things he could say next. It felt deafening, and I wondered if he could hear it. My mind had already slipped into worst-case-scenario mode, and I worried for my friend's safety even though he'd said she was technically okay.

Without even flinching at the pain I must have been causing, he said, "She's the one who called it in."

CHAPTER 5

Once Adam informed me that Rina had been the one to call in the death, my mind—and the room—began to spin. Half of what he said was lost, and all I heard was "fatal head trauma," "detaining her," "no known witnesses."

He kissed me on the forehead and reminded me he needed to leave. I nodded absently, mumbling a goodbye and promising him that I was okay. Clearly, I wasn't. But it's not like he could stay and console me. He was taking lead on this situation, and they needed him at the scene of the crime ASAP.

I took a few deep breaths to steady myself, trying to slow down my thoughts so I wouldn't plummet off the anxiety cliff. I was beyond worried. And I wanted to know what the hell had happened.

Taking myself back to those first moments of waking up and hearing Adam's baritone voice rapid-fire over the phone helped me regain focus. I remembered him asking if there were any neighbors who'd heard an argument take place. And I had the answer to that: no.

Then he'd hung up, promising to be quick, and immediately rummaged around the room for his clothes and shoes. Slowly the conversation was replaying through my mind. He'd said to me that Rina had claimed to be in the shower, loud music had been playing, and she hadn't heard anything. But when she'd come out of the bathroom, Gavin was laying crumpled on the living room floor, his head soaked in blood from what appeared to be the result of him falling backward onto his coffee table.

The wannabe detective in me wanted to know what kind of coffee table, but the restaurant manager in me wanted to hurl.

Kikko watched me expectantly, and I gathered from the hyperactivity of her tail that she thought it was tinkle time. I glanced over at the clock: 3:47 a.m. I swung my feet over the edge of the bed, wiping the sleep from my eyes. "Come on, dog, we're not going back to sleep any time soon."

The air was crisp and fresh, and a light coating of frost blanketed the grass, which crunched under Kikko's paws as she paced back and forth searching for that perfect spot. I stared out into the darkness, its consistence broken by patches of light from the sparse streetlamps. It was eerily quiet for a Friday night, when even at this hour there were usually cars coming in and out.

Kikko snorted in frustration. She wasn't a fan of the cold weather, and frankly neither was I. She pulled on the leash, heading back toward our apartment.

Probably because it was so late and I hadn't had much sleep, I was having a difficult time thinking. I felt like I was in a fog. All I could do was run over the last moments before Adam had to leave. What could have happened? And how many times would I ask myself that question? Would I know tomorrow? Would Adam tell me anything? Or did I have to wait until I talked to Rina, and when would that be?

I let us back in to the apartment, removed Kikko's leash, and pulled out a treat from the bag we keep by the door. She pranced around and spun in a circle. An idle wish that I could bottle my little companion's energy passed through my mind.

It was now 4:10 a.m., according to the microwave clock, and even though I felt out of it, I didn't see myself falling back asleep very easily. I decided to make some coffee and hang out on the couch for a while.

The smell of coffee was comforting, and I stood next to the counter watching the rich umber liquid drip into the pot. I felt impatient. I needed action.

Once my coffee was done brewing, and I was snuggled under a throw blanket on the couch with my dog in the crook of my leg, I attempted to truly relax. I knew I wasn't going to be any good to anyone—including myself—if I couldn't pull myself together.

I'd have to wait until later in the morning to find out anything truly useful. My biggest question was what Rina had been thinking going back to his apartment. It wasn't like her. At least not the Rina I knew.

We hadn't been friends all that long really. She'd only moved to Cleveland a little less than a year ago after her own sister and brother-in-law had been murdered. Which I assumed made Gavin's death doubly hard for her.

After the death of her sister, she'd gone through what many do and surmised that life is too short to not follow your heart. So without overthinking any of the details, Rina moved to get away from the chaotic life she'd created for herself in New York City. Cleveland was a different pace, and she'd craved reinvention. Her younger sister, Isabelle, had taken those same steps to find something outside of the hustle and bustle of the big city and it had given Rina the motivation she needed to do something she'd wanted to do for a long time: open a business.

Of course, me being me, I had encouraged her to do so. I'd helped her search for an apartment and plan the move, and I was her welcoming committee. She'd promptly opened the cosmetics store across the way from Ho-Lee Noodle House. In it, she sold popular Asian cosmetics and skincare brands like Shiseido, Amorepacific, Skinfood . . . the list went on. And if those weren't enough for you, she also carried other more common, but still prestigious lines. With her cute Hong Kong–style shop, it was no wonder she was a huge success.

In fact, whenever I glanced at Megan's and my vanities, I couldn't help but wonder if the two of us weren't solely responsible for footing the bill for Rina's lavish downtown loft.

All she'd wanted was a sense of normalcy after the tragedy of losing her sister, and I'd damn near promised it to her. Yes, I'd been thrown into an upheaval of goings-on in this city, but I also knew that wasn't the standard. Maybe my idealistic mind wanted to continue thinking of the bad parts of life as uncommon. Or maybe people have a way of brushing over the tribulations of their life.

I heard the creak of Megan's bedroom door as she opened it and poked her head out into the living room. With a raspy voice, she asked, "What are you doing awake at this dreadful hour?"

"Feeling guilty . . ." I craned my neck over the couch to face her. "I have some news."

"Uh-oh," she replied, sounding more awake. She padded over in her fluffy bunny slippers and plaid flannel pajamas à la Victoria's Secret. "What's happened now?"

I filled her in on the nugget of information I knew so far. Mid-story she got right up and went to pour herself a cup of coffee without saying a word. She stayed silent the entire time I spoke. My guess was that she was still trying to process the information, much as I had tried to do after being abruptly woken up.

"Wow," was all she finally said when I'd finished.

"Yeah."

"So, wait . . . why do you feel guilty? Because we threw the event, or . . . ?"

"Because I'm the one who told her it was a good idea to move to Cleveland. If I'd never butted in like that, she could still be in New York without all this craziness hanging over her head."

"Oh, Lana." Megan shook her head. "No way, don't put this on yourself. You can't be responsible for something like that. Or even the fact that we hosted the event. She's a grown woman. She didn't have to go home with this guy. Which, by the way, can I just say . . . holy wow. I didn't know she had it in her. She's always seemed a bit straitlaced to me."

"Normally she is more on the conservative side when it comes to things like dating. I'm happy to see her getting out there, but my concern is that it's not safe," I replied. "She doesn't know him. And with all the weird stuff that happens nowadays, well . . ." My brain threw up a caution sign. *Am I starting to sound like my mother?*

"What do you think happened?" Megan asked.

I stared into my half-empty coffee cup. "I have no idea, to be honest with you. I keep thinking it's a giant mistake. That Adam is going to call any minute and say he had the names wrong."

Megan frowned. "Sweets, it would have happened already. You said he left over an hour ago."

I sighed. "I know."

Megan patted my leg and sprung off the couch. "Never fear, it's nothing that Riley and Lee can't handle." She placed her hands on her hips and jutted out her chin, embodying the Wonder Woman pose. "For justice and the American dream . . . or whatever those people say."

I rolled my eyes. "Calm down, Diana Prince, we don't even know that our services are needed in this instance."

My best friend groaned. "I think both Linda Carter and Gal Gadot would be very disappointed in you."

CHAPTER 6

It was a good thing it happened to be a Saturday, because after Megan and I blithered on for another hour and drank up all the coffee, I passed out on the couch. I ended up sleeping until almost eleven o'clock and woke up to Kikko snorting and nuzzling her way under my hip. I kept one eye closed and watched my dog attempt to retrieve whatever I was laying on for a full minute before she realized I was staring at her. She let out a high-pitched yip.

"Okay, okay," I grumbled, reaching underneath my leg to find her stuffed squirrel sans stuffing. She'd gutted the poor thing ages ago, but it was her second-favorite toy, and I couldn't bring myself to throw it away. She gave it a good chomp and took it to the opposite side of the couch.

I stretched my arms and legs lazily, not wanting to get up. I had to do something with myself, but I didn't know what, and clearly mine and Adam's plan to get some Christmas shopping done was out of the question. That was the hazard of dating law enforcement—you never knew when they were going to be whisked away by the job.

Megan was nowhere to be seen, and I didn't hear her rummaging around in her room. When I finally made my way to the coffeepot for what seemed like the eightieth time that day, I found a Post-it stuck to the lid of the water reservoir. It said, "Went to the gym, be back soon."

A twinge of guilt ran through me as I remembered that—after a promise to Megan to start working out on a regular basis—I'd also signed up for a gym membership but had only gone one whole time. With all the running around I did at the restaurant, you'd think I was pretty fit . . . but you'd be wrong. Shanghai Donuts was most likely to blame for that.

After I downed a cup of coffee while aimlessly staring out the living room window, I realized I needed to take advantage of having the day off from manager life and do a little detective work. It was all I could think about, and Megan was right: we needed to help Rina if we possibly could.

The first thing I did was call Rina's cell phone. No answer. Then I tried to call Adam for the hell of it. Went right to voice mail. I sighed. Not like he was going to tell me much anyway, but it would have been nice to hear his voice.

I kept thinking about that angry woman who'd shown up at the speed dating event. What the heck was her name? I'd said it only this morning and was drawing a complete blank. That told me I needed more coffee.

"*B* something . . . ," I muttered to myself after I'd refreshed my mug. Tapping the side of my cup, I paced the living room. "Brandi!" I yelled after walking the length of the room a few times.

Kikko's head jerked up and she gawked at me as if to say, *What the heck is your deal, woman?*

I gave my dog an apologetic shrug and headed for my bedroom. This situation called for my trusty notebook. Setting my coffee mug on the nightstand, I got down on my knees and dug under the mattress for the tattered notebook that had become my official detective brain dump.

For a while I'd considered burning it—and one day I was sure I'd have to—but after a private detective I'd worked with a few months ago had said she was quite impressed with the notes I'd kept, I opted against it. She encouraged me to keep it even though the cases had been solved. *"You never know when something you've thought in the past might help with something in the present."*

However, the poor spiral notebook was on its last legs, and it would need replacing pretty soon whether or not I chose to light it on fire.

Taking my coffee and notebook back out to the living room, I plopped down on the couch and opened to a fresh page.

At the top, I wrote down Gavin's name. I didn't know much about him, but I wrote down what I did. He was roughly five foot eleven from what I could tell last night. His hair was short and brown. He was pretty thin, he didn't appear to have much muscle, and he wore glasses.

He was also a musician. In my personal experience, that way usually led to trouble.

Something had gone down with that Brandi girl that made her angry enough to cause a scene. I wrote that down. I included a speculative note—"Bad breakup?"—and circled it. He'd had a story ready for Rina at the appropriate time, and it was plausible, but I wasn't so quick to buy it.

Women tend to know these sorts of things, whether we

admit it to ourselves or not. And we can read the pain on a woman's face pretty well because chances are we've felt those same feelings at one time or another. I'd yet to meet a woman who hadn't suffered some type of heartbreak.

And from what I'd read on Brandi's face, this wasn't a fly-by-night sort of "relationship." This was something that took up a bit of her time. She felt used . . . as if her time had been wasted to such a point that she wasn't afraid to cause a scene in a *very* public place.

I tapped the pen against the paper, trying to recall anything else that might be useful. What I needed was my iPad. I should have checked the news right away to see if anything had been reported since the morning. I didn't even know if Rina was still detained or not.

I found a small blurb on Cleveland.com that talked about a homicide taking place in Fairview Park. A man had suffered blunt force trauma to his head and was dead when officers arrived on the scene. The small paragraph promised more details as the story developed.

Great. So they didn't know anything either.

I decided to get dressed, and texted Megan to see how much longer she would be. Heading up to Asia Village seemed like the best option. Not only could I find out what the gossip was there, but the ledger I'd kept with all of the participants' info was in my office. And of course, I needed my partner in crime.

While I was attempting to contour my face with the new kit I'd bought from Rina's shop, Megan replied to let me know she was on her way home, and would be more than happy to come with me.

I finished applying my makeup and tilted my head left

and right to see if I noticed more defined cheekbones or a fantastic jaw line. I couldn't see a difference.

Kikko waddled into the room while I dug around in my closet for my favorite skinny jeans. Her curly tail wiggled, and I knew she was waiting on me to take her outside.

"Come on, little dog, let's take you on a walk before Megan gets back. I've got places to go and people to see. The game is afoot!"

"So, when we get there, who are we questioning first?" Megan asked.

We were making our way down Center Ridge Road . . . slowly. We'd managed to hit every traffic light from the moment we'd left the house. The road was busy with weekend shoppers weaving in and out of the strip plazas we passed along the way.

"I don't know. It's too late to run into the Mahjong Matrons. At this time in the afternoon they're usually downtown playing mahjong. As much as they love gossip, they definitely wouldn't want to be interrupted during game time."

"What about Kimmy?"

My eyes bulged at Megan's suggestion. She wasn't exactly Kimmy's biggest fan. "You really want to stop at China Cinema and Song?"

"It's for the greater good," Megan replied.

"Remember you said that when we see her."

"Uh-huh."

Fifteen minutes later we arrived at Asia Village. The place was packed with cars, and it made me happy to see the plaza's business beginning to pick up for the upcoming holidays.

When we entered the enclosed shopping center, we were greeted by a bustling crowd and noisy chatter. Everyone seemed so happy, and I couldn't blame them. Shopping indoors on cold Cleveland days was definitely a bonus.

"Let's stop at the restaurant first," I said, directing Megan toward Ho-Lee Noodle House. "I want to see how business is going and grab that list of names."

We passed China Cinema and Song on the way, and I craned my neck to see if Kimmy was behind the cash register. But the only person in sight was her mother. Hopefully Kimmy was in the back.

I started to reach for the door handle of my family's restaurant when Megan grabbed my arm and pulled me away. "What?"

"Look," Megan said, pointing in the direction of the Ivory Doll. "Rina's shop is open."

CHAPTER 7

My mind fluttered with questions as Megan and I made our way across the plaza to Rina's cosmetic shop. Why hadn't she answered when I called? Why hadn't she called, period? She would have to know that *I* knew something was up, considering Adam was the lead detective on the case. Was she afraid? Or maybe she was embarrassed of what we would think? We had all told her not to get involved with this guy and clearly she'd gone ahead and done it anyways.

But when we entered the Ivory Doll, we discovered it wasn't Rina who had opened the shop. It was Kimmy.

"What are you doing here?" I asked, skipping over the pleasantries.

Kimmy was in the middle of testing out bronzers in a mirror near the cash register. "What's up, ladies?"

"Where's Rina?" My eyes traveled past Kimmy to the entrance of the back room that housed the extra stock and Rina's office. "Is she here?"

Kimmy laughed. "Ha! Come on, Lee. You should know

better than that. She was only released from police custody this morning. She didn't call you?"

"No!" I replied, slightly offended. Why had she called Kimmy and not me?

"Oh, well, she called me this morning and asked me to come open the shop. She said she needs all the money she can get her hands on to pay the attorney fees this whole debacle is going to end up costing her." Kimmy shrugged. "So I told my parents that I needed to help out and they were cool with it. And now here I am."

"Did she tell you anything?"

"You know, Lana, it would serve you well to at least pretend like you care how I am. Like, 'Oh hey, Kimmy, how are you doing today? Do you need any help running the shop? Do you need a pee break?' and so on."

I pursed my lips. "Are you serious?"

"Yes, of course I'm serious. I know your mother raised you better than this."

Megan groaned. "Kimmy, cut the crap already. You know this is a big deal."

Kimmy rolled her eyes at Megan. "Yes, Blondie, I know. But it would still be nice to be acknowledged."

"Fine, fine," I said, shaking my head. "Are you doing okay? Do you need a bathroom break?"

"Actually, yes, yes I do."

No one was in the shop besides the three of us. I couldn't imagine what someone listening in would think of this ridiculous conversation. "Well, go on then."

Kimmy turned up her nose and walked out.

Megan gawked at me, incredulous. "This girl is something else. We're here to find out what happened to Rina and she has managed to make it all about herself."

I sighed. "You know how Kimmy can be sometimes. Let's ignore it and hope when she comes back we get some answers. I'm dying to know what happened and why she called Kimmy and not me."

Megan glanced around the store. "I might as well buy some stuff while we're here. Help Rina out with these lawyer bills."

"Any excuse to buy makeup," was my response.

While Megan ambled around the store, I stood near the cash register in a daze of speculative thoughts. So Rina had to get a lawyer involved. Interesting. She was definitely a suspect then. I mean, why else would you need legal representation?

Five minutes later, Kimmy came back. "Ah, much better. Now where were we?"

Megan circled back over to where we were standing. She had a concealer tube in one hand and a palette of smokey nude eye shadows in the other. "You were going to tell us what the hell is going on."

"I really can't believe that Rina didn't call you herself," Kimmy replied. "Don't you think that's weird? You guys are so much closer than her and I."

"Kimmy." My tone was curt. I was done with this tiptoeing,

"Okay, okay. Geez." Kimmy flipped her hair over her shoulder. "Rina went to that dude's house after they hit up some bar in Lakewood. I guess the place was small and crowded. She said by the time they left she was a sweaty mess. Well, they got back to his place, and things were getting pretty hot and heavy." Kimmy winked at us for emphasis. "She felt gross and wanted to take a shower. So she did. He was blaring music . . . something from his band's newest album, like real heavy metal stuff, ya know? She came out of the shower, and *blam*!—he's on the floor next to the coffee table. Rina goes to check his pulse and he's deader than dead."

Megan gasped. "That's horrible! Was there any sign of foul play?"

Kimmy shook her head no. "All that Rina noticed was that the door was unlocked. But she couldn't remember if the door was locked to begin with. I guess *that* really pissed off your boyfriend, Lana." She turned to me and raised an eyebrow.

"I know Adam," I said, sounding a little defensive. "He was probably upset because if she could remember that the door *was* locked, then he could surmise that someone entered and left, leaving the door unlocked on their way out."

"Well, he could speculate that anyway."

"He can't protect her just because I'm his girlfriend."

"Either way, you know she didn't do it," Kimmy stated, folding her arms over her chest. "And now we gotta help clear her name."

Megan held up a hand. "Whoa, whoa, whoa. *We* don't have to do anything. Lana and I will take care of this."

Kimmy's jaw dropped. "What? No way. She's my friend too. I can't sit by and do nothing while the two of you save the day. No. Definitely not."

"Okay," I gave Megan's arm a squeeze. "Let's not argue

about this right now. We can all contribute one way or another."

Megan glared at me, and I shrugged.

"What do we do first?" Kimmy asked. She clapped her hands and rubbed them together in excitement.

"We have to figure out who this guy is," I began to explain. "And then we've got to find out who would have a motive to kill him."

Megan nodded in agreement. "Suspect list, here we come. I have to say, though . . . I can see where Adam's coming from. It's not looking too good for Rina. We better move fast."

Kimmy furrowed a brow, studying Megan's face, which was filled with concern. "Why do you say that?"

"Because there is no proof of anyone else being around. Rina claims she was in the shower and came out to find him lying dead on the floor. No signs of a break-in. And she just so happened not to hear anything going on?" Megan's shoulders fell. "It's all a little too convenient."

I promised Kimmy I'd be in touch soon about how she could help us clear Rina's name. There was no longer any question that we needed to get involved, and for the first time in a long time, Megan didn't have to convince me to take action.

Our next stop was Ho-Lee Noodle House. I still needed to get the list of participants from the speed dating event.

Vanessa Wen, my teenage helper, was standing at attention behind the hostess station. Color me surprised. It was probably the first time in maybe forever that I hadn't caught her in the middle of fluffing off.

"Hey boss," Vanessa said with an exaggerated smile. "What brings *you* in?"

Narrowing my eyes at her, I replied, "Why? What are you up to now?"

She held her hands up in defense. "Nothing, I swear."

Glancing around the restaurant, I attempted to find something out of order. There were a few tables occupied with parties of four, and a couple of single customers at the two-seater tables we had near the front of the dining area. But nothing seemed askew.

Megan whispered into my ear. "She's messing with you."

Vanessa stifled a giggle. "I am. I had a heads-up that you were in the plaza, so I wanted to razz you a bit."

"You're trying to make me paranoid? You want me to try and find something wrong? Aren't you worried that I'll actually come up with something? Assuming that you were in fact slacking before someone warned you I was popping in."

Her cheeks turned red. "Well . . . I didn't really think about that."

"You know what else you didn't think about?"

She tucked in her chin and gave me her best puppy dog eyes. "No . . ."

I leaned over, putting my elbow on the lip of the wooden lectern. "That I am completely and totally messing with you right back."

Vanessa's eyes widened and a burst of laughter escaped her glossy lips. "Ha! Boss, you totally got me that time. I must be rubbing off on you."

"Let's not go crazy," I replied with a smirk.

I would admit to no one but myself that sometimes— only sometimes—Vanessa was growing on me. Don't get me wrong, she still drove me crazy ninety-nine percent of the time, but she didn't irritate me as much as she did when she first got dragged into working here. Maybe both of us were growing up.

"But seriously, boss," she said, the smile dissolving from her face. "Why *are* you here? Is it because of you-know-who being involved with the you-know-what?"

I raised an eyebrow. "You're aware of that, huh?" I was caught a little off guard by her question, but to be totally surprised would have been naïve. This was Asia Village, after all. Rumors spread like wildfire in this place.

Vanessa nodded. "A few people have been talking about it ever since Kimmy opened the Ivory Doll this morning. Yuna told me she heard from Jasmine who heard from one of the Mahjong Matrons who said *she* heard it from Cindy who heard it from Penny at the Bamboo Lounge who said when she was talking to Freddie that he said Rina is mad at you and Megan because you're the whole reason she went to this speed dating thingy to begin with."

Both Megan's and my jaws dropped.

Megan blinked rapidly. "Wait . . . my brain is not computing. Yuna is the receptionist at the hair salon, right?"

"Right," Vanessa replied.

Megan turned to me. "And Jasmine is the gal that does your hair?"

"Yup," I said. "And she's also Yuna's boss."

Megan inhaled deeply. "Okay, so one of the Matrons comes into the salon and gabs because she was talking to . . . Cindy . . . who is that again? The name is familiar, but I can't place her."

I laughed. "She runs the bookstore."

"Okay, got it. Then Penny . . . she owns the lounge, I remember her. . . . Now who the heck is this Freddie person?"

I widened my eyes, giving her that knowing look that best friends often share. As if to say, *duh, you know exactly who he is.*

"Ohhhhh." Megan clapped her hands together. "I know. He's the one you had the hots for when Ian revamped the community center. Right?"

Vanessa gasped. "What?! You did?"

"Megan!" I groaned. "Are you kidding me? Blab it to the world."

"Oops, I thought all you guys had a crush on him when he first started showing up here."

Vanessa covered her mouth, and blushed again. "*I* did. I mean he's totally old, but he's still a super hottie."

Megan snorted. "You think he's old? Kid, you've got a long way to go."

Megan and I both laughed. Freddie was only a couple of years older than us, just a touch over thirty.

"Anyways," I said, pointing a finger at Vanessa, "don't tell anyone about that. It's a secret, and besides, it no longer applies."

Vanessa gave me a salute. "Yes ma'am."

"And try not to gossip about what's going on with Rina either. This is going to be a delicate situation. You wouldn't want to be responsible for making things worse for her."

"Hold on a minute," Megan said, putting her hands on her hips. "I forgot what we were talking about while we went through the chain of gossip. Did you say that Rina is blaming Lana and me for what happened to her?"

Appearing slightly uncomfortable, Vanessa nodded. "That's what was said."

I shook my head. "That doesn't sound like Rina at all. She doesn't play the blame game like that."

Megan tilted her head. "Well, that would explain why she called Kimmy to help out and not you."

"Yeah, but that makes no sense. We were the ones who told her *not* to go out with him. She can't hold us responsible for what happened just because we held the event." I could feel the frustration rising all the way from my gut. The feeling would most likely stick with me until I confirmed that this was a poorly translated game of telephone. And there was only one way to do that.

"Wait right here," I said to Megan. "I'm going to grab the list off my desk really quick, then we're heading to our next stop."

"Oh? Where are we going now?"

"Rina's apartment."

CHAPTER 8

Katrina Su—whom we lovingly knew as Rina—was a New York City girl through and through. Sometimes Megan referred to her as "Carrie" from Candace Bushnell's *Sex in the City*. Rina hated the reference because she liked to think herself as a more down-to-earth type of woman, but most of us agreed that she fit the bill of glamorous and chic, packed with expensive taste. And the loft apartment she'd chosen downtown was testament to that.

In order to help make her transition to a new city a little easier, I'd helped with scouting for apartments since I'd lived here all my life. Figuring it would be easier for me to sift through the rental listings with my knowledge of the neighborhoods' different personalities and quirks, I quickly put together a list of potential options. However, after going back and forth with Rina over the phone, I'd quickly learned I wasn't thinking *large* enough.

I can't say I wasn't a little apprehensive when she explained to me what she was searching for when it came to her new home. I'd tried my best to calculate expenses for her, taking into consideration that she would be starting a new business. A new business, I might add, that might or might not do well. But she assured me that I was worrying for nothing. So adjusting my search, I only matched her with apartments that were considered "luxury."

Her loft at the Euclid Grand cost more than I made in a month. It had been so long since we'd discussed her family that I couldn't remember if they'd come from money, or if the cosmetics shop was really doing that well. If so, what was I doing wrong with *my* life? But either of those options still left me wondering why she had complained about money to Kimmy. If she was handling her finances well enough to afford basically name-brand everything and high-end living quarters, then why was she so concerned about closing the shop for a day?

I turned onto the bustling Euclid Avenue and headed for the Playhouse Square district. Truly, Rina had settled on a great location. Not only did she live in one of the most picturesque areas of Cleveland, but she was less than fifteen minutes away from basically everything the city had to offer. Asia Plaza, the east side counterpart to Asia Village, was less than five minutes away from where she lived.

"I feel like we're dressed like hobos," Megan said as I pulled into a nearby parking garage. "I haven't been here yet; it's a lot fancier than I thought."

"Don't worry about it," I replied. "I don't think anyone will be paying attention to what we're wearing."

Entering through the main doors, we were met by a spacious lobby outfitted in neutral-toned, modern décor. Enlarged photographs of historic Cleveland covered the walls and offered a romanticized view into days long past.

Megan froze for a moment, her eyes skimming over the surroundings with a sense of awe. "Makes our apartment seem like a slum."

I chuckled, my eyes darting over to the concierge staffing the lobby. I could feel her watching us, and it seemed she was eavesdropping on our conversation. She quickly turned away when she noticed she'd been caught staring, reverting her focus to whatever she was doing on the computer in front of her.

Ignoring her, we headed for the elevators and made our way to Rina's floor, where Megan stood behind me as I knocked on our friend's door.

"Thank you! Leave the food outside the door," Rina yelled.

"It's us, Rina," I said in a harsh whisper. I didn't want her neighbors to hear us.

"Lana?" Rina asked, sounding confused. "Who's with you?"

"Megan. Let us in," I said, leaning my face closer to the door.

A moment passed and I imagined Rina standing on the other side with her hand hovering over the dead bolt, wondering if she wanted to let us in and deal with our questions.

A few seconds later, Rina opened the door a crack. Her puffy eyes were filled with sadness and worry. It was obvious she'd just gotten through crying. "Maybe you could come back later. I'm not feeling much for guests right now."

"We won't stay long," I promised. "We wanted to check on you and make sure you're okay."

Finally, Rina fully opened the door and stepped aside to allow us entry.

Megan gave Rina an awkward smile and squeezed her arm.

Once Rina had shut the door and locked the dead bolt, I opened my arms for a hug and she collapsed against me, letting out heavy sobs. "Lana, I don't know how this happened. Why did I have to go over there?"

I gave her a reassuring squeeze. "It's okay; you couldn't have known."

"But you warned me," she said through a wail. "You warned me."

Rina started to hyperventilate, and I pulled away from her, holding her by her arms. "Come on, let's sit on the couch. Take some deep breaths."

We made our way through the narrow loft. The open floor plan touted a state-of-the-art kitchen with marble countertops and stainless-steel appliances to the right with a small dining area for a table of four to the left. Beyond that was the living room area and stairs to the single bedroom and master bath on the second floor.

"I'll make some tea, yes?" Megan asked.

Rina nodded as she collapsed onto her leather sofa. "Tea bags are above the sink."

I sat down next to Rina, placing a delicate hand on her leg. "Have you been like this all day? Maybe you shouldn't be alone."

There was already a tissue box on the side table, and she grabbed at it, plucking a tissue out and wiping her eyes. "Pretty much. I can't stop seeing it in my head. He was just lying there, Lana . . . staring at the ceiling. I've . . . I've never seen anything like it." Another sob escaped.

I gently rubbed her back. "I know. Unfortunately, I've seen it myself. It's a hard thing to swallow."

"What have I done in my life to warrant all of this . . . tragedy?"

"Nothing," I reassured her. "Not a damn thing. Don't blame yourself for what happened to Gavin."

"The cops think I did it. They think . . . they . . ." She burst into tears.

"Shhh, it's okay," I said. "Let's not talk about it right now. Try and calm yourself down first. You don't want to make yourself sick over this."

The apartment was silent for a few minutes. The only thing to be heard was the tea kettle hissing from the heated coils of the electric stove and Rina's intermittent snuffles.

Once the tea kettle began to whistle, Megan poured the hot water into a teapot and brought it over on a tray with three small teacups. Setting the tea service down on the wooden coffee table, she filled the cups almost to the brim, and the three of us sat staring at the steam coming off the hot liquid. To say the silence was awkward would be putting it mildly. I could feel harsh waves of energy coming off of Rina like a tsunami.

I picked up a teacup and handed it to her. "Drink some of this. It'll make you feel better."

"They think things got out of hand and I pushed him as I was trying to leave." The words came out robotic. She held the teacup in the palm of her hand as if she were a hand model displaying a product. "They told me if I claimed self-defense that they'd go easier on me."

"Were you . . . ?" Megan asked, barely above a whisper.

Rina's eyes opened wide. "Was I what?"

"You know, did he try something he shouldn't have?" Megan answered.

"No!" Rina shouted. "It was nothing like that. He was a perfect gentleman."

Though I was having a hard time imagining that anything about Gavin was gentlemanly, I kept my mouth shut. Sarcastic commentary from yours truly wasn't going to help the situation. "What *did* happen then?" I asked, trying to keep my voice neutral. In truth, I was beginning to feel a bit impatient. I needed to do something constructive. I wanted her to say the magic words so I could have my aha moment and solve the case, and live happily ever after in a place where nothing bad ever happened. Yeah, they call me a daydream believer.

Rina took a slow sip of tea, her gaze traveling off to the far side of the room. It made me wonder if she was reliving the previous night. "I hate having to keep retelling this story." She exhaled deeply. "We went back to his apartment. I felt gross from the bar we went to, plus the drink that was spilled on me earlier in the evening was making me feel sticky. I asked to use his shower. When I came out, there he was. After checking his pulse and not finding one, I called nine-one-one. And that about sums it up."

"What about before that?" Megan wanted to know. "Did anything strange or unusual happen while you guys were at the bar?"

"Not really," Rina replied slowly. "Well . . ."

"Well, what?" I asked.

Rina exhaled deeply again. "He was getting a lot of text

messages, and he seemed kind of irritated. When I asked him about it, he shrugged it off and said that it was business."

My mind instantly traveled to the perturbed woman who had confronted him during speed dating. If I hadn't had interjected when I did, I don't know that she would have left of her own accord. So maybe she wasn't finished saying what needed to be said and decided to continue the conversation via text.

Rina glanced at me, studying my face. I imagine she saw determination set in my eyes. It was already in my mind that I would figure this out if it was the last thing I did. So when she said, "I don't want you getting involved in this," I had to admit, I was a little surprised.

"But why?" I asked. "Megan and I do have some experience investigating, and we can't leave you out to dry on this."

Abruptly she stood up from the couch, tea spilling from her cup. "I said I don't want you to get involved."

Megan's eyes bulged as she stole a look in my direction.

Rina began to pace. "If you start digging around, it's going to seem like I have something to hide and you have to clear my name. And I don't want that. I don't want any of this!" She slammed her cup on the table and stormed up the stairs.

As far as room exits go, it wasn't that impressive considering there was no door to her loft bedroom. A few seconds later, we heard a door slam after all. *The bathroom*, I thought.

Megan set her teacup on the tray, held out her hand for my cup, and stood up. "I think it's time we go."

Once everything was put in the sink and we were ready to leave, I asked Megan to give me a second. I jogged up the steps and saw the closed door on the opposite side of her surprisingly spacious bedroom. Knocking gently on the door, I said through the crack, "We're going to head out now. If you need anything, call me. Don't shut us out. You don't have to handle this alone."

No response.

I shrugged to myself and made my way back down the stairs, giving Megan a nod that it was time to leave.

Once we exited the apartment and were halfway down the hall, Megan turned to me and said, "I know she's our friend and we love her dearly, but she is totally hiding something."

CHAPTER 9

When we arrived home, Kikko was doing the tinkle dance by the door, so I rushed back outside while Megan agreed to make us some coffee for a snooping session. I was anxious to get the last name of that Brandi girl off the speed dating list. My gut was telling me she was somehow involved.

Naturally, because I felt a sense of urgency, Kikko did not. She took her sweet time smelling individual blades of grass while I tried to calm my nerves.

Back inside, Megan greeted me at the door, hands on hips. "Do you realize this is the first case we've worked on in Fairview since you've started dating Adam?"

I removed Kikko's leash and opened the treat bag, plucking out a miniature slice of bacon. "No, I hadn't really thought about it."

"How do you think he's going to feel with us meddling?" she asked, padding back into the kitchen. "I don't see it going well."

I shrugged, following behind her. "We can't worry about it. This is too important."

"I know, but . . . well, if they are looking into her, I feel like that means there's a reason for that. Don't you? And not to mention how she was acting today."

"Maybe. But we both know that things aren't always as they seem. So . . . she's gotten herself into one of those situations. And we're going to help her get out of it. Whether she likes it or not. Besides, we're not even clear on whether Gavin's murder has anything to do with the speed dating event at all. The whole thing could be a total coincidence."

"Do you really believe that, though?" Megan grabbed two coffee cups off the counter and handed one to me. It was already prepared the way I liked it—a little bit of sugar, a lot of cream.

I thanked her and we moved to the kitchen table, our base of operations. "Not entirely, but it is something we have to consider. Unfortunately, right now, it's the only starting point we have."

My laptop was already waiting for us, so I slid it over to where Megan was sitting and let her navigate. Megan was always better at digging up info on people than I was.

"We've gotta be quick about this," I told her. "Adam texted me a little bit ago and told me he'd be over in about an hour."

"Right," she said, turning the laptop on. "Are we going to act like we didn't do anything involving this today? Or are you going to do that whole 'being honest' thing you guys go on about ad nauseam?"

Instead of answering, I sipped my coffee. I really didn't know how to respond. Adam and I had talked about honesty at length, especially when it came to my interfering in police matters. However, at this particular moment in time, I didn't want to hear his discouraging theories about Rina and the predicament she'd found herself in. And I certainly didn't want to hear that I wasn't capable of figuring things out just because I was a "civilian." In my heart, I knew it wasn't just about *those* things. It was also about my safety. But when I'm being stubborn, I don't like to admit that. Rather than voicing all of that to Megan, I answered with a simple, "We'll see."

Digging in my purse, I pulled out the list of names and skimmed over it, remembering my excitement at how well the event had gone. Megan and I had such high hopes that halfway through the evening we'd discussed potentially making it a monthly offering. But now, in light of how things turned out, I didn't think I wanted the added stress. Plus, once this circulated a bit more around town, would anyone even want to do speed dating? I mean, what a bad reputation this whole thing would give the entire event.

I hadn't even talked to my dad yet. I knew I wasn't going to hear the end of it.

"Here it is," I said to Megan. "Oliver. Gavin Oliver."

Megan typed the name in the search bar, and I watch her eyes zigzag over the results.

Turning my attention back to the list, I said, "And that woman's name was Brandi Fenton. I guess it's good she caused a scene so her information stuck—"

"Holy crap, Lana!" Megan shouted. "Check this out."

"What?" I twisted in the chair to lean in her direction as she turned the laptop to face me. "What am I looking at?"

"Read the third listing."

The headline was an article from *Cleveland* magazine: "Gavin Oliver Named One of Cleveland's Most Eligible Bachelors."

"Open that," I said.

Megan turned the laptop back around and opened up the article.

"What does it say?" I was literally on the edge of my seat.

"Wait a minute," Megan said, her eyes narrowing. "This was posted a week ago."

"That can't be right. If he was considered such an eligible bachelor, why would he need to go to a speed dating event?" I asked. "Wouldn't he basically have women trailing after him?"

"Well, he definitely would have after this article," Megan replied. "It says here that he was also chosen as this year's 'Top 30 in their 30s.' Not only is he the guitarist and lead singer in a local band that apparently does really well for itself, but he's also a successful businessman. They don't disclose the name of his company here, but they say that he's the leading regional sales manager of some hoity-toity financial group."

"Hoity-toity?" I asked with a laugh.

"Okay, I added my own commentary," Megan admitted. "The word they used here was 'renowned.'"

"Interesting." I pondered whether this was relevant or merely simple happenstance.

"Do you think there's any chance that Rina could have known about this when she met him?" Megan sipped her coffee, watching me over the brim of her mug.

"I would assume that he told her. He didn't seem like the bashful type to me."

Megan shook her head. "That's not what I mean."

I tilted my head in response. "What do you mean then? I'm not following."

"Like, do you think she knew *who* he was when she sat down with him?"

"Are you insinuating that she targeted him specifically?"

Megan shrugged. "You have to admit this whole thing is strange. When's the last time you've seen Rina look twice at a musician, or any type of artist? If the man's not in Armani, she's not interested. Sure, he's a big shot, but he certainly doesn't present like one at first glance. At least not that night, he didn't."

"She liked Freddie from the plaza's community center," I reminded her. "*He's* not a fancy-pants."

"Oh come on, Lana." Megan rolled her eyes. "Freddie is pretty well off from what you've told me, and he's friends with Ian who runs in a wealthy social circle. She had plenty of time to learn about him. But Gavin, well she picks him after two minutes and he just so happens to be one of Cleveland's Most Eligible Bachelors?"

Ian Sung, Asia Village's property manager, came from a well-to-do Chinese family who traveled in very elitist social circles. It *was* true that Freddie had been a longtime friend of Ian's. And though he was pretty secure in the financial department, he didn't flaunt his wealth like Ian. You could say he was mostly down-to-earth. But, of course, since he was an employee at Asia Village everyone knew his business, so his wallet wasn't really a secret to anyone. Megan was right on that point.

Megan interrupted my train of thought and said, "There's a Q and A Gavin did here with the reporter. And he talks about the kind of woman he finds most attractive. It says, and I quote, 'I like a woman with a little bit of edge and sass to the way she looks. Someone who shows a little skin and isn't ashamed of it. And definitely pouty lips. Sleek class and a little badass.'" Megan groaned when she finished reading. "Who says this kind of stuff?"

I didn't like the direction my mind was traveling in. I thought back to Rina's unprecedented appearance at the speed dating event after telling us that she thought it was borderline ridiculous. Then the fact she had dressed totally out of character; I'd never seen her show that much cleavage in the time that I'd known her. And mix that with my curiosity about her concern for keeping the shop open at all costs because she suddenly couldn't afford to be closed for even one day. To me, that said money issues, which I'd never known her to have. To top it all off, her outburst demanding Megan and I not get involved seemed a bit overly dramatic.

Granted, this was all speculation and there could be a perfectly good reason for all of it. But I was having a hard time seeing that good reason at this particular moment in time.

Though I felt guilty about it, I decided to entertain Megan's train of thought for a few minutes longer. "Okay, suppose she did orchestrate this whole thing. Wouldn't she want to keep him around? She still doesn't have a motive."

"We just haven't figured it out yet," Megan replied. "We need more time to find out what, but I'm telling you, she's hiding *something*. Who knows, maybe he rejected her and out of desperation she pushed him . . . and it was a lot harder than she thought she did."

"It seems kind of weak to me," I said, still not wanting

to believe it. "Plus, we're forgetting, how would she have known where he was that night?"

Megan held up a finger. "Let me check this guy's social media pages; I bet you that he talked about his whereabouts that night. That would also explain how Brandi found him. Maybe it wasn't a casual run-in like she made it seem. You know how people are in this day and age, they can't take a pee without informing half the free world."

While Megan searched social media, I excused myself to the bathroom. When I shut the door, I took a few deeps breaths. It felt like our investigation was going in the completely wrong direction. We weren't supposed to be finding reasons to solidify Rina's guilt. We were supposed to be finding things to exonerate her. How this got so turned around was beyond me.

I ran the faucet and dabbed some cool water on my neck with a washcloth. This whole situation was making me anxious, and I didn't like it. When I got back to the dining room table, I would tell Megan that we needed to redirect our attention back onto Brandi Fenton. Right now, she was the *only* person I wanted to set my sights on.

But my plan was quickly kiboshed. As I opened the bathroom door to exit, I heard the doorbell ring followed by yips and whines from Kikko.

Megan's eyes widened as I re-entered the living room area. She closed the lid to the laptop. "Detective Hottie is here."

"Shhh," I scolded as I went to let him in.

Adam stared back at me as I opened the door, my leg held out to the side to keep Kikko from running out. My boyfriend narrowed his eyes and said, "What do you have up your sleeve?"

Yeah, that poker face I'm always going on about and would love to have? Still a work in progress.

After we'd kissed and said our hellos, Megan tried to deter him with small talk, her arm protectively covering the laptop. Adam's eyes drifted casually back and forth from the laptop to me as he played along, answering her questions.

I scuttled away, busying myself in the fridge pretending to search for a bottle of his favorite beer even though it was right there staring me in the face. I had hoped to avoid the subject of Rina for a little while longer, but it didn't look to be going that way. I mean, who was I kidding? As if he wouldn't assume I'd be interested in this whole thing. Rina had become one of my closer friends, so of course I'd want to help prove her innocence.

I pulled out a beer bottle, removed the cap, and handed it to him.

He studied my face as Megan prattled on about a documentary she recently watched on the effects of the pharmaceutical industry in the United States. By the expression in his eyes, I didn't think he'd heard a word she'd said.

"It's okay, Megan," I said. "We might as well 'fess up."

She exhaled deeply. "Oh good, because I really had no idea what I was talking about. I slept through half that documentary."

Staring down at the table, I said, "We've been delving into Gavin Oliver's personal life, trying to figure out what he had going on that might have caused . . . his untimely demise." I decided to stop there. I've learned in recent times, the less you offer, the better.

Adam groaned and slumped down in the dining chair across from me. "Babe, I can't have you doing this while I'm running an investigation."

"It's not like we're telling anybody," Megan chimed in. "Just some casual back-seat snooping. What's the harm in that?"

He turned his attention to Megan. "It's basically saying that I'm not able to perform my job."

Megan glanced at me for some backup.

"That's not it at all," I replied. "We're trying to see if maybe there's something we can find that's different from what you're looking at. I mean, we can do things on an unofficial level. You can't."

"It's been one day, Lana."

I folded my arms across my chest. "So? I'm impatient. And are you even considering anyone outside of Rina for this? Kimmy already gave me the third degree on you talking to Rina as if she was clearly guilty."

Adam rested his elbow on the table and massaged his temple. "Oh, Kimmy Tran. Of course she would throw in her two cents."

Megan nodded. "Right? That's what I said."

He lifted his head. "Not that it's either of your business, but we are checking out two other leads. Can we leave it at that? I'm finally off of work, and I don't want to talk about this anymore."

"Two more leads?" I asked. "Are we allowed to ask who?"

Megan and I shared a glance.

"You know you aren't," he said. "Don't act like this is news to you, doll face. I can't give up my leads."

Megan's face perked up. "But if we guessed correctly, would you tell us then? That's technically not you giving up anything."

He shook his head and took a long sip of his beer.

I knew there was a slim-to-nothing chance that he'd say anything more. But it was worth one last shot. "Well, what *can* you tell us?"

"I've already said what I can say, which is nothing," was his reply. "We're looking into it. The end."

"Just tell us this: Does it have anything to do with his financial status? Or the fact that he was titled as one of Cleveland's most eligible bachelors?"

The raising of his eyebrows gave him away. I'd piqued something in him to break the lack of expression on his face. I was sure it meant he was impressed with the direction I was going.

Megan bounced in her seat. "Okay, so right before you came, I was getting ready to tell Lana what else I found online. We were trying to figure out if anyone knew where he was that night, and turns out," she said, directing her attention to me, "he *did* plaster it all over his social media. Which is now making me wonder if that's why we did so well with attendance that night. He posted that he was going 'incognito' but then took pictures of himself standing outside Asia Village."

"What? How is that going incognito?" I asked.

Megan shrugged. "Exactly. Weird. He captioned the photo, 'Looking for an honest woman who knows nothing about me,' but clearly that is not what he was doing. And it also makes sense why there were so many latecomers and that most of them were women. Usually for us at the bar, the ratio of men to women is about three to one. That night I'd say it was reversed."

I tapped my chin. "So that means, it *is* within reason that his murder happened that night specifically because someone knew where he'd be."

Adam smirked. "*You* said it, not me."

Megan's eyes slid in Adam's direction before returning to mine. "I imagine a guy like that has a few stalkers. He basically gave the killer an itinerary on where to find him."

I appreciated that Megan didn't divulge the fact that she was hyper-focused on Rina as the person she was referencing. It wouldn't look good to Adam if we admitted we were contemplating our own friend as a viable suspect.

"Or it gave them a great way to pin the murder on someone else," I offered. Someone like Rina.

CHAPTER 10

It bothered me the rest of that evening that the topic of Brandi Fenton never came back up. I tried to replay how we'd gotten so off topic. Did Megan really believe that someone like Rina could be responsible for Gavin's death? And more importantly, what did Adam think?

These thoughts kept me up long after Adam and Kikko had begun snoring. I listened to the pattern the two sounds created, their breathing periodically falling in sync.

I tried my best to relax and fall asleep, but the fact that I had to go about my business the next day and have dim sum with my family as if it were any other Sunday was making me feel stifled.

When I finally woke for the day, it was safe to say that my mood was a bit on the grumpy side after such a restless night. Things not on my wish list for the day were: spending time with my sister, getting lectured by my parents, and pretending I wasn't constantly thinking about who Gavin's killer might be.

I was already halfway through putting on my makeup

when Adam finally stirred. He rolled over to face me and stared at my reflection in the mirror. "Come back to bed. Can't we cancel today?"

I twisted in my seat to face him. "You know we can't. My mother will throw a tantrum."

He buried his face under the pillow. "Can I call in sick?"

"No." I got up from my vanity stool. "You may not call in sick. I need you there for moral support." I jumped on the bed and grabbed his pillow, tugging it from his grasp. "Get up and go shave, we have to leave in a half hour."

"You're no fun," he said, pretending to pout.

"You'll get over it." I started to rise from the bed, but before I could get both feet on the ground, he wrapped an arm around my waist and pulled me back.

"Oh, will I?" His fingers traveled down to my midsection and he started tickling me with one hand while holding me down with the other. "Will I get over it, Miss Lee?"

I loathed being tickled. Smacking at his arm, I tried to slither away but he was much stronger than me. "You're messing up my makeup!" I yelled in between uncontrollable giggles.

He burst out laughing, and let go, allowing me to wriggle free. "Okay, okay. Just trying to lighten the mood. I know this is hard for you."

I laid back down, gingerly placing my head on his chest without endangering my foundation-covered face. "Can't we have normal lives like other people do? You know, where we spend the day doing frivolous things."

"Apparently, no." He kissed the top of my head. "If I could make this go away, I would."

"I can't let this go, you know."

Now it was his turn to sigh. I felt him shifting to sit up, so I moved. He reached for my chin and held it delicately in his large hands. I could feel the calluses on his palms. "Babe, I love you. And I know. Please do me a favor. . . . Don't tell me about it . . . and don't let me catch you in the act. Let's pretend just this once that I'm a clueless guy who has no idea what you're up to."

I smiled at him. "You'll never be the wiser."

Li Wah's is a fantastic restaurant in our own shopping center's competitor, Asia Plaza, that's been around since the 1990s. Cleveland has voted it the best Chinese restaurant in the area. If you're talking to my mother, it's wise to emphasize "area," because otherwise she will correct you and then disown any association she has with you. According to her, *we* are the best the city has to offer—but on our side of town, of course. My mother has a profound amount of respect for Li Wah's and its owners. That's why our family spends most every Sunday gathering there for dim sum.

Adam parked the car and watched me from the corner of his eye. "You ready for this?"

"Ready as I'll ever be." I checked my lipstick in the mirror. I'd chosen a deep mauve color and I was starting to regret it. "Does this make me look more yellow?"

Adam snorted. "You're not yellow."

I wrinkled my nose. "Yellow-ish. Mellow yellow."

"Ha!" He slapped my thigh. "Come on, silly lady, let's get in there before your mom yells at me for us being late."

We entered the restaurant and said hello to the hostess. We knew each other well enough to exchange pleasantries, so I was just beginning to ask how she was when my mother screamed my name halfway across the room. She didn't need a microphone, that was for sure.

I blushed, smiled again at the hostess, and scrambled over to my family's table before my mother could call out for me again.

This was how a majority of our exchanges started. Nearly three decades of being yelled at from across a public area. I've tried many a time to explain to her—my dad has too— that it isn't necessary, and she can try waving or something less abrasive, but her response is always the same: *"I worry you will not see me."*

One of my New Year's resolutions was going to be attempting to not correct my mother at every turn. I wish she'd return the favor.

There were two empty chairs between my grandmother and my sister. I decided to sit next to my sister, Anna May, and spare Adam the discomfort. Last time I lost track of their conversation and caught the tail end of it where she was questioning him on whether he was the marrying type or not. I put a cork in that one real quick. Adam and I were happy the way we were at this moment in time and we didn't need any pressure from outside sources, especially not my sister.

Taking a seat next to my sister, I gave her a playful shove on the shoulder. She faked a smile and fiddled with her chopsticks.

When you put the two of us together, you wouldn't know we're related. We are polar opposites. Where she is reserved, I am rebellious. Where she is prim and proper, I am inappropriate.

Her frizz-free, non-chemically treated black hair shines

with health and vibrancy. Mine has been covered with dye and could use a moisture treatment sooner rather than later. She chooses to apply her makeup in such a way that you're not aware she has any on. I, on the other hand, can smoke an eye like nobody's business. Her nails are perfect, her skin glows with radiance, and she *is* good at math.

For all intents and purposes, she is the ideal of an Asian daughter, and that is something that my mother tends to hold against me from time to time.

"You are late." My mom glanced down at her watch. "A-ma is hungry."

My grandmother perked up and beamed at Adam and me. She patted his arm lovingly and then asked my mother if we could start ordering.

They began their back and forth in Hokkien, and my dad and Adam went on a ramble about something they'd both seen on the History channel while I scrutinized my sister. She'd barely said hi.

"What's your deal?" I asked. She was sitting with her arms crossed over her chest and her head slightly turned away from the table. I was waiting for her to comment on my lipstick. That's what we do: we see the other wear something new and say something smarmy. The fact that she hadn't said anything was the third sign of the apocalypse.

"No deal." Her voice came out flatter than tap water.

I couldn't help but crinkle my eyebrows at her. Leaning in her direction, I replied, "Yeah, right."

She turned toward me, her eyes blank, her expression stoic. "I am fine."

"Oh man." I leaned back in my chair. "You are so not fine."

Suddenly, I realized everyone at the table was staring at us, but no one was saying anything.

I addressed the table. "What did I miss?" Something was going on and I wanted to know what it was.

"Everything is okay," my mother said, avoiding eye contact.

Now I knew something was up.

My dad grabbed Adam's attention again with another anecdote, and my mother twisted in her seat to summon the man rolling around with the dim sum cart.

Okay, so no one was going to talk.

My mom went about ordering some of our usuals: turnip cakes, rice noodle rolls stuffed with shrimp—my personal favorite—spring rolls, steamed pork dumplings, scallion pancakes, sticky rice wrapped in lotus leaves, BBQ spareribs, and some gai lan—also known as Chinese broccoli—in oyster sauce.

Everyone continued to act strangely as we dug into our food. I couldn't say that I wasn't happy because, let's face it, I'm always at least a little bit happy when rice noodle rolls are around, but it was still weird. I wanted to know what had happened to make everyone act so on edge. My only guess was that whatever it involved, they didn't want to discuss it in front of an outsider—meaning Adam. Asian families are notorious for never wanting to air their dirty laundry in public.

Twenty minutes into stuffing our faces in awkward silence, Adam's phone rang, and he excused himself to take the call. Usually he only did that for the chief.

When he returned, my guess was confirmed. He was being called away. It didn't happen all the time, but when it did, it seemed we were always in the middle of doing something.

"Gotta go, babe. Duty calls." He kissed the top of my head and thanked my parents for inviting him, throwing in a quick apology.

When he was out of earshot, my mother leaned forward and hissed. "Do you think he is leaving because something happened with Rina?"

"I don't know, Mom, you know as much as I do right now."

Anna May huffed. "I guess I'll take you home."

I was thirty seconds away from giving her lip and saying that if she was so put out because she had to drive slightly out of her way to take me home, I'd take an Uber. But then I realized that being alone with her would be the perfect opportunity to find out what the heck was going on, so instead all I said was, "Thank you."

My mother continued on as if Anna May had never spoken. "What do you think will happen to Rina? She has no family here, no one to help her."

"I don't know what will happen, but she'll be fine, Mom." I waved her concern away with my chopsticks. "She didn't do anything, so there's nothing for them to find. She's innocent."

"I hope you are right."

We finished the meal with baked pineapple buns and red bean coconut pudding. While we lounged with the dessert, my mother questioned me about the ongoing redecoration plans for the restaurant. We had been at a standstill for what seemed like an eternity. Most of it was due to the fact that our styles differed so greatly, but part of it was because it seemed like I never had a moment to breathe. There was always something going on or someone getting into trouble.

Though I didn't want to talk about that subject either, it was better than going on about Rina and her problems. My mother could become quite judgmental when it came to the younger generation.

After the bill was paid, we moseyed out into the parking lot and said our goodbyes, heading in opposite directions.

Since Anna May had started interning at the law firm, she'd changed quite a bit. Everything she owned was now high-end designer brands, and if she hadn't been an elitist before, she definitely was now.

After a night spent wondering about Rina's income, I now couldn't help but wonder about my sister's. I didn't think the internship paid much, if anything, and I knew how much she made at the restaurant helping out. It was less than *I* made. I could only imagine how she was able to afford a Valentino handbag. And of course, I was thinking all of this to myself as we got into her brand-new Audi S5 Coupe. Though I loved a fancy car, I didn't know much about them except whether I liked how they looked or not. But I knew enough to know that this particular model was upward of fifty grand.

My guess on how she was acquiring such lavish objects was only two words long: Henry Andrews. He was Anna May's new beau and a high-powered attorney who made a pretty penny.

Drawing comparisons between Rina and Anna May, it wasn't lost on me that perhaps Rina's motives were as simple as finding a man who could provide her with the finer things in life.

I knew that my sister wanted the "whole package" when it came to a romantic relationship. I suspected that Rina felt the same way.

"Nice car." I shut the door and grabbed blindly for the seat belt.

"Thanks."

"Okay, what the heck is going on with you?" I couldn't hold it in anymore.

She rolled her neck and turned the engine on. "I'm actually surprised that you don't already know."

"Know what?"

"About what Mom and Dad saw in the newspaper this morning."

My stomach churned. "What did they see?"

Anna May gripped the steering wheel with both hands and stared straight ahead. "A giant photo of Henry . . . with his wife."

CHAPTER 11

If we were cartoon characters, I would have had to pick my jaw up off the ground. "His *wife*?"

Anna May was quick to reply. "They're not technically together." She pulled out of the parking spot and headed toward the exit.

Now all the secrecy was making sense. The gut feeling I'd had that something was off when she first started seeing him was officially validated. I remembered Megan and I digging for information on him but coming up dry. Originally, I thought that he was somehow crooked in his legal dealings, so we must have been putting our focus in the wrong places.

"I knew something was off," I blurted out.

"Sorry I can't stack up to your perfect relationship with Adam." The words came out bitter.

"But to date a married man?"

"It's not so black-and-white, you know."

I leaned back in my seat and stared at the cars in front of us. "Then explain. I'm willing to listen."

She inhaled deeply through her nose. Her thumbs tapped rapidly on the steering wheel. "When we first met, he was in the middle of moving his stuff out of their house. He thought the divorce would be cut-and-dried. They don't have any kids and don't own a whole lot together. They have a house, an oceanside condo somewhere in Florida, and a boat. She's getting it all."

"Okay . . ."

"He figured if he gave her all of their assets, he could walk away from the marriage. It's not like she's destitute or anything."

"What does she do for a living?"

"She's also a lawyer." Anna May turned to me for a split-second while braking at a stoplight and I could see the desperation set in her eyes. "The whole thing was supposed to be over already. Neither one of us anticipated her dragging it out like this."

"So what's the problem?"

"She wants more. And she's also claiming that this is incredibly embarrassing for her because she comes from a pretty well-to-do family. According to her, she hasn't even told her family yet. That's why they went to the charity auction together . . . to save face."

I didn't like the sound of this whole situation. It stunk of lies, and I didn't know who the bigger liar was, Henry or his wife. Privately, I was agitated that my sister would let herself get wrapped up in drama like this. But I knew two things that kept me from speaking out of turn. One of them being that sometimes, you can't control the outcome of these sorts of things. And two, my sister was hurting and this was no time for a lecture. I chose my words carefully as I questioned her. "Can I ask why you would even put yourself in this situation? I mean, Anna May, he's a married man and the whole thing sounds overly complicated. What if he suddenly decides he doesn't want to divorce her after all? You're the one getting hurt in this situation. Not him."

My sister had turned her attention back to the road, but her profile betrayed the fact that her lower lip was quivering. I didn't want the girl to burst out into tears while driving. "Don't you think I've thought of that? But you can't help who you love, Lana."

"You love him for sure?"

She nodded.

"What did Mom and Dad say?"

"That I should be ashamed of myself, and that I'm hurting their marriage. But it's not me that caused the divorce, Lana. It's not. This was going on long before I came around."

It almost sounded as if she were trying to convince herself, and I began to wonder about the reality of the time line. I also had to wonder if Henry was being totally honest with my sister. Had he genuinely been planning to divorce his wife? What kind of couple were they really? There were always the on-again, off-again types. What if Anna May had caught them during one of their off-again periods?

We pulled into the driveway of my apartment complex, and I knew that once I got out of this car it would be the end of this subject. My sister was infamous for keeping her mouth shut when it came to her personal life.

She pulled into the lot that was connected to my building and put the car in park. "Please don't share this with anyone."

"I'm not going to, but people are going to start putting two and two together. Do you want to come in and talk some more?" It was a weak attempt to keep my sister talking before she totally closed herself off. It wasn't often that my sister came over just to talk, but I felt bad letting her leave this way. Clearly she was struggling with her emotions.

Anna May shook her head, turning her face to look out the driver's side window. "No, I have some paperwork to do and then Henry and I are planning to meet later on tonight."

"Okay, well if you need anything, you know I'm here for you." I reached for her forearm and gave it a gentle squeeze. "Anything."

Her eyes traveled down to my hand before meeting my eyes. She acknowledged the gesture with a delicate smile. "Thanks, little sister."

I got out of the car and watched my sister drive away. I couldn't believe it. Anna May—the perfect daughter—had truly gotten herself into a bind.

"She's *what*?" Megan screeched. The news of my sister had shocked Megan so much she literally jumped out of her seat at the kitchen table.

"I want to see this picture my parents saw," was all I said in return.

The laptop was already on, and Megan sat back down to type in the search. In times like this I wish we did get the newspaper because then maybe I wouldn't have been the last one to know about this. I was curious as to what my mother was really thinking about this whole situation. In her eyes, my sister could do no wrong, and I was expected to live up to the standard that Anna May carried. I had no doubt they were now thinking that they'd miscalculated things a bit.

"Here it is," Megan said. "Henry and Heather Andrews. Ew, that's kind of annoying . . . Henry and Heather?" She made gagging noises.

The picture of the couple was understandingly upsetting for the eyes of people like my parents. And I could imagine for Anna May as well. They were an attractive pair. Heather was flawless with deep-set, brown eyes, pouty lips, and cheekbones that any woman would kill for. She smiled wide for the picture, showing a perfect set of teeth. Her cheek was pressed up against Henry's and his smile reached all the way to his eyes. To anyone who didn't know them, they appeared to be a happily married couple.

"They could be acting, but they look genuinely happy to me," Megan commented.

"They do." That rock in my stomach reappeared. "They really do."

"So now what?"

I shrugged. "No clue. Anna May mentioned she was meeting up with him tonight. I don't know if that's to talk about this or not."

"Do you think this Heather woman knows her husband is seeing someone else?"

"If she does, it doesn't seem to faze her."

"You don't think they're swingers, do you?"

"I'm guessing not. Usually people are pretty open about that. I don't see him hiding it from my sister if that were the reality."

"Well, do you want to hear what I've been up to since

you've been gone? I've got something to distract you from family drama; it involves the case."

"Lay it on me. I'm happy to have the diversion."

She wiggled in her seat. "I finally got around to searching for Brandi, and would you believe she's a flippin' model?"

"Really?"

Megan nodded. "So now we have two people who could have the pick of the litter and are doing things that don't make sense. I mean, no offense to Gavin, but is he really all that? I don't see it."

I shrugged. "People always want what they think they can't have. Plus, we don't really know what happened with the two of them. If they were in something serious then—"

"They can't be that serious considering this girl is surrounded by men. Why she would get hung up on him and act a fool in public, I don't know. I combed through her social media, and she posts a lot of . . . revealing photos. Men are constantly commenting and asking her out. I'd be so lucky to have that many options."

"Maybe she was amping things up to try and get a rise out of Gavin. You know, thinking if she's highly coveted by others then he'd want her more."

Megan leaned forward, resting her hands on the table. "Oh no, she's been quite the attention seeker for a while, like consistently for three years. From what I can tell, she's remained persistent about posting these types of photos before, during, and after she was involved with Gavin."

"You searched that far back?"

"I couldn't help myself. It was like watching a soap opera. And I think I figured out the time line for her and

Gavin seeing each other. Or at least their height of communication." Megan typed away on the computer and pulled
up Brandi's Instagram page.

She wasn't exaggerating. At least fifty percent of the
photos were of Brandi half nude. "She's definitely comfortable with herself," I concluded.

"So this photo here is the first one I found Gavin liking."
Megan tapped the screen. "Then from here on out, he likes
every single photo, comments on some of them, and then
suddenly it stops about three weeks ago. I can't find him on
anything of hers. I checked to see if they still follow each
other. She follows him, but he doesn't follow her page anymore."

The woman in question was posed on the front of a yacht
with her head tilted to the sky in a large, yellow straw sun
hat. The barely there bikini she modeled was equally as
yellow and complemented her bronzed skin. The caption
read: *Yachts, bikinis, and bellinis. What more could a gal
ask for? @ Whiskey Island Marina #thegoodlife.*

"What do the comments say?" I asked. "Anything revealing?"

"Not really. There is one where Gavin says he's a lucky
guy, but other than that, nothing to show they're involved.
Mostly generic stuff commenting on her looks."

"Does she say anything back worth noting?"

"Everything says 'thanks babe' and then a kissy-face
emoji. But that seems to be her staple reply. She says that
to a lot of men."

"Damn, I was hoping there was something professing her
love to him or vice versa."

"Me too. Or some blatant jealousy on her part. I checked

his page against the time line I constructed on hers, and there's nothing revealing there either."

"Has she liked or commented on anything on his page in the last three weeks?"

"No, but oh!" She smacked her forehead. "How could I forget this gem? She *did* comment on his band page. Which . . . also lame, his band is called Razor Blade Thin."

"What did she say?"

"Well, this is where it gets interesting." Megan typed in a few words and pulled up the page for Razor Blade Thin. She tapped on the last photo posted, which was a close-up shot of Gavin himself, strumming the guitar in a violent pose and screaming into a microphone. "The caption references a Carly Simon song."

"Let me guess," I replied. " 'You're So Vain.' "

"Bingo. And at least four women commented on it thinking it was about them. But the most interesting comment was from Brandi and it's the only communication they visibly had in the past three weeks."

"What did she say? I'm on pins and needles over here."

"*I want my hat back.*" Megan leaned back in her chair and threw her arms up as if to claim victory.

"I don't get it."

"The song, Lana, I looked it up, and the first verses talk about someone walking into a party as if they were walking onto a yacht and mentions a hat dipped below their eye. The yacht photo. The ridiculous yellow hat . . ."

"So the post was really directed at her?"

Megan clasped her hands together. "Yes! It has to be. If not, that is the biggest coincidence on the planet. Clearly Brandi got it too, because she asked for her hat back."

"I am so confused. He is the man scorned? That doesn't explain why she would act the way she did at the speed dating event."

"Obviously we're missing something here. I'm not saying that Carly Simon's song is going to break the case or anything; there's clearly some kind of history here, and hurt feelings. She's mad about something and I want to know what it is."

"Does this mean that you're done traveling down the road of Rina's guilt?"

Megan tilted her head. "I think so . . . at least for now. There's still something that bothers me there, mostly the way she acted when we stopped by her place. But her behavior could be misconstrued, and I don't know her like you do. Up until she didn't want our help, I was sure she had nothing to do with it. I guess I let myself get blindsided with what I felt are the facts. In my heart, I know she couldn't be capable of something like this. It's just . . ."

"Just what?"

"Well, she has to be hiding something. Don't you think?"

"Sure. In the long run, everyone's got something to hide," I replied.

"And that's where I currently stand. There's something not being spoken here, but I am more inclined to think that we're just getting signals crossed."

I felt a wave of relief. "Good. Now that that's out of your system—for the time being—and we're on the 'suspicious of Brandi' train, I have a proposition for you."

"That sounds ominous. What are you getting me into now?"

"While my family was being all awkward and silent at

dim sum, I was thinking to myself that we really should go to the scene of the crime. You know, scope out the lay of the land and see if maybe we can run into a neighbor or something? It's a long shot, but I'd like to see if it kick-starts anything."

"Oh girl, is that all?" Megan laughed and swatted my arm. "I thought you'd never ask."

CHAPTER 12

Megan and I agreed there was no time like the present, so after she got dressed, we headed to Gavin's apartment. For someone who was pretty well off and often seen in the public eye, his address was rather easy to find. That either spoke to the ease of information access in this day and age or that he hadn't been too worried about privacy. Taking a guess from the things he posted about himself on social media, I concluded it was probably a mixture of both.

It was a quick drive to Gavin's apartment development, and I was surprised to find how close it was to Asia Village.

As I pulled into the entrance, Megan said, "This isn't how I pictured it. I was expecting a fancier living situation."

She was right. I had carried the same expectations of something more high end. Especially if he was making the kind of money that was insinuated by the magazine article.

The buildings were unassuming with tan aluminum siding that could use a bit of spot repairs. The grounds left something to be desired with overgrown patches of crab grass and poor attempts at complementary shrubbery. It wasn't to say that the landscaping was wretched, but it definitely wasn't the property management's first priority.

The apartments were stacked neatly side by side, and going by the amount of windows present, there were twelve units in each building. The address we'd found said he lived in building thirteen.

Megan pointed out the window. "Here it is. Number thirteen." She turned to me. "Do you think this is his current address?"

"It's got to be," I replied, pulling the car into a parking spot. "Unless he moved somewhere else in Fairview Park, but the murder definitely happened within the city limits if Adam is the one investigating."

"It seems kind of plain, no?"

"Maybe outwardly fancy stuff isn't his sort of thing." I scoped out the building for any signs of activity, but there were none. I still didn't know what we were going to do, or what we were going to say. Or even who we were going to talk to, for that matter. I tend to live eighty percent of my life doing things on the fly. In situations like this, it wasn't a very helpful way to live.

Megan seemed to read my mind. "What's next? We should have been delivery people or something. Acted like we were dropping off a package for him."

It was too late for that now. "What about friends from out of town? Or a sibling?"

"Scratch the sibling thing. On the off chance that people in his building actually know him they would know we were liars before we even got started. Let's do the friend scenario. We're from Michigan and passing through town."

We got out of the car and headed toward the door of building thirteen. A small black dog in a bottom-floor window barked at us as we approached. The entrance was a tiny vestibule with mailboxes on one wall and an intercom on the other. I skimmed the names for "Gavin Oliver."

"Oliver" was marked as living in 1305. I took a minute to calculate which apartment would be below his, figuring they'd be the most likely ones to hear a disturbance. I pushed the button for apartment 1301. The name read "P. Colletti."

A woman's voice responded. "Hello?"

"Hi, we've been trying to reach Gavin Oliver, but we can't get him to answer. Do you know where he is?" I felt silly talking to the wall. I checked the ceiling for a camera, but there were none to be found.

"Did you say 'Gavin'?"

"Yes, we're friends of his and are only in town for a few days, so we'd really like to see him before we leave. Do you know him?"

There was a long pause before she said, "You better come in. I'll buzz you. Come down the stairs, I'm the first door on your left."

A terrible sound vibrated in the vestibule and the lock released. Megan and I took one last affirming look at each other before heading down the stairs. We were usually pretty good at playing off of each other in these situations. Which probably came from how close we had become over the years. Eye contact could almost always tell the other everything we needed to know about how to proceed.

The door to apartment 1301 opened and a petite woman with shoulder-length, raven black hair stepped out into the hallway. She was dressed casually in yoga pants, a hooded sweatshirt, and large gray slippers trimmed in white fur that together read Sweet Dreams. Her eye makeup was smeared at the outer corners and I wondered if we had woken her from a midday nap. "You'll have to excuse me, I'm kind of a mess today."

"That's okay. Thanks for letting us in," I replied. "I'm Lana, and this is Megan. We've been trying to get ahold of Gavin without any luck. Sorry to catch you at a bad time; we didn't know what else to do."

"Nice to meet you both. I'm Pamela. And don't apologize at all, I didn't want to yell through the speaker of the vestibule about what happened." Her eyes darted to the other doors in the hallway. She had left her own door ajar, and behind her I saw the black dog from the window that had been barking at us. It stuck its nose through the opening, sniffing and letting out grunts of disapproval.

Megan pretended to be confused. "What do you mean? What happened exactly?"

Her gaze traveled down to her slippers. "I don't know how to say this, so I'm just going to say it. There was an incident at Gavin's apartment two nights ago and it turns out he was murdered."

Megan and I both gasped a bit too dramatically. But how else were you supposed to act when you're hearing this type of news "for the first time"?

"That's terrible!" I covered my mouth with my hand for effect and wished I had the ability to cry on cue. "Do you know how it happened?"

Pamela scratched the back of her neck, still avoiding eye

contact. "He had some kind of head trauma. I guess he was pushed on his coffee table." Her eyes watered as she said it.

"Do you think it was accidental?" I asked. It was something that had been weighing on me in the back of mind. I believed that Rina was innocent, but there was that tiny part of me that worried there had been roughhousing of some kind . . . things got out of hand, et cetera. It could happen. I didn't like to think it, but it could happen.

She shrugged. "The cops don't seem to think so based on what I've heard from some of the other neighbors."

Megan feigned shock. "But who on earth would want to kill Gavin? He was such a nice guy."

Pamela finally made eye contact. I don't know if I was imagining it, but I swore I saw contempt flash in her gaze. "He was with someone at the time, so I know the cops are interested in her. But . . . well . . ."

"But what?" Megan asked.

"No offense to your friend, I'm sure you guys knew a different side to him, but he was kind of a ladies' man. A player, really. And he had a constant string of women coming in and out of that apartment. I can see there being a lot of people not happy with him. Plus, the other stuff he had going on."

"What other stuff?" I needed to sound genuine in my curiosity, so I added: "He hadn't mentioned anything to us."

"Well one strange thing that happened was I heard him get into a fight with a man not too long ago. I think it was a bandmate . . . maybe. He had the same three guys over almost every night. The one I'm thinking of was probably his closest friend from what I could tell—at least he was here the most. He used to stop me outside the building all the time and told me they were in some kind of death metal band or something. I don't know . . . I'm not really sure actually."

"Death metal?" I asked.

"Yeah. He asked me to come see them play some time, but I never went. That's not really my thing."

"Do you think it's possible it was this guy?" As soon I said it, I realized it must have seemed strange. Wouldn't I know who 'the guy' was if I was a friend of Gavin's? I decided to improvise and include, "We didn't know much about his band because we knew him before he started it."

Pamela shrugged but did not elaborate. Instead, she visibly inched toward her door.

Something about what was said seemed to unsettle her.

Megan's expression betrayed concern, and I knew exactly how she was feeling. We didn't sound like we knew 'our friend' at all.

Megan blew a raspberry. "Gosh, I feel like it's been forever since we've seen Gavin. It's almost like we didn't even really know the guy. Who would have any idea all this was going on? Are you as shocked as I am, Lana? I mean . . . geez. And there was more going on besides what you've already told us?"

I started to get a little anxious that Megan was going overboard with her performance. When she's nervous she tends to ramble, and if you don't stop her she'll go on until she's nearly out of breath. Thankfully I was standing close enough to nudge her in the side without it being obvious.

Pamela hesitated for a moment, watching the two of us,

and then leaned against the wall outside her door. "I don't know for sure, but I think he lost his job or something. I overheard him having a conversation and he was yelling, *'Why me? Why is this happening now? I've done so much for you.'* Then after that, I noticed that his patterns changed. He seemed to be around a lot more."

As I suspected, she seemed to overhear a lot. Thin walls in apartments were nobody's friend. I wondered what other things she had overheard that she wasn't sharing with us that could be relevant. Did she know more about the night Gavin was killed but was afraid to speak up? I also had to wonder if Adam had spoken with her, and if he had, what had she told him?

Megan elbowed me in the side. "Well, we're so sorry to have taken up your time with this. We should probably go."

"Right," I agreed. "Sorry again."

Pamela produced an insincere smile. "No problem. I'm sorry for your loss. It's such a shame he had so much trouble in his life."

We said goodbye and headed up the stairs to leave. I waited for Pamela to shut her door and then I jogged up the steps to the next floor leading to Gavin's apartment. I made sure that my steps were heavy and I bounced a little on each step to hear the sounds they would create.

"Can you hear that? I asked Megan, who had stayed below.

"Oh yeah, loud and freakin' clear."

Satisfied with my confirmation, I trotted back down the steps, making as much noise as I had going up. "Come on, let's go."

I didn't know what I was feeling about the information we'd learned, but I did know that I now regretted the whole exchange. If we were Gavin's friends from out of town, I couldn't exactly leave my information with Pamela and have her contact me should she remember anything significant about that night. What leg did we have to stand on at this point?

As we got into the car, I expressed my concerns.

Megan fastened her seat belt. "We'll have to take what we can get and hope it's enough. She did give us a little bit of a lead in a few areas. We now know for sure that he was involved with several women and had them over to his apartment frequently. We also know that something potentially happened with one of the guys in his band. That's an avenue we should explore ASAP. And the job comment . . . I don't know if that's a job thing Pamela overheard . . ."

"Why do you say that?" I pulled out of the parking spot and headed in the direction of the main road.

"Based on what she said, that could also apply to a relationship. Especially if he did a lot for say . . . a certain model we've recently stumbled upon."

I took my eyes off the road for a moment to acknowledge what Megan was saying. "You think he was talking to Brandi?"

Megan held out her hands, palms up. "It's very possible. Maybe he was helping her with her glamourous lifestyle and then she didn't need him anymore. Or it could be something to do with the band."

"Like he was saying that he's done so much for his bandmate?"

"Bingo." Megan made an invisible check mark with her

index finger, looking satisfied with herself. "There's something to what she told us, Lana. I can feel it. Try not to get discouraged. I think we've made some great progress today."

I let out a long sigh. I really wished that I shared in Megan's moment of triumph, but I wasn't quite feeling it.

CHAPTER 13

When we got home that afternoon, I felt so completely over-loaded with everything that still needed to be done, includ-ing things in my personal life, that I did what any sane human being would do. I took a nap.

I slept for about two hours—an hour longer than I intended—and when I woke up, I heard a man's voice com-ing from the living room. It took me about a minute to realize that it was Adam.

Kikko stirred from underneath the blankets—forever my nap companion—and popped her head out, ears raised at attention. No doubt she had heard Adam's voice as well.

We both got out of bed at the same time, and when I opened the door to my bedroom, she shot out to greet our visitor.

In the hallway, I could hear Megan's voice more clearly and she was defending Rina's innocence. It was a relief to hear that she had definitely decided Rina wasn't guilty. Before I stepped into the living room, I heard Megan say,

"You know she's innocent and it's total bull that you won't admit it."

Adam's voice was level and sounded very official. He responded with, "I like Rina too, but I have to consider the facts. Innocent until proven guilty, but I have to follow the evidence. You know this by now."

When I entered the living room, they both stopped talking and turned in my direction. Adam looked worn around the eyes and I could tell he'd had a long day. I went to sit next to him on the couch, kissing his cheek as I snuggled up next to him. I was still groggy from my nap and didn't know if I was in the mood to get involved in their conversation.

"Lana," Megan started. "Would you tell your boyfriend that he is being totally unreasonable about this? He doesn't need to keep digging into Rina's personal affairs when there are so many other worthy suspects out there." She widened her eyes and jutted her head forward as if to say, *Back me up*.

It put me in a tough position. I knew that Adam's job was to find answers no matter what that meant in areas of personal opinion. He didn't have a choice, and neither Megan nor I could change that. I battled with admitting to him that we had talked to Pamela earlier that day. What would he think of that? Would it cause an argument? I knew that Megan was hinting at me informing him that we'd learned about some things that might make the police—specifically him—look in a different direction. But before I could decide what to say, Adam put his hand on my thigh and gave it a gentle squeeze. "Lana already knows my position in this, and she knows I can't play favorites. End of story."

Megan rolled her eyes. "Yeah, but we—"

Before she could rat us out concerning what we'd learned

only a few hours earlier, I decided to cut her off. "I think what Megan is trying to say is she's concerned that you're putting too much focus into one person and maybe not as much energy into other aspects of his life that might have caused this."

Adam turned to face me and narrowed his eyes. "What do you know?"

I tried to feign innocence, but in truth, it wasn't something that I was very good at. "I don't know anything specific, it's just a generalized comment."

"Lana Lee, if you think I believe that for a minute, you're kidding yourself." He folded his arms and gave me what I've come to reference as "detective face." That's when he scrunches his eyebrows in disapproval and his jaw gets so tense I know his teeth are clenched—maybe even grinding together. If his jaw starts clicking, then I know he's really frustrated with me.

Megan huffed. "This conversation is going nowhere. I'm ordering Mexican. Do you guys want anything?

Adam shifted his glance in Megan's direction. "I want a steak burrito and tortilla chips, but don't change the subject. What have you guys been up to that I don't know about?"

Megan looked to me for guidance.

With reluctance, I decided to confess. "We might or might not have gone to Gavin's apartment complex and maybe talked to one of his neighbors, who possibly told us some information about the goings-on in his life right before being murdered. Maybe."

Adam covered his face with his hand, massaging his temples. "Please tell me you didn't actually do that."

"I said maybe."

Megan held up a hand. "Lana, Mexican or not?"

I nodded. "Get my usual." Which consisted of a beef quesadilla, rice, beans, and a whole lot of sour cream.

She gave me a thumbs-up and began typing away on her phone. The joys of modern technology were definitely not lost on either of us. Especially when it came to ordering takeout.

Adam was silent, shaking his head. "Who did you speak with while you were there?"

"His downstairs neighbor, Pamela," I said.

"Ah, Miss Colletti. And who exactly did you say you were?"

My cheeks were getting warm. "Friends of Gavin's . . . from Michigan."

He inhaled deeply through his nose. "Did it ever occur to you that she might call the police department and mention that two of his friends from out of town stopped by after he was deceased? And that if she described what you two looked like and the chief found out, he would have my head on a platter?"

"No . . . why would she do that?"

"Lana, think about it. If someone came to ask you questions in a similar scenario and claimed to be someone's friend, wouldn't you think it was odd that they didn't already know he was deceased?"

Megan had finished ordering, and she set down her phone and chimed in with, "We covered that base. We're old friends who happened to be passing through town . . . a total coincidence."

"Right . . . days after he is found dead?" Adam retorted.

I squirmed in my seat next to him. "Yeah, but it could happen."

"Would *you* believe it?" he asked. "I mean, days after he's murdered? You wouldn't at all think it was suspicious and that these people might be digging for information? Or think for a minute that the main suspect in question is Asian and might find it odd that an Asian woman came by a few days later."

Megan leaned forward. "Wait, are you implying that this woman saw Rina that night?"

Adam nodded. "She certainly did. She saw them when they were entering the building. Miss Colletti even commented that Rina smiled at her from the top of the stairs. She was able to make a very accurate description."

My stomach was starting to hurt.

Megan snorted. "Well, Rina and Lana aren't the only two Asian women in the community. It's not like she would automatically assume they would know each other."

I wrapped my arms around my stomach. "No, but the community is small in Northeast Ohio in general. And if she wanted to speculate, like we do, she could have assumed that we were there to find out what's what in order to see if there was any proof that Rina was guilty."

Adam rose from the couch, cracking his knuckles.

Megan flopped backward. "That's a huge if, Lana."

Adam reached for the empty beer bottle that had been in front of him and made his way over to the kitchen. "You guys better hope so. If word gets back to the chief, there's only so much I can do."

*   *   *

After we finished our Mexican, the three of us decided to watch a stand-up comedy show to lighten the mood. I needed a good laugh. So for one hour we blocked out the rest of the world with some Tom Segura.

Adam flinched when the comedian made a few Asian jokes, but loosened up when he realized I was laughing right along with the audience. One thing my mother taught us growing up that stuck with me is never to take ourselves too seriously. She took great care in guiding my sister and me on navigating the differences between joking around and mean-spirited comments.

Thanks to her, I could joke with the best of them. But if someone happened to be a bully or took things too far, I was well equipped to handle myself in that situation too. My mother definitely didn't raise us to keep quiet, I can tell you that.

The evening was winding down and Adam and I said our good nights to Megan after we finished taking Kikko for her evening tinkle. Within minutes of his head hitting the pillow, Adam was sound asleep, snoring in sync with Kikko.

I, however, was awake. My mind was moving a thousand miles a minute and I tried to think about anything other than Rina's situation and what had really happened to Gavin.

Though it might have ended up being a risk on Megan's and my part to visit with Pamela, it had been necessary. We needed something. I didn't know if we could trust what she'd said now that Adam had informed us that Pamela had seen Rina with her own eyes that evening, since I felt slightly suspicious that Pamela hadn't mentioned it when we'd talked with her. But then again, if we were Gavin's friends, why would she?

I tried to organize my thoughts, thinking that maybe if I had a solid plan going forward, I might be able to sleep better. I inhaled deeply and tried to start at the beginning.

Megan and I needed to somehow meet with Brandi Fenton. As much as it pained my spur-of-the-moment personality to come up with a plan, it might serve us well to know in advance how we would handle Gavin's former flame. Especially if she recognized either of us from the speed dating event. Not enough time had passed where the possibility of her forgetting us was plausible.

At some point, I needed to check on Rina and how she was doing. I'd texted her a couple of times since last I saw her, but she had yet to reply. I wondered if she would be at work tomorrow morning or if she would ask Kimmy to fill in her for again. That thought spurred me to make a mental note about talking to Kimmy. Even though I didn't want to involve her, it could work out for the best. For whatever reason, Rina was shunning everyone but Kimmy. It was possible that I could turn my outspoken friend into a useful informant.

And then there was the matter of getting in touch with Gavin's bandmates. I concluded that it would be fairly easy to find information on who was who. Even if it took Megan and I contacting every single one of them, I'm sure neither one of us would have a problem with it.

I contemplated how to handle Gavin's supposed work situation and thought maybe I should leave that for last. I'd need to learn about the dynamics of his company and the best way to snoop around. I would be lying if I said pretending to apply for a job at his company hadn't crossed my mind. It felt a little over the top, but I included it on the backburner of my thoughts as a potential tactic.

While I started to finally drift off to sleep, my brain skimmed over the list of things that needed to be done. I had to deal with scorned women, plus work problems, and maybe a falling out with a close friend that resulted in death. All of this was riding on the fact that someone had entered Gavin's apartment, killed him, and then left again all while Rina was in the shower. The odds were slim, and I felt overwhelmed beyond belief, but I was still holding on to the notion that my friend was innocent.

Chalk on the necessities of everyday life, maintaining my relationship with a detective—the detective—and jumping through whatever hoops my family might cook up for me in the meantime. It was all beginning to feel like too much.

CHAPTER 14

I could probably count on my fingers and toes all the times I've been excited for a Monday morning in the twenty-eight years I've been on this planet. Thankfully today, I still had a toe to tack this rare occasion onto. I could hardly wait to get this day started.

Though "excited" wasn't even the right word for what I was currently feeling. It was more along the lines of anxious. And strangely enough, that stemmed from the minimal amount of chatter compared to the overabundance of activity that normally took place in the Asia Village gossip mill. For a minute, I entertained the thought that maybe the sparse ear bending was out of respect for Rina. But a moment later I realized that respect had never stopped anyone at the plaza from dishing out juicy tidbits or ridiculous speculations.

I didn't want to have an awkward interaction with Rina at the plaza. My worst fear was upsetting her to the point of tears and retreat as she'd reacted when Megan and I went to visit her. But we needed to talk this out . . . alone. I'd tried calling her sporadically throughout the weekend so we could avoid a public outburst, but I'd gotten her voice mail every time.

Not only was it frustrating to the case, it was also a bit disheartening that she was shutting me out. I would think as close as we'd become in the short time we'd known each other, she would know that I was only trying to help. After all, it had been me that helped bring her sister and brother-in-law's murderer to justice.

Adam had slipped out about an hour before I rolled out of bed. I vaguely remembered him kissing my cheek and whispering he loved me before I acknowledged the door to my bedroom opening and closing.

He'd left me a note telling me that our time together this week would be shortened due to the investigation and he'd text or call during his free time. By now I was used to this sort of thing, but it didn't make it suck any less.

I felt exhausted, even though I'd slept a decent seven hours. It was going to take more than one cup of coffee to get me functioning at normal speed. I dillydallied at the kitchen table with my coffee and a copy of *Woman's World* before heading back to my vanity.

With a critical eye, I studied my features in the mirror. Putting on makeup can be something of an art form. You need patience, precise lines, blending capabilities, and most important, a steady hand. Something that I currently didn't have. Even with my elbow resting on my vanity for balance, I'd either had too much coffee too quickly or it was the tension I felt boiling in my stomach that was causing my hands to shake.

Trying not to rush, I applied my eye shadow, blended, and

then added eyeliner and mascara. My skin was starting to pale from lack of sun, so I added extra bronzer to define my cheekbones. I spent a full minute tilting my head up and down to investigate whether or not I was acquiring a double chin. My face seemed rounder than normal, and I promised myself that this week, I would try not to eat any doughnuts. Okay . . . well, maybe one. But that was it. Cross my heart.

Megan was sound asleep, and I left a Post-it on her door, wishing her a good day. I let Kikko out for her morning tinkle and left with five minutes to spare.

Traffic was reasonable and I felt at ease as much as I realistically could considering how much was on my mind. I didn't want to think about Rina's situation anymore. While stopped at a traffic light, I chastised myself for not being able to mind my own business. But the enabler sitting on my left shoulder argued, *"Well, how can you sit by while all these injustices happen?"*

The enabler had a point. I couldn't sit on the sidelines. It wasn't in my nature.

By the time I reached Asia Village, I had gone from beating myself up to giving myself a pep talk. Everything was going to be okay. I had to keep telling myself that. They say that if you tell yourself something often enough, it becomes true. I was going to put that theory to the test.

The plaza was quiet upon entering, and the door closing behind me echoed throughout the building. Shop owners were starting their day, unlocking doors, lifting gates, and making finishing touches on organizing their merchandise.

After I said "good morning" to Mr. Zhang at Wild Sage herbal shop, my attention traveled to the opposite side of the plaza where Modern Scroll resided. It had been a while since I'd stopped in to purchase more books, so I made a mental note to swing by sometime before Friday. I used to go once a week at the very least, but things had become so hectic in my life. Between managing the restaurant, preparing for the speed dating event, and juggling time between my family, my best friend, and my boyfriend, I'd been slipping on some self-care items, like perusing a bookstore at my leisure. It was one of my favorite things to do. There is no better place to cast out all your worries. Some people like to walk in nature, some prefer losing themselves in sports. But me? Well, in my eyes, there was no happier location than a brick-and-mortar bookstore.

Before I unlocked the restaurant, I noticed that the lights in Rina's store were still off. But I reminded myself that wasn't completely unusual because I was often one of the earliest to arrive. I'd have to check again once Peter showed up for the day.

After I dropped off my purse in the back and switched on all the lights, I went around the dining room and tidied up any areas that appeared to need it. I stood in the center of the restaurant and turned a three-sixty as I assessed the dining room and what changes I'd like to make. I thought it would be nice to have everything redecorated before the new year. A fresh beginning for Ho-Lee Noodle House.

My thoughts were interrupted by Peter knocking on the double doors of the restaurant. He waved to me through the glass, and I acknowledged him with a head nod before making my way to the entrance.

"Hey dude. Mornin'." He glanced over his shoulder as he passed through the doors. "Did you see Rina is here today?"

I followed his line of sight and saw my friend scurry to her shop, unlock the doors, and disappear into the darkness.

"I think that's the first time she's been at the plaza since you-know-what." He shook his head. "I feel bad for that chick. She's had it rough."

We walked back to the kitchen together, and I asked, "So you think she's innocent then?"

He tilted his head back. "For sure. You don't? She couldn't hurt a fly. Plus, that dude was into some shady stuff. Shady people, shady dealings. Just all out Shady McShaderson."

"You knew Gavin Oliver?"

Peter raised his shoulders and tilted his head. "Sorta. I'd see him around. We weren't best buds or anything. I've seen his band play before. They weren't that great. And the crowd he hung out with at metal bars . . . they were all trouble."

"Do you think it's possible that one of those people killed him? Like maybe a band member or an association from the bar?"

He'd finished switching his black baseball hat out for another black one that he deemed his work hat. When he adjusted the brim over his eyes, I noticed he was giving me the stink eye. "No way, man. I do not condone you getting knee-deep in this situation. Can't you take a break? Go shopping or do some crafts . . . or whatever you girls like doing."

"Not all women like to do the same kind of stuff, Peter." I folded my arms over my chest.

"So you don't like either of those things?"

I paused. "Well okay, I'm a bad example."

He snickered. "Exactly. Now try and stay out of trouble. Aside from stressing me out, you're going to give your boyfriend gray hair with all this meddling. I know this is *his* case and all."

"He can handle it."

"Okay, fine. You're giving *me* gray hair. How about that?"

"Shall I buy you some hair dye?"

He turned away from me. "What am I going to do with you?"

"It's simple, tell me what you know. You know I won't shut up about it. We're stuck together for the next eight hours."

Peter turned on the grill. "Fine. Dude got hella drunk all the live long night. He'd make an ass out of himself while he was out. Hit on girls, start fights, all that kind of stuff. I can't tell you how many nights I'd bump into him and he'd get kicked out or they'd plain out stop serving him alcohol."

I tried to envision this behavior in my head. Gavin Oliver seemed to be two people. When I'd met him, I didn't expect to hear this kind of information. Then seeing his apartment building and that not being what I anticipated either was just adding to the confusion. Tack on the fact that he was a successful businessman and pretty well known in the city, I didn't know what to make of it all.

Of course, I believed every word that Peter told me. He'd have no reason to lie or exaggerate.

It seemed as if Gavin was trapped between two different lives. One of success and prestige. And then another who ran with a rough crowd and got so wasted he was kicked out of bars.

I wasn't anyone to judge, considering I wasn't the biggest fan of adulthood myself, but it did sound to me as though he was holding onto his youth a bit too tightly. The fact that he was able to accomplish all that he had in the condition he ran his life was, in a way, actually quite impressive.

"And that's about it as far as what I can tell you. He was not a good dude. I don't know how he got all those women. How Rina zeroed in on him instead of one of the other fifty guys that showed up that night, well, damn, I can't wrap my head around that."

I nodded. "I agree. What was so special about Gavin?"

"All I can think is that it's because he's loaded."

The topic of Gavin's finances made my stomach hurt. Was it really enough motivation for Rina to disregard the rest of his personality? Then again, I'd felt he was pretending to be something he wasn't when he'd wooed my friend. Maybe she'd really fallen for the charmer.

Checking the clock on the wall, I saw there was still about twenty minutes before the restaurant would open and our first customers of the day, the Mahjong Matrons, would arrive. I decided it was enough time to quickly approach Rina at her shop. Maybe suggesting a few drinks after work over at the Bamboo Lounge would be the best route to take. I could act like her situation was the furthest thing from my mind and that I only wanted to relax and socialize. It felt a little conniving to think that maybe if I loosened her up with a cocktail or two, she'd be more forthcoming with me. But at this point, I didn't know how else to get her to talk to me.

"I'll be right back," I told Peter.

"Ugh! I can't get you to stand still for five minutes. What are you up to now?"

"Nothing. Just want to welcome Rina back and offer to take her out for some drinks after work."

"Uh-huh."

I stuck my tongue out at him and left the kitchen. I needed to make this quick. The Mahjong Matrons would not stand for being made to wait.

The front half of the shop was still dark, and I spotted Rina toward the back near the cash register. When I knocked on the glass door, she jumped, pressing her hand to her chest and closing her eyes.

A few moments later, she unlocked the door and moved to the side so I could enter. When she said hello, she didn't even try to smile.

I did my best to pretend that her mood wasn't affecting me. "Welcome back to work!"

"Thanks." She turned and walked back over to the sales counter. "I have a lot of catching up to do. Is there something you need?"

I hadn't known Rina for all that long or anything, but I'd never seen this side of her. Even at her sister and brother-in-law's funeral, she'd been more pleasant than this.

Part of me wanted to question how much catching up she really needed to do. She'd only missed Saturday since she wasn't open on Sundays except during the holidays. But it probably wasn't a good idea to poke the bear.

I kept the awkward smile on my face. "I thought after the last few days, maybe you'd like to grab a drink with me after work or something. It's been a while since we've gotten together."

Rina's eyes fell to the invoice on the counter. "I have plans after work. Maybe we could go another time."

"Would tomorrow be better then?"

Without looking at me, she nodded. "Yeah, I suppose that would be fine."

"Great, I'll meet you at the Bamboo Lounge around five thirty?"

"Sure."

"Okay, see you then."

Rina nodded again, never taking her eyes off the invoice on the counter. I said goodbye and headed back over to the Noodle House. I couldn't help but wonder if she really had plans after work or if it was an excuse to stall sitting down with me. What was she so afraid of? I wanted to feel one hundred percent positive that she was innocent, but when people started acting out of character you really had to wonder what they were hiding. This wasn't the Rina I thought I knew.

As I made my way around the koi pond, I met up with the Mahjong Matrons. Not only did the four elderly women always order the same dishes every day, they also always walked in the same formation: two women in front and the other two directly behind them. In a way, it reminded me of the "buddy system" back in elementary school.

Helen was the first to greet me. "Good morning, Lana. We are so glad to see you." Her eyes slid in the direction I'd just come from. "We have much to talk about."

CHAPTER 15

The Mahjong Matrons settled into their usual booth by the window that provided a nice view out into the plaza. It was the perfect place for them to enjoy their breakfast and a little people watching at the same time.

I went into the kitchen to prepare their tea and inform Peter that they had arrived. I didn't need to tell him what they wanted, because he already knew.

When I returned to their table with a teapot, they turned their cups over in unison. Helen, being the oldest, mothered the other women and always poured out their first cup of the day.

Pearl was the outspoken one in the bunch. She was not shy in her quest for gossip. "Tell us what is happening with Rina Su. We have heard so many stories."

I didn't want to point out the fact that they had caused some of those stories to circulate. "I don't know much, to be honest with you. She isn't really speaking to me right now."

Wendy's brows furrowed. "But we saw you coming from her shop."

"Yeah, I'm trying to get her to have drinks with me," I explained. "Every time I try to talk to her, she runs away." I could hear the defeat in my voice, and it annoyed me.

Helen shook her head, taking a sip of her tea. "This is not a good sign."

It didn't seem like agreeing with her would be a good idea. The last thing I needed was my name being dragged into one of their gossip sessions at the plaza's salon, Asian Accents. I could see it now: *Oh yeah, even her own friend thinks she is hiding something.*

Sadly, depending on the day of the week, it seemed, it was kind of true. There was nothing I despised more than being wishy-washy about something I was feeling. I wanted Rina to be innocent, but she wasn't acting like someone with nothing to hide.

"I think she needs a little time," I said, hoping to sound confident in my words. "Finding someone dead isn't an easy thing to handle."

"Yes, you know this well, Lana," Opal replied, barely above a whisper. Pearl's younger sister, she was a slip of a woman, small, somewhat fragile by appearances, and when she spoke, you had to really concentrate to hear what she was saying. "Perhaps this is the way to help her open her heart to you."

Now why didn't I think of that? If I wasn't standing in front of these four ladies, I probably would have smacked myself on the forehead. But I nodded in agreement as if that was my plan this whole entire time.

Opal clucked her tongue, "Ai-ya, let us not forget why we wanted to talk with Lana."

The other three women nodded in agreement, mumbling

to each other in Mandarin—of which I only knew a few words.

Helen took point, and shifted gingerly in her seat. I started to feel a bit nervous and could only guess at what they might be ready to bring up. Finally, she said, "We have heard some things about Anna May that do not sound too good, and we would like you to tell us if they are true."

Pearl leaned forward. "Yes, is it true that she has stolen someone's husband?"

Opal winced. "This cannot be true. This is not the Anna May we know."

My stomach dropped and the kitchen bell rang at the same time. Thank goodness for Peter. "Uh, I'll be right back." Before they could say anything further, I zipped away to get their food.

My first thought was how the heck did anybody know that my sister was involved with Henry? And my second thought was that I was going to kill whoever had leaked the information. The only people I'd ever mentioned anything to were Megan and Adam, and I knew they hadn't told anyone.

It was simple though. I would go back out there and tell them it wasn't true. And really it wasn't. My sister was not a husband stealer. Not to her knowledge, anyway. I knew that she believed Henry's story. I could see the devastation on her face when she talked about the feature piece in the *Plain Dealer*. It had been a blow to her.

But the problem was, it wasn't the whole truth. I wasn't very good at lying to strangers, let alone to people who knew me. I had tells. I know I did. My eyes got shifty and usually I could be caught biting my lip.

It was still a work in progress. Granted, with the practice I'd had recently, it was getting a little easier to lie as long as I felt it was justified in some way. I don't know if that was a good thing, but it certainly came in handy.

Peter had been talking to me the entire time I went through the situation in my mind, and I hadn't heard a word he said. I was lost in my inner dialogue. He hadn't seemed to notice, and I threw in an "uh-huh" before I left with the Matrons' food.

The four women sat at attention, their eyes on me the moment I walked through the swinging doors. I noticed that Helen was tapping her foot.

I set down the plate of pickled cucumbers first. "Where did you hear this information about my sister?"

Helen smiled. "Lana, you know we do not like to tell where our secrets come from."

Wendy let out a childlike giggle. "Then no one would tell us their secrets."

So whoever told them was someone that they highly respected. In certain situations, they'd told me their sources, but clearly this was someone they were loyal to.

Next, I served the plate of Chinese omelets as I said, "Well, I can tell you it's not true. Whoever told you must have heard it wrong."

The four women regarded one another, all of them appearing skeptical. I narrowed down my suspicions to someone they really, really respected and who had fed them accurate information in the past.

Wendy confirmed it. "This person is never wrong."

I shrugged as I set down a large bowl of rice porridge. "No, I'm sorry, they must be this time. My sister is single.

You know she's been working at that law firm as an intern. Maybe someone there liked her, but she would not get involved with a married man." Except when she does and the story sounds like a bunch of baloney so her younger sister has to cover for her. Minor details.

The women seemed unconvinced and spoke without words to one another—as Megan and I have been known to do.

Opal smiled sweetly. "It is nice for you to protect your sister." Her eyes traveled across the table to her own sister. "Family must protect family. We should not have bothered you with this."

Helen waved away the suggestion. "Ah, but we must. Because we want to help your family save face. This will be embarrassing for your mother if she has a daughter like this. You must tell Anna May to be careful."

They must have picked up on my confusion, because what the heck was my sister supposed to do to be careful when someone was starting these rumors about her? Wasn't that kind of out of her control? Even I had her back on that one. Pearl cleared it up by saying, "You must tell your sister to find a new boyfriend for everyone to see and then they will know this story is not true."

I set down their final platter of century eggs and smiled. I didn't know what to say to that.

Before I walked away, Wendy grabbed my wrist. "Please, Lana, tell her before it's too late."

After the Matrons left to undoubtedly occupy themselves with other rumors, I texted Anna May and asked how many people knew about her and Henry outside of our family.

Then I texted Megan and Adam to make sure that they hadn't let it slip to anyone they knew. They both confirmed that they hadn't said a peep about it, but my sister never answered.

The rest of the day was uneventful. Nancy, Peter's mother and one of my mother's best friends, showed up at eleven for her split shift. I slipped away into the back room and handled some managerial duties before eating a quick lunch. I craved something different than I normally ate so I had Peter whip up some shrimp lo mein.

While I sat in our tiny break area shoveling noodles into my mouth like I'd never eaten a day in my life, I couldn't help but think about Rina. It was still bugging me that she might have been lying about having plans after work. Before long, my paranoid mind had convinced me that the best possible solution to gain some clarity on the matter was to follow her after she left work.

I had a moment where I thought maybe I was going a bit overboard and should just believe my friend, but my mind wasn't satisfied with simply letting it go. I needed to confirm that Rina wasn't hiding anything. Following her and seeing proof with my own eyes was the only way I could do that.

At 4:50, I told Nancy and Peter I had to run because Megan needed me to drop off her cell phone charger at work. It was probably one of the flimsiest excuses I'd come up with in recent times—surely someone would have one she could borrow—but thankfully neither one of them thought it through and I hightailed it out to the parking lot to wait in my car.

Rina always closed the shop promptly at five. She never

stayed late on a Monday, and if she was telling me the truth, she would be in a hurry to get wherever she was going.

I'd turned on the car and was singing along to an Alkaline Trio song to quell my impatience. I despised waiting, especially in the car, and was beginning to regret not stopping in the bathroom before taking off. I always had to pee at the worst times.

A few minutes later, I saw Rina exit the plaza and slip on her sunglasses before scanning the parking lot like they do in the movies. I was immediately suspicious.

I watched her get into her car, and a couple of seconds later, she started to back out of her parking spot.

This wasn't my first rodeo. I should have been ashamed to say that I've tailed someone before, but oddly enough, I wasn't.

I pulled out of my spot but took a few moments before I followed her out to the street. I had to time it perfectly so I wasn't sitting behind her car at the stoplight.

When I saw the light turn green, I punched it through the remainder of the lot and noted that I saw her car make a left. With a second to spare, I made it through as the light was turning yellow.

My heart was already racing—and nothing had happened yet. I followed behind her, heading west on Center Ridge Road, keeping a distance of two cars between us so I had a little cover.

She took us down to Clague Road and made a left. The only place I could think of that we were going would be the freeway. Sure enough, a couple of minutes later, we were turning left onto I-480 east.

Quickly, I went through the possibilities in my head.

We were moving in the direction of Brook Park, Parma, and Parma Heights. I was doubtful she would take this way to go downtown, because I-90 wasn't all that far from Asia Village, and that was a much quicker way to go. The other possibility was that she was hopping onto I-71 and going into Middleburg Heights, Berea, or Strongsville. Of course, there were many other places we could be going, but these seemed like the most likely.

The mystery was solved when she merged into the I-71 lane. We headed south and she signaled as she was getting off at the Pearl Road exit. Two more cars had gotten between us, and I worried that I wouldn't be able to follow as well when we exited the ramp.

She made a left onto Pearl Road and before I realized it, she was turning into a strip plaza parking lot. I was familiar with the area and knew there was another entrance into the lot, so I passed the one she entered and turned into the next driveway, parking my car at the opposite end.

I caught a glimpse of her getting out of her car and watched as she did another scan of the parking lot before entering the Islander Bar and Grille.

My heart had begun to race again. It was thumping so loud I could hear it in my ears. *Breathe, Lana, Breathe. This isn't a big deal*, I told myself. *Walk into the bar and see what you can see. You can have a panic attack later. And see? She did have somewhere to go. Maybe it'll all be fine.*

As I attempted to walk casually down the sidewalk, I considered the fact that my personality really wasn't right for this line of work. Being a restaurant manager was much easier on my mental health.

Reaching the door of the Islander, I said a silent prayer that she would not be facing the entrance. If she was, I'd be busted immediately. I opened the door slowly, trying to get a good view before actually going in, but it was difficult to see since it was so dim in the bar. I took a dainty step in and willed my eyes to adjust to the change in lighting. All I knew for sure is that the bartender was staring at me as if I were an alien.

I smiled awkwardly and quickly surveyed the room, spotting Rina on the opposite side of the bar. But I couldn't see who she was with. Where she was sitting afforded me the luxury of staying in her peripheral, so I gained a little confidence and walked up to the bar, positioning myself slightly behind two men who were deep in conversation. Noticing my presence, they both turned to look at me.

The man to my left, who wore a ball cap touting the Ohio Buckeyes, pointed at the space between him and his friend. "You need to get in here?"

I let out a nervous laugh and shook my head. "Oh no, I'm okay, thank you."

The man shrugged and the two guys continued their conversation. I set my attention back on Rina and whomever she'd come here to meet. I could see that it was a woman, but her face was turned away so I couldn't see who it was.

A few minutes passed and I was starting to come off as a real weirdo. I felt frozen in place. The bartender had come by, and I avoided eye contact, so she'd kept moving but had a bit of an attitude about it. And the two men occasionally paused to acknowledge that I was still standing there.

Guilt washed over me. Maybe I had overreacted by

following her here. It was entirely possible that she was simply meeting someone for an innocent drink after work. And here I was . . . jumping to conclusions that she was secretly trying to ditch me.

As I was getting ready to contemplate my next move, the woman next to Rina turned to get the bartender's attention. I was finally able to get a full view of her face.

I gasped.

The two men whipped their heads in my direction, the Ohio Buckeyes' fan asking me, "Are you okay?"

I nodded, mumbled a thanks and rushed to the exit.

A few people took notice of me as I jogged back to my car, but I was too inside my own head to care what they thought.

Once the door was shut, I pulled my cell phone out of my purse to call Megan.

She answered after the third ring. "Hey, I'm at work, can I call you back?"

"I'm in Middleburg Heights at the Islander," I said, ignoring her request.

"Is everything okay?"

"I followed Rina here because she said she was too busy to meet with me and I had a feeling it was a lie, so now I'm here—"

"Lana, chill. What happened? Is anybody there with you?"

I took a breath. "No, I'm by myself. But Rina is here."

"Okay . . ."

"Megan . . . she's here with Brandi Fenton."

CHAPTER 16

Thirty minutes later I was back in North Olmsted on a bar stool in the Zodiac, the bar that Megan has worked at for longer than they've deserved her. The past few months her new position as manager has made things more bearable because she's calling most of the shots. With how much she worked, it had turned me into a barfly of sorts. Something both my sister and mother nagged me about.

I sat at the end of the bar, on my usual stool, with a vodka and Coke to calm my nerves. My current outlook was grim, and I felt like the walls were closing in on me. Megan had stepped away to help some customers, because one of the bartenders had called in sick. I stirred the ice cubes in my glass trying to sort out the thoughts rolling around in my head. I couldn't make sense of why Brandi and Rina would be meeting for drinks. And in Middleburg Heights. Not that it was particularly far or anything, but it was out of the way enough to make me think that it was intentional. She wouldn't run into any of us at the Islander on a Monday night.

Megan returned with a frown on her face. "Are you sure

they didn't know each other prior to the speed dating incident?"

I jabbed at one of my ice cubes, pushing it to the bottom of the glass. "Not that I know of. But . . ."

"But what?"

I shook my head. "I don't want to say it out loud."

"I'll say it for you," Megan replied. "But what if they were in on this whole thing together."

I cringed. "It's just . . . odd."

Megan leaned against the bar. "It is odd and opportune. Think about it. Rina gets the date, and she was really gunning for this guy. I mean, come on . . . he's not even her style. She gets him to invite her home and then leaves the door unlocked. She needs to shower." Megan's face went flat. "Lana, who showers at a guy's house on the first night they meet? So she's got an alibi. Oh, innocent me, I was in the shower. Meanwhile, Black Widow Brandi is slipping in the apartment to exact her revenge."

I returned her scenario with a wry grin. "Black Widow Brandi?"

"It's fitting."

"I came to that same conclusion on the way here. I hate that I did. It has to be a misunderstanding." A few months ago, I would have immediately assumed I was totally off the rails for such a theory, but then a situation happened with the shop owners of the now closed Yi's Tea and Bakery that had me second-guessing everything I thought I knew.

"It very well could be, my friend. But it's not looking good for Rina. And it continues to get worse."

"Why would she be willing to go along with something like that though? Let's say that Brandi wants to murder

Gavin for being a terrible guy to women, especially her. Why would Rina get involved?"

"Who knows? I'm open to other reasons they would meet three cities away in Strongsville at a bar that none of us goes to. Because you asked her out for drinks, and she said no. She had every opportunity to tell you what she was really doing."

"Maybe the location was convenient for Brandi? We haven't tracked down where she lives yet."

"I'll give you that. Perhaps. But Rina still didn't come clean about where she was going or who she was meeting. And before you say it's none of our business and she doesn't have to tell us every little thing, I will say I agree. She is an adult woman. *However*, considering she's under investigation right now, should she really be meeting with the deceased party's ex-girlfriend when they had no prior friendship?"

"Well maybe she didn't want me to know because she thought I would want to tag along and get information for the case."

"I don't know, Lana. We can make excuses for her all day, but we're not going to know until one of us confronts her and gets an honest answer. You're meeting with her tomorrow after work, right?"

I nodded.

"See if she 'fesses up then. If she doesn't after the fact when there's no opportunity for you to supposedly interfere, then you know she's hiding it intentionally."

I took a sip of my drink, which had started to turn mostly into water. "I should go home. I still need to shower and I'm exhausted."

"Before you leave, I wanted to bring something up about some next moves we should take."

"I'm listening."

"We need to infiltrate Gavin's workplace. How do you feel about going on a fake interview?"

"A fake interview?" I groaned. I may have already had the same thought, but now that Megan had said it aloud I knew she wouldn't back down. "How are we going to pull that one off?"

Megan shrugged. "I'll figure out the details."

"I'll consider it."

"Okay, then next is the situation with his bandmates. I was thinking we need to meet them somehow. You said Peter would see them around—can you ask him tomorrow morning specifically what bars? We could accidentally run into them. But that's all I've got for the time being. I still don't know how we're going to actually get at Brandi. I can't figure out where she works or if she even does."

"We'll work around it for now. I'll ask Peter about the band in the morning. Can I go now? Between tailing Rina and worrying about my sister's pending dishonor in the Asian community, I've had it with this day."

Megan patted my wrist. "Anna May can handle her own. The Rina thing will work itself out one way or another. You know these things always have a way of doing that."

That night when I got home, I walked Kikko, showered, and collapsed into bed with my hair still wet. I knew I would regret it in the morning, but at the moment I didn't care. I was asleep the second my head hit the pillow and I slept like a rock the entire night.

When I woke in the morning, it was exactly as I suspected: my hair was a disaster. I spent extra time straightening the annoying waves out with my flat iron set on the highest setting possible. Steam drifted from my scalp as I went back and forth from root to tip. You'd think being Asian I would have that nice silky, straight hair that everyone else has. But you don't get that luxury when you're mixed—unless, of course, you're my sister. Why she got the good hair genes and I didn't, I'll never know.

I set out for work trying to keep my expectations for the day low. It wasn't something I could normally pull off, but my new thing—which I still struggled with—was trying to eliminate preconceived notions. Putting too much pressure on the day usually led to much disappointment and unhappiness.

The parking lot was mostly empty when I arrived, and I scanned the cars to see if Rina had gotten there yet. She hadn't. I headed inside and went about my usual morning routine of wishing Mr. Zhang a good day as I passed; waving through the window at Ruth Wu, who owned Shanghai Donuts; and admiring Modern Scroll's window displays from across the pond.

My favorite part of the workday is when I first open the restaurant. There is a sense of calm in the darkened dining room before the clattering of utensils and murmured conversations take over. I like that I have this little slice of peace all to myself.

There was a little time before Peter arrived to prep the kitchen, so, as I usually did, I went over paperwork—receipts from the previous night and pending shipments of food that might be coming in that day—until he showed up.

Peter handled all the delivery arrivals, but I made sure that orders were placed and everyone got paid accordingly.

I heard Peter knocking on the front door twenty minutes later and he mumbled a hello as he trudged through the dining room toward the kitchen.

"Late night last night?" I asked as I followed behind him. Like myself, he wasn't much of a morning person, so I thought it better to hold off on any questions concerning Gavin's band this early in the day. It's not like I wouldn't be with him all day long.

He groaned. "One too many shots of tequila. I don't know how Kimmy can drink as much as she does. I can't keep up with her."

I laughed. Kimmy was a beast when it came to who could drink whom under the table. I'd never met a woman with such high tolerance to alcoholic beverages. "Where'd you guys go?"

"We went to Delmonico's Steakhouse over in Independence. I even offered to spring for a bottle of fancy champagne. But she wanted to drink tequila shots. Go figure."

"Ooh la la, Delmonico's. That's pretty fancy. Any special occasion?"

"It was an anniversary dinner or whatever. Uh, I think we've been together a year or something. Kimmy keeps track of all that stuff. I'm just . . . you know . . . glidin' along."

"Congratulations, I didn't realize you guys have been together that long." I tried to calculate the timing and how long Adam and I had been dating. Had it been a year? We were always so wrapped up in what was going on that time seemed to slip away from us.

"Thanks. Who knew I could settle down with a lady for this long?"

I rolled my eyes. "It's not like you've ever been a wild man or anything."

"Yeah, but dude . . . I'm like a free spirit and stuff. You know I like to do my own thing. Chill. Sit back. Kimmy is the furthest thing from chill."

"This is true," I said with a chuckle. "But opposites attract. You guys make a great couple."

As he switched out his hats for the day, he said, "Right on." And that was the end of that.

I left him to his own devices and went back out to the dining area, making sure everything was aboveboard before I officially opened the doors for the day.

The Mahjong Matrons arrived on schedule, and as I prepped their tea, I began to wonder if I could float through my days half-asleep since my life always felt as if it were on repeat.

The perils of repetition I felt were squashed when fifteen minutes into their breakfast, Anna May walked into the restaurant. She appeared stern, her shoulders back and her head lifted as if she were looking down at everyone else. The resolve in her eyes told me she was on the hunt and I groaned as she marched up to me at the hostess stand.

"Lana," she spat. "May I speak with you in the back please?"

"I have customers," I said, jerking my head in the direction of the Matrons.

My sister sneered. "Peter can watch over them if that's really necessary."

"What is your problem?" I folded my arms over my chest. If she thought she was going to cop an attitude with me first thing in the morning, she had another think coming.

"Meet me in the back."

I let my sister go ahead of me, took a few deep breaths, and remembered that I could be a patient person when I put my mind to it.

Feeling as calm as I was going to be, I headed back to meet my sister in *my* office. As I walked past the Matrons, Helen let out a "Psst!"

I turned to her and she said, "Tell us what happens with your sister."

All I could do was shake my head.

My sister was sitting in my desk chair when I walked in and I noticed that she had her power suit on. By that, I mean she wore shoulder pads. The navy pantsuit was well fitted to her figure and she did indeed resemble a lawyer. The white dress shirt she had underneath her suit jacket had a plunging neckline, and she was showing a bit more cleavage than I was used to.

"You maybe want to button up one more," I said, touching my own chest.

"Knock it off, Lana."

"What is your beef with me? You're too high and mighty to say good morning these days?"

Anna May burst into tears, setting her head down on my desk. "Everything is a mess, Lana. I walked in this morning, and everyone was staring at me, giving me dirty looks."

I ate a piece of humble pie. Never mind she was in my

spot, in my office, giving me attitude—she was my sister, and she was really going through something. I sat in the guest chair and made a mental note to get better seating arrangements because these plastic chairs were awful. "I've been meaning to talk to you about that. Did you get my text yesterday?"

She nodded without lifting her head. "Yes, but I was doing damage control . . . or at least trying. I got so many calls yesterday. Donna Feng called me, Lana. Donna Feng."

Donna Feng was what my mother liked to refer to as the "head honcho." She was the property owner of Asia Village and several rental properties around Cleveland. Her own husband, rest his soul, had an affair—a long time ago—with Peter's mom, Nancy, and it turned out that he was Peter's dad. Talk about a soap opera.

With that background in mind, it made sense to me why news of my sister's secretive relationship would cause some conflict for the now widowed woman.

"What did she say?" I asked.

"She wanted to know if it was true." My sister said in between sobs. "I said that nothing happened between us, and our relationship was strictly professional."

"Um . . ."

My sister lifted her head; her mascara had run down her cheeks. I handed her a tissue box from the corner of my desk. She wiped her eyes. "What?"

"Well, Anna May, you're sporting a new fancy car, plus some really expensive jewelry along with a totally different wardrobe. I'm pretty sure your closet could be an Armani outlet store."

"So?"

"So, an intern who puts in a few hours a week at her family's restaurant can't afford those types of things."

My sister didn't respond.

"Look, I'm not here to judge you. I believe you when you tell me what is going on with him and his wife. But it seems bad from the outside. And you know everyone around here likes to be judge and jury."

"What do I do?" she asked.

Thank goodness I was sitting down because the day that my sister asks me for advice is the day that hell has frozen over.

"Really, I don't know. Have you talked to him about it?"

She shook her head. "No, it's embarrassing. I don't want him to think my whole life is filled with drama."

"It's kind of his fault though. He should have never put you in this position to begin with. He couldn't wait until things were finalized with his wife first?"

My sister was never willing to say a bad word against Henry, so I wasn't surprised when she dismissed the question and moved on, saying, "I want to know who let it slip that we were seeing each other. Even if I do suddenly have nice things, how would anyone know or even think that they came from him?"

"I have some suspicions."

Her eyes smoldered. "Tell me."

"Well, I was talking to the Matrons yesterday. They asked me if it was true. Of course, I told them no, but they weren't quick to believe me, which made me think they heard it from someone they would trust without question. Someone like Esther Chin."

"How the heck would Esther know?"

I pursed my lips at my sister. "I mean, really?"

Esther was my mother's best friend and confidante. How could my sister not put two and two together? I knew she was upset, but had her brain totally fallen out of her ears?

"I hate to say it, but I think the culprit is Mom."

CHAPTER 17

Before my sister left, she cleaned up her face so she would be presentable for work. I told her about the suggestion from the Mahjong Matrons that she needed to find someone to be seen with socially so that this new rumor would die down.

Anna May wasn't too happy about the suggestion, but she said that she would think about it. She didn't say so, but I knew she was worried about what Henry would think if she started spending time with another man.

When I returned to the dining area, the Mahjong Matrons had finished breakfast and were waiting on their check. I apologized for the delay, but they were more interested in what happened with my sister.

"Is there anything we can do to help?" Opal asked.

"Actually, there might be. Is there any way you can spread it around that my sister is involved with someone else?" What better way to dissolve a rumor then with another rumor, I thought. "Just say you heard from someone that she was out with a black-haired man, and they looked like they were together."

Helen gasped. "Does this mean then that the affair is true?"

I cringed. Maybe my off-the-cuff plan wasn't the best. "No, but the truth sounds like a lie."

The Matrons appeared skeptical.

"This would really help her," I urged. "And my family. Donna Feng called Anna May yesterday and lectured her about it. She was crying in my office a few minutes ago."

The women tsked and shook their heads. Wendy was the first to reply. "Do not worry, Lana. We will help any way we can. We would not want this dishonor to fall on your sister. Your family has always been good to us. *You* have been good to us."

I wanted to say that they shouldn't have partaken in this particular rumor mill at all if that were the case, but I didn't want to disrespect my elders either. It was a tough spot to be in. I thanked them for their help instead and cashed out their bill.

I considered texting my sister and letting her know what I'd done, even going so far as to type it all up. But before I sent the message, I deleted it and decided it would be best to wait. See how things panned out first.

A few minutes later, Kimmy Tran barreled into the restaurant and scanned the dining area. I was still cleaning up the Matron's booth, and I waved her over. "Lee, we need to have a discussion."

"About?"

"I thought we were working together on this whole Rina thing, and I haven't heard squat from you." She leaned to the side and planted her hands on her hips. "You wouldn't be trying to cut me out of the action now, would you?"

Holding my breath, I replied, "No Kimmy, I wouldn't dream of it."

"Is that sarcasm?"

I finished piling the dirty dishes onto my serving tray. "I haven't even talked to Rina. The only thing that's happened so far is Megan and I went to check out Gavin's apartment." I left out the part about talking to his neighbor, Pamela. I could already feel her eyes burning holes into me.

"Well," she clapped her hands, "let's get this show on the road. Time is tickin' and I'm ready to play good cop, bad cop."

The doors to the kitchen swung open and Peter stepped out, holding the doors in place with his hands. "I thought I heard you causing a ruckus out here." He snickered as he said, "Can't you wait until after lunchtime? It's kind of early for all this."

"You be quiet over there, Peter Huang. I have words with our gal, Lana."

"Girl talk?"

"Yes," Kimmy and I said in unison.

He shut the doors and disappeared back into the kitchen without saying anything else.

"I'm serious, Lana. Don't shut me out."

"Okay, okay, I won't. I actually have something you can do for me."

Her face lit up. "Oh yeah? Like what?"

"I need you to find a way for us to get in touch with Gavin's band. Peter told me that he's run into them while he's out and about. Have you ever been around when that's happened?"

Kimmy tapped her chin. "I don't know. Maybe? Gavin

didn't look familiar to me when I saw him here. But that doesn't mean we haven't run into him at some point."

I lifted the tray of dirty dishes. "I was hoping we could bypass asking Peter anything because I know the moment I say anything, he's going to know I'm up to something."

"I'll take care of it," she replied. "I won't do it now because he knows we've been gabbing. I'll stop by a little after lunch and act more natural. You know I'm good at that."

"Uh-huh." I started to turn away. "I've got to get back to work—"

She held up her index finger. "Um, just one minute. When are you going to confess that you've told me a half truth?"

"Huh?"

"I ran into Rina in the plaza's parking lot and asked her if she wanted to get drinks, but then she told me she was already getting drinks with yourself."

Oops, busted. "It totally slipped my mind."

Kimmy pursed her lips. "Well, no problem, I invited myself. So I'll see you after work. Maybe I'll even sing tonight."

As my cheeks reddened, Kimmy beamed with accomplishment and blew me a kiss before she walked out the door. I guess stalling Kimmy's involvement hadn't lasted as long as I hoped.

Five o'clock came before I knew it, and I was anxious to sit with Rina and maybe find some answers. Something that would completely exonerate her—at least in my mind, if not the police department's. Figures that when I thought I'd already accomplished that, she had to go and meet with Brandie, my favorite suspect for the crime.

I found myself agitated with Kimmy though. I was trying to shake it because I knew she meant well and only wanted to help, but I would have liked to talk to Rina one-on-one. I surmised that I'd have to see how today went, and depending on the outcome I might have to steal away some alone time that Kimmy couldn't impede on.

Trying to brush off the irritation I felt, I said goodbye to Vanessa, Lou—our evening chef—and Nancy before heading out.

If you like to sing your heart out to classic Chinese songs, then the Bamboo Lounge is the place for you. I'm not a singer by any means—not unless I'm in the car or shower and no one can hear me—but I like to go for the ambiance. Plus, sometimes you can catch someone with a really great voice. Like Nancy. Man, does she have a set of pipes on her.

When I stepped out into the plaza, Kimmy was passing by. Across the way, I saw Rina locking up shop. Most days she kept the store open until nine o'clock, except on Sundays, Mondays, and Tuesdays when she closed at five. Very rarely did she take a day off. The rest of us had suggested she think about hiring some help, and she'd agreed, but had yet to do anything about it. I didn't know if her reluctance had something to do with the expense or with trusting a stranger with her livelihood. The shop was all Rina had and I knew that it was very important to her.

Kimmy paused when she saw me and said out the side of her mouth. "Are we acting casual or is this an intervention?"

Rina had noticed us across the pond and waved.

"Act natural," I said to Kimmy while I acknowledged

Rina with a smile. I waved back to her, and we all headed toward the Lounge.

"Hi ladies," Rina said in lackluster sort of way.

"I could sure use a drink. Am I right?" Kimmy replied grinning.

If she'd picked up on Rina's void of enthusiasm, she didn't let it show. Then again, Kimmy was much better at playing along than I was. Everything I felt and thought lived directly on my face. As much as I continued to work on it, I really had to think to stop it from happening.

When we entered, Penny Cho—the karaoke bar's owner—greeted us from behind the bar. The place was fairly empty and business probably wouldn't pick up until closer to six o'clock. There was a group of businessmen who liked to come in and belt out Chen Lei—a famous Taiwanese singer—songs every Tuesday night. It was always entertaining to watch their progression as they continued to drink throughout the evening. Their "Asian flush" gave away how much alcohol they'd consumed. I was very fortunate I didn't have that telltale marker. Kimmy, much as she could drink, was not so lucky.

"Nice to see the three of you," Penny yelled from halfway across the room. "Have a seat wherever you like, and I'll be right over."

A few people sitting at the bar turned to glance in our direction.

Penny didn't typically wait on tables unless she was short on staff, but because it was us, she always took the time to at least come over once.

We found an available booth near the windows facing the

parking lot and away from the few people that sprinkled the tables around the main area of the lounge. A lot of people liked to sit closer to the stage, so they had a good view. From where we were sitting, you mostly stared at the side of heads and a large speaker, but at least you could hear your friends speak.

Kimmy and Rina sat on one side, and I sat opposite them.

The three of us had yet to say anything to each other outside of "hello," so I decided to start the conversation. Nice and slow.

"So, how have things been at the shop?" I said, directing my attention to Rina.

She looked tired and a little less put together than she normally was. Her hair was tied back in a loose ponytail and the only makeup she wore was some mascara and lip gloss. It wasn't like her not to have on a full face of makeup. Especially with working in a cosmetics store, she always made it a point to put on products that she sold so when customers asked what she was wearing, she could point to the shelf.

"It's been pretty slow." Her attention traveled around the room.

"Same at our shop," Kimmy added. "A big ole snooze fest."

"Things will pick up," I replied. "The holidays are right around the corner."

"Aren't they always?" Kimmy rolled her eyes. "I feel like I'm perpetually waiting for the holidays, wishing away the few summer months we have to enjoy in the meantime. But the winter months are when we make our cash."

Rina turned to face Kimmy better. "I haven't asked in a while, but are you still working at that gentleman's club to help make ends meet?"

Kimmy let out a groan. "Yes, and I'm getting sick of it. The money is really great, but it's exhausting keeping it from my parents. I'm always lying about why I'm tired or where I am."

"Where do they think your extra money comes from?" I asked. "They barely pay you anything at the shop."

Kimmy's stint as a cocktail waitress at a local gentleman's club was the best kept secret in town. The only people that were privy to that information were myself, Rina, Megan, Peter, and Adam. Kimmy had picked up the side job as a way to help make ends meet. It was meant to be temporary, but she'd grown accustomed to the quick cash she received from generous tippers. If her parents ever found out, they'd lock her up and throw away the key.

She shrugged. "They don't ask, I don't tell."

We fell silent after that, and I began nervously drumming my fingers on the tabletop. The conversation felt forced and artificial. None of us were saying what we really wanted to say. We might as well have been commenting on the weather or some random local event for all we cared about these topics.

The tension at the table was about to reach a level four when Penny came up to our table. "What'll it be, ladies?"

Each of us ordered a cocktail and then some sake for the table. I probably didn't need it since rice wine went straight to my head, but I felt that I needed to unwind. I'd been so stressed over the past couple of days it was beginning to manifest as knots in my neck and shoulders. Adam had promised to give me a massage, but I hadn't seen him since Sunday.

Penny returned with our drinks, and while waiting we had partaken in more idle chitchat. I had started tapping my foot, becoming impatient with how things were starting out.

I considered what Opal had said the previous morning about relating to Rina's predicament of finding a dead body. That's when I realized that I could use Kimmy's presence to my advantage. It was time for me to set the stage.

"You know . . ." I paused to take a sip from my drink, attempting to appear casual about what I had to say. "It's kind of funny that the three of us are sitting here together. We have something in common with each other that most people don't."

Kimmy seemed to pick up that I was up to something. "Oh yeah, like what?"

Rina remained silent.

"We've all had the unfortunate experience of finding a dead body. Isn't that so weird?" It wasn't hard to feign the bizarreness of it all because it really was strange.

A little too dramatically, Kimmy responded with, "Ha! We should have our own club or something. And this is our therapy . . . every week for the rest of eternity." She held up her glass as if to toast the idea.

Rina's attention drifted around the room again. If I had hoped for some kind of dialogue, it wasn't happening.

Switching gears and trying to get Rina to participate in the conversation, I said, "I'm so glad we could all get together today. I guess it worked out that you were busy yesterday since now Kimmy was able to meet up with us too." I kicked Kimmy under the table.

Kimmy glanced over at me and winked. "Yeah, that is lucky. What did you have going on yesterday? Like do people actually accomplish stuff on Monday evenings?" She threw in a laugh, but it sounded fake. Apparently Kimmy was a bit off her game.

Rina finally turned her attention to the both of us, her eyes sliding back-and-forth between us. "I had a doctor's appointment I had to get to after work," she said plainly. Then her eyes darted around the room again.

Kimmy and I shared a look, then Kimmy said, "A doctor's appointment? Is everything okay? You're not sick, are you? You seem okay to me."

I already knew that she was lying, but of course I hadn't gotten to tell Kimmy about where I'd seen Rina the night before. And now I'd become even more suspicious than before. Why was she lying about meeting with Brandi?

Rina nodded half-heartedly and took a sip of her drink. "Yeah, I'm fine."

Kimmy turned to me and seemed to ask with her eyes, *What now?*

Suddenly, Rina dug around in her purse and pulled out her wallet. "All right guys. I don't know what's going on here, but it's pretty odd that you're clearly trying to manipulate this conversation into talking about what happened with Gavin. I don't want to talk about it, and I want to be left alone." She threw some money on the table. "That's for the drink and some tip. I have to go."

Kimmy and I were shocked at the abrupt behavior and

sat there speechless as Rina stormed out of the karaoke bar. After she'd walked out of the restaurant, Kimmy leaned backward in her seat and shook her head in bewilderment. "What the hell just happened?"

CHAPTER 18

I felt compelled to fill in the missing details about Rina's actual whereabouts the day before so Kimmy had an idea of what theories were rolling around in my head.

Kimmy was stunned to say the least. "So wait, girlfriend was really having drinks with this Brandi woman? That same chick we had to boot out of your restaurant?"

"The very same."

Her shoulders sagged. "Man, that does not look good at all. Especially because she lied about it. Like, why lie unless you have something to hide?" She took a sip of her sake. "None of this makes sense."

"I know. I want to believe she had nothing to do with this. That what we're thinking is all wrong and we're going to laugh about it one day. But the more time goes on, the more I question everything."

"We need to get moving on these high-ticket items." Kimmy wiggled in her seat. "I'm ready for whatever we have to do. And you'll be happy to know that I talked with Peter about Gavin's band during lunch."

"Oh yeah? How'd that go?"

"Better than I expected. At first, I thought he was kind of suspicious. Like why am I even asking about this dude? But then I added that I thought one of the band members was a friend of Peter's and wondered if he was devastated by what happened."

"And he bought it?"

"Girl, I can sell ketchup popsicles to an Eskimo."

I held in an eye roll.

"He told me I was confusing Dan with Joey. So then I was like, oh the guy we saw at the Beachland Ballroom? And he was like, nah, those guys like to hang out at the Grog Shop."

I had to admit that I was impressed with her tactics and nodded with approval. "Now we have some place to scope out." Finally, I felt like something was going our way. It might lead to a big nothing, but it was better than what we currently had, which was a big *fat* nothing.

"Tomorrow night, you, me, and Blondie are heading out for the evening. There's a local band playing, and I have a feeling those guys are going to show."

"Wow, you actually want Megan to come? That's definitely something new."

She shrugged her shoulders and winked. "What can I say? Sometimes I try to be the bigger person."

When I finally got home that evening, I was more than ready to get into my pajamas, veg on the couch with pizza, and catch up on some reading. But instead, I found that Megan was home and she had other plans for me.

She bounced in her seat at the kitchen table as I walked through the door. "I got you an interview."

"What?" I hung my keys on the hook and set down my purse, giving Kikko a scratch behind her ears as I bent forward. "An interview for what exactly?"

"You have an interview for a receptionist position at Border and Main Financial this Friday. Do you think someone can open the restaurant for you? The appointment is at nine thirty."

"Um . . . what?" I felt like whining that I didn't want to go undercover, but I curbed it. Without sounding too much like I was complaining, I asked, "Why do I have to go and not you?"

"Because I have to work until two a.m. Thursday night— you know I won't get home until three. And I don't want to mess this up by oversleeping or something stupid. I can't think of other ways to get into Gavin's workplace to ask questions. Having you go seemed like the obvious solution."

I sat in the chair across from my best friend and contemplated my new task. "Well at least it's something I can actually sound like I know about. If you had gotten me an interview for Gavin's position, we'd be in big trouble. I don't know squat about financial anything."

"I actually tried that first. But his position was already filled."

That piqued my interest. "It was?"

"Yup. I was also surprised. I called in and asked to talk to Gavin Oliver, and they 'regretted to tell me' that he was no longer with the company. I asked what happened to him and they said there was a tragic accident."

"So how did you find out he was replaced? I can't see them offering it up."

"I pretended to be a client of his. I said my name was Julie Smith. I figured it's a common enough name that if they looked it up, they might actually find something. But I didn't have to worry about that because right away the receptionist told me that someone by the name of Randy Jeffers was handling the transitioning of Gavin's former accounts and asked if I wanted to speak with him. So naturally I said yes, and then as the transfer was going through, I hung up."

"Interesting." My mind calculated whether or not Randy Jeffers could be a person of interest. If he stood to gain something by favoring a certain employee, it would absolutely be a solid motive.

Megan had her laptop in front of her and she turned it so I could see her screen. "I did a search on Randy Jeffers, and this is him. I think he's going to end up being the guy who interviews you. His profile says that he handles new hire onboarding and transferring of clients."

Randy was maybe in his early forties and had the beginnings of salt-and-pepper hair. It was a standard headshot, something a company would mandate, and his closed-lip smile was pleasant yet slightly self-assured. Clean shaven and dressed in a crisp, long-sleeved shirt and tie, he was exactly what I thought of when the words "company man" came to mind.

"You're really asking me to accomplish a lot during this interview. Not only do I have to pretend like I'm interested in this job, but then I also have to try and turn the conversation into something that has nothing to do with the position itself. No pressure or anything."

Megan spun the laptop back around. "You'll do fine. Don't worry so much. You'll be in and out of there before you know it."

"I have to find someone to open the restaurant that morning. Vanessa's back in school so she can't help. If money wasn't so tight, I'd suggest hiring another server. But my mother has already squashed that idea in the past."

"Can Kimmy swing it? She *has* been asking for ways to help."

"That reminds me," I said. "We're heading to the Grog Shop tomorrow night to try and run into Gavin's band. You don't have to work, do you?"

"I do, but I can see if Robin can work. She owes me a favor considering I've come in for her about five times in the past two months." Megan reached for her phone and started typing up a message.

"You're not going to believe this, but it was actually Kimmy's idea to invite you along. She found out from Peter where the guys would likely be."

Megan's phone slipped from her hand onto the table. "You're kidding? Kimmy Tran extended an invite to me?"

"I know, I was equally surprised."

"Hell must have frozen over."

"I said that same thing this morning," I told her. "My sister asked me for advice on her drama situation. When have you ever known Anna May to ask my opinion on anything in her life?"

Megan blinked rapidly. "Truly, is there a full moon coming?"

"Ha! More like an apocalypse."

CHAPTER 19

The week was shaping up to be filled with a lot of things I didn't want to deal with, and when I woke up on Wednesday morning for work, I was overcome with a sense of dread. Much like Kimmy, I was tired of wishing the days away so I could get to the next objective, whatever it might be. Why was living in the moment so difficult for me? Was it something in modern society that caused this affliction? I didn't have the answers. What I did have was an increasing anticipation for Saturday.

Saturday would mean this was all in the past: that we'd already gone to the Grog Shop and I'd completed my fake interview at Gavin's former place of employment. I promised myself that if I could make it through these next three days, I would let myself sleep in as late as I wanted and wear pajamas all day long. Hell, I wasn't even going to comb my hair.

When I got in the car, I turned on a motivational podcast. Clearly, I needed it. By the time I got to work, I was feeling more positive and less like the world was closing in around me.

I said my hellos as I passed through, unlocked the restaurant, and started my day with a renewed sense of hope. And maybe that really is what made all the difference. My day went smoothly, and if there were any hiccups that had planned to throw me off course, I somehow avoided them.

The Matrons informed me that they had dutifully spread the new rumor about my sister being seen with an unknown man. Helen told me that they made him sound "extra handsome," whatever that meant.

Kimmy stopped into the restaurant a few times and expressed how excited she was to head over to the Grog Shop that evening. I wished I felt that same excitement, but my mind was rife with the various scenarios that could take place. Anxiety at its finest. But, I reminded myself, at the very least, it would serve as a night out with the girls.

Arriving home, I found Kikko annihilating her stuffed duck on the couch and Megan in the bathroom hogging the best lighting in the apartment to apply eyeliner. She was dressed all in black and her straight blonde hair was set in relaxed beach waves. She turned to face me, and I could see she was smoking out her eyeliner.

"Look at you gettin' all fancy," I said, leaning against the threshold of the door.

She smirked. "We haven't gone out a lot lately, I think I'm overcompensating."

"When's the last time we took a vacation?"

"It's been an eternity."

I straightened and turned to head into my room.

Megan followed. "What are you going to wear tonight?"

Opening my closet door, I scanned over my options. "No clue. I was thinking black too. You can't go wrong in black."

While I sifted through the black clothing that I owned, which was quite a bit, Megan disappeared back into the bathroom to finish up her makeup. I pulled out a pair of distressed black jeans with pre-made holes in the knees and a black stretchy tunic that had an angled cut at the neckline and at the bottom.

After I smoked out my own eyeliner and applied enough lip gloss to last me until next Sunday, I teased out my hair to give it a little more volume. I added a leather cuff bracelet and some heeled boots before finally being satisfied with my outfit.

Megan let Kikko out while I finished getting ready, and by the time I was gathering my purse and keys, they were back, and we were ready to go. Megan offered to drive us. As she put the key in the ignition, I said, "Don't forget we have to pick up Kimmy. She's on the way anyhow."

Ten minutes later we were in front of Kimmy's apartment building waiting for her to come out. Megan, growing impatient with waiting, honked the horn after we'd been sitting for a few minutes.

"I swear, this girl takes forever to get ready. I mean, you think *we're* bad? This is way worse."

I chuckled. "You know she likes to get a little extra when we go out."

That was putting it lightly. When Kimmy walked out of her building, I think both Megan's and my mouths dropped. She'd chosen a shimmery miniskirt that might have the word "micro" attached to the front of it, a sleeveless black top with a severe plunging neckline that was exposing a jewel on her bra, and stiletto heels that I wouldn't even attempt.

Kimmy opened the back door and struggled to get in. "I can't even sit in this damn thing. Eyes forward ladies, or you're going to get a free show."

Megan twisted in her seat to face her. "Kimmy, you know the Grog Shop is kind of like a grunge bar, right? You're a little glammed up for where we're going."

Kimmy waved away Megan's comment. "We need to draw these bees in with a little honey, and I knew neither one of you was going to show enough skin."

Megan turned back around and put the car in drive. "I think you went beyond a little honey."

The Grog Shop is in Cleveland Heights and about thirty-five minutes from North Olmsted. It's a reasonable distance to travel for an evening out, but you'd think we were being dragged halfway across the United States with the way Clevelanders acted about venturing to opposite sides of the city. I, myself, have complained a time or two whenever the occasion has risen. But I do love what the east side of Cleveland has to offer. It is the home of Little Italy, the Coventry area—which is where we were heading—and many of the city's historical sites. There is a ton of great food, mom-and-pop shops, and quaint bookstores that I'd gladly spend hours in.

It was after six, so street parking was free, and Megan was able to find a decent spot not too far away.

Kimmy cursed as she got out of the car. "Of course we have to walk the night I wear these shoes."

Megan groaned. "I said I would drop you off at the entrance. And you shouldn't have worn those shoes. I told you this wasn't the place for it."

Kimmy gingerly stepped down from the curb, lifting her arms up for balance. "They're going to pay off, you watch."

The three of us made our way to the entrance, walking through groups of people milling around waiting for the show to begin. Kimmy stuck out like a sore thumb amidst the T-shirts and Converse. There were a few whistles and catcalls thrown her way. She acted indifferent to it, but I could tell that she was enjoying the attention.

After we'd shown our IDs and had our hands stamped, we made our way to the bar to get some drinks.

While Megan ordered for the three of us, Kimmy and I tried to casually scout out our surroundings. The place was gritty and industrial with an exposed ceiling of metal piping that zigzagged the length of the room, brick walls displaying photographs of previous concerts, and a cement floor that was stickier in some places than others. The stage area was lined with speakers and had a background of red curtain on two sides.

Kimmy leaned in so I could hear her over the noise. "You know who to look out for, right?"

I nodded. We were hoping to run into Dan the drummer, who would stick out the most since he was about six foot five, Shane the bassist, whose teased-out, long hair would give 1980s hair bands a run for their money, and Derek the other guitarist. Frankly there was nothing that stuck out about him. He was pretty plain with shaggy brown hair, no visible tattoos like the others, and I guessed him to be a little below average height for a guy.

The bar was starting to fill up faster as it neared seven

thirty. Megan handed us our drinks and we migrated near the front of the stage to see if we could get a better view. Kimmy, in her stilettos, had some height on both of us.

People were starting to gather on the stage, checking equipment and readjusting placement of the microphones. I chewed on my straw while I attempted to play it casually cool—as if I were there to have a good time.

I nearly spit out my drink when Kimmy elbowed me in my side. "There!" She pointed across the room. "There's Dan!"

Megan grabbed Kimmy's arm and pulled it down. "Don't point. You don't want us to look obvious."

I followed the direction that Kimmy had been pointing in and sure enough there was a guy who was taller than everybody around him. His hair was a dirty-ish blond color and hung below his chin. He tucked it behind his ears as he bent down to talk to someone standing in front of him. His thin lips curved into a mischievous smile, and he nodded with amusement. I couldn't see the person he was talking to, but with a facial expression like that, I imagined it was a woman.

"Let's head over that way," Kimmy said, taking point.

We followed behind like ducklings chasing after their mother. As we got closer to where we'd spotted Dan, we noticed the two other guys were nearby, all three of them talking to women who seemed to be fangirling over their presence.

I stood off to the side behind Megan and Kimmy, and as I was trying to think of how we were going to approach them in a natural way, Kimmy surprised me by going front and center, reaching for Dan's rather large bicep and pulling him away from the woman he'd been talking to. Kimmy's smile was coy and playful, her lips curved in a seductive smile. The other woman appeared annoyed, and she burned daggers into Kimmy with her eyes, but my friend paid no attention and pulled Dan closer to our group.

"Hey there, little lady," the bassist replied. "I like a girl that's direct."

"Are you the guy in that one band, Razor Blade Thin?"

"The one and only." His chest muscles flexed as he said it.

Kimmy squeezed his arm. "I have such a thing for drummers. I probably shouldn't say that." She added a girly giggle to the end of her sentence.

"It's the best instrument in my opinion," Dan replied.

The other two guys from the band noticed Dan chatting with us and strutted over. Well, okay, only Shane the bassist did the whole strut thing. The unsuspecting guitarist, Derek, more accurately ambled over in obligation.

Behind me, I felt a shift in the room as the lights dimmed even more, and I knew that the band was about to start playing.

The bassist and guitarist introduced themselves, and we all took a moment to smile and nod as we said our hellos and gave our names. Shane seemed to gravitate toward Megan and was asking her what she did for a living, while Derek had stepped back a little after the main introductions. He wasn't as outgoing as the other two men appeared to be, and instead stood observing the goings-on. One hand was stuffed into the pocket of his jeans and the other clutched a beer bottle that he swigged from rapidly. It reminded me of someone trying to get themselves drunk, so they had a bit of liquid courage.

In this moment I felt he was the perfect target to question. He didn't seem too interested in being flirtatious so I could potentially spark a more worthwhile conversation. Kimmy seemed to be holding her own and they were discussing the nuances of being a drummer, while Megan and Shane were having a round of small talk. I could hear the idle chatter of "Where are you from?" and "Where do you like to go out" . . . along with "What do you do for a living?" . . . It was beginning to feel more like we were out to pick up guys—which was so not the case—versus trying to get some intel on Gavin.

I decided to make my move and slunk over to stand near Derek. His eyes slid in my direction, and he gave me a curt nod before taking another swig from his beer bottle.

"How are you doing tonight?" I asked.

He shrugged. "All right."

I tried to relax my shoulders and smile a little. I felt tense. "Call me crazy, but you don't seem like you want to be here tonight."

Derek smirked. "What gave it away?"

"Let me guess, you got dragged out by your friends?"

"You got it."

I nodded. "Same here."

"The guys are trying to act like everything is normal, but we just had one of our band members die. Not cool, man. I am not about the bar life right now. Ya know?"

"I totally get it. And I'm sorry to hear that. That must be so hard. What happened, if you don't mind me asking?"

"We actually don't know for sure yet." He brought the beer bottle to his lips, but before he took a sip he said, "There are some weird circumstances."

"Oh?" I didn't want to seem overly interested in what he was saying. But it was hard to keep my cool. This was going easier than I thought it would, and I was anxious to get more out of him before the conversation turned.

"Yeah, some chick might be involved, but who knows at this point. Our boy Gavin had a lot of skeletons in his closet. Or he's plain stupid." His posture relaxed and he tipped his beer bottle in my direction. "So that's my story, what's yours?"

"What do you mean?"

"Why'd *you* get dragged out?"

"Oh." I stumbled on my thoughts. I wanted to ask why he thought Gavin was stupid and was not at all thinking about anything else. Quickly I came up with a generic story. "The girls were restless. We haven't done much in a while, so they thought, let's go out, have some drinks, and unwind."

"Your friend over here looks like she's ready to hit up West Sixth."

West Sixth is a popular street of downtown Cleveland lined with upscale restaurants and nightclubs where they were a little more particular about the dress code. It's where in the dead of winter you can find a gaggle of twenty-something girls outfitted with stilettos and sequined mini-skirts acting as if "wind chill" wasn't in their vocabulary. I'd shivered with the best of them, but the closer I got to thirty, the heavier my winter coats became as my concern for fashion over warmth decreased.

"She likes to go to the nines," was my explanation.

"My buddy Dan digs that sort of thing. He's in the market for some arm candy. But it only feels right to warn you that you might want to tell your friend he isn't someone to take seriously."

My stomach tightened. If Peter found out about this somehow, I knew I would be the one to get an earful. "I don't think she's really interested in anything either."

Derek shrugged. "Better that way. No offense, but women are trouble."

"Is that why you think a woman was involved with your friend's death?" It was my attempt at bringing the conversation back to Gavin.

He twisted his neck in Dan's direction to see if he was listening. Seemingly satisfied with his friend being preoccupied, he turned to face me directly so his back was to the drummer. "I don't know, to be up-front with you. All I know is that Gavin seemed to have a lot of problems with women. And he and Dan got in a fight over some skirt like a week or something before Gavin ceased to exist."

"Who was this skirt?" I asked, borrowing his terminology. "A serious girlfriend?"

"Nah, I don't think so. Gavin wasn't serious about much. Well, his day job. But women were an expendable commodity to him. I don't fly with that. You treat a woman with respect, or you keep to yourself. It's not hard."

"So what happened with Gavin, Dan, and this girl?"

Derek tapped his beer bottle with his index finger. "Not entirely sure, but the band almost split up over the whole thing. This chick, Brandi . . . she wasn't worth it at all. Dan got loud over it. Said that Gavin stole his groupie. Like, get over yourself, man. But that's Dan, his ego is as big as he stands tall. You didn't hear it from me though."

"Do you think the two guys had it out?"

He sucked in his cheeks. "I don't know if I'd say all that. But if you ask me, that Brandi girl was involved somehow. Hey, you want a drink? You're kinda empty." He gestured to my glass.

"I'm okay, thanks."

"Suit yourself. I'll be back, I'm gonna get another."

After he'd walked away, I took a moment to consult my thoughts. Was he just unwilling to speak up against a fellow band member? What about Brandi made him think she'd naturally be involved somehow, rather than the imposing Dan?

The band onstage was playing at full force, and my ears were starting to ring. I looked over to my friends and wondered what sort of information they had dug up.

CHAPTER 20

Though the guys had meandered around the bar to talk to other women and friends, they all came back around throughout the evening to make small talk. But my interest in putting on airs had dwindled, and Derek stopped coming around after a while. He didn't seem to be the pushy type, and that was fine with me since I wasn't on the market to begin with.

We left around eleven, and from the look of things, I was the only one worn out. Megan was used to keeping late hours during the week, and Kimmy seemed to be on some sort of high from her acting role. She waved a torn piece of paper in front of us as we walked to the car. "And I got his phone number. Still got it, ladies."

Megan laughed. "Who writes their number down anymore? That's so old fashioned."

I shook my head at both of them. "Who cares? It's not like you're actually going to call him. You better get rid of that before Peter finds it. He'll go ballistic."

"What's got your panties in a twist?" Kimmy asked. "Are you going into cranky toddler mode?"

"Sorry, it's been a long day and I'm ready for bed. Plus, I'm a little disappointed at how all this turned out."

"But at least we have a way to talk to them again. This might come in handy somehow. Although, I have to say, he didn't say much at all about Gavin. All he said was that their band was taking a hiatus until they found a new lead singer." Kimmy tucked the paper in her purse. "He didn't seem heartbroken, that's for sure."

"What did you find out, Megan?" I asked.

We had reached the car, and as Megan unlocked the doors, we hurriedly got in to get away from the wind that was beginning to pick up.

Shutting the door, Megan responded, "Not much more than Kimmy. Shane was a touch more on the upset side. He had this pained expression on his face when it came up. But he didn't dwell on it much. He said sometimes life throws these curveballs at you. Then he turned the conversation to hobbies right after."

I put on my seat belt and leaned back, allowing my hair to get ruined by the headrest. There was no reason to worry about my appearance at this time of night. I stayed quiet while Megan and Kimmy went back and forth about the night's events. If I didn't know any better, I'd say they were bonding.

Meanwhile, I found it interesting that Dan hadn't appeared too upset that Gavin was gone. It made me wonder how much he actually cared, which in turn caused me to consider the fact that he could be involved somehow. Was it possible he'd shown up at Gavin's apartment, confronted him, and gotten into a physical altercation all while Rina was in the shower? He was definitely physically capable, and did have a motive . . . though I didn't know how strong. He couldn't be that torn up over Brandi if he was so quick to chat up Kimmy.

We dropped Kimmy off in front of her apartment and I told her we'd talk more in the morning about what would be next. With only Megan and me in the car, she began to talk more freely about her thoughts.

"My impression from Shane was that Dan is kind of the ringleader. At least now that Gavin is gone. He said at times he and that Derek guy feel like they're just along for the ride."

"I got that same feeling too," I said. "Derek seemed a little worried that Dan would overhear our conversation."

"So what are we supposed to do with this?" she asked.

I looked out the passenger-side window as we pulled into our apartment complex. "I have no idea. I suppose make note of what happened and keep it movin'. Tonight feels like a giant waste of time."

"Did Derek bring up Brandi at all?" Megan pulled into an empty spot and put the car in park.

"He did actually. And he made his feelings apparent that she was more trouble than she was worth."

"Shane brought her up too. He made a comment that he wouldn't be surprised if she brought bad juju into Gavin's life."

"It says something that they both think she was involved, yet she wasn't even there. Rina was."

"That's a good thing then, right?"

"Yeah, I think so. But it doesn't help that I saw Rina with Brandi."

"Brandi is the common denominator in all this mess," Megan said, opening the car door. "While you're rehearsing for your interview that's coming up, I'll try to find a way for us to conveniently run into Brandi."

Thursday evening after work, I was on the hunt for business casual attire. I had my fake interview the following morning and wanted to get a new top to wear. Any excuse to shop, right? I decided to head to Westfield Mall in North Olmsted and hit up Express for a new button-down. And maybe a couple of other things that weren't necessary either.

I was standing in front of Auntie Anne's debating on whether or not I needed a sour-cream-and-onion pretzel before heading home or if it was me eating my feelings. My hand subconsciously traveled to my waistline. Maybe I could skip my daily doughnuts tomorrow and then this whole thing would be a wash.

Before I could fully come to a decision, someone tapped my arm. "Excuse me."

Here I was standing in the middle of the walkway without a care in the world. "Oh, I'm sorry, I—" But when I turned to apologize to the passerby, I realized I recognized her. It took me a moment to put two and two together. I was standing in front of Pamela, Gavin's neighbor.

The short, dark-haired woman regarded me with confusion. "Didn't I just meet you a few days ago? You and your friend were at my apartment, weren't you?"

I thought about lying, but didn't think I had it in me to

pretend it was a case of mistaken identity. "Oh . . . um, Pamela, right?"

"Yeah. Okay . . . so what are you doing here? I thought you and your friend were only in town for the weekend?"

I was starting to sweat at this unplanned encounter. Did I say that the trip was extended because of Gavin? Would she even believe we'd stay for someone we clearly hadn't seemed so close with? What were the chances of me running into her, of all people?

My lack of response was making it worse, and I could see the suspicion starting to accumulate in her stare.

She took a step back. "Wait a minute, don't tell me you came up with that lame story of being his friends from out of state because you're really one of his women or something." She smacked her forward. "I am so naïve."

I waved my hands at her, signaling no. "No, I'm sorry, I'm caught a little off guard. No, neither one of us are his women."

"Then who are you? Are you a reporter? FBI?"

"FBI?" It was hard to hold back my shock. First, how could anybody mistake me for an FBI agent? Even if I were undercover, there was nothing official about me or my attitude. And secondly, why would the FBI be investigating Gavin Oliver?

"Sorry, sorry," she replied. "My mind tends to get a little conspiracy driven. I'm sure you have a more mundane answer than I'm concocting."

I swallowed hard. "Can I buy you a pretzel? I was thinking of getting myself one."

She tilted her head. "Um . . . I'm okay, thanks."

"Why don't we sit down and I'll explain."

There was a wrought-iron bench a few feet away for people to leisurely enjoy their salty baked treats. We both sat down, placing our shopping bags at our feet.

"My name is Lana," I began. "Our friend was there the night of the murder."

Pamela's face blanched. "So that's why you're so interested in this?"

"Yes, I know it seems kind of strange."

"I was wondering about the person who called the cops. The neighbors I've talked with didn't know anything for sure, and the property management is refusing to tell us any details."

"We're trying to help clear her name," I explained. "Even though she's not guilty of anything, the cops are still investigating her, and my friend—the one you met the other day—and I are trying to find something to exonerate her beyond a shadow of doubt, as they say."

"You must really care about your friend," Pamela commented. There seemed to be a touch of envy in her voice.

"My friends are like family to me. I do whatever I can to protect them, even if it is a bit unconventional."

"I see. And have you found anything yet?"

"Not really. We've talked with his band to see if anything would come of it, but I'm sad to say it wasn't very helpful. Can I ask if the name Brandi sounds familiar?"

She shook her head. "No, who's that?"

"Never mind. I don't want to take up your time, I can see you're busy and you probably already think I'm crazy." My eyes slid down to her shopping bags. "But I was wondering if there was anything helpful you could tell me? Anything at all. Even if you don't think it's important. It might help."

Pamela tapped her foot and looked off into the distance. "Not really, I'm afraid. I think you'd probably not want to know that I didn't hear anyone coming or going after they came back from wherever it was that they were."

"You were listening?" I asked.

She rubbed her neck. "I haven't been sleeping that well. He was always blaring his music at all hours of the night, and I don't sleep as hard as I used to. I could hear everything. Forget the fact that others have to get up early for their jobs, he partied almost all night long. Sometimes I don't get to sleep until almost four in the morning. So yeah, I was up . . . listening against my will."

"That's terrible, I'm so sorry."

"Eh, it's okay. It's in the past now and it's been a lot quieter this week. Maybe these bags under my eyes will start to disappear."

"So is it possible that you didn't hear someone else show up because his music was so loud?"

"Not unless they were delicately opening and closing the main door. I don't know if you noticed when you stopped by, but it creaks when it opens and slams pretty hard when it closes."

I sighed. If someone was coming over to get into an argument with someone else, I doubt they would take care in tiptoeing through the entrance and up the steps. Then again, someone who knew this information might put in the effort if they didn't want to be found out . . . or find another way in. "I appreciate you sitting with me and talking this out. I know it seems kind of weird that we're doing this."

Pamela started to reach for her bags. "I won't lie, it's a

little bizarre, but I get it. You want to protect your friend. If you don't mind a bit of advice though?"

"Not at all."

"Tell your friend to get a good lawyer."

We parted ways after I thanked her again and asked her not to inform the authorities that she'd bumped into me or that we'd ever met at all. The last thing I needed was for her to tell Adam or one of the others at the Fairview Park Police Department that I was trolling around prying for answers.

As I left the mall, I replayed the conversation I'd just had with Pamela and wondered if it meant anything. Maybe she was remembering it wrong, and there really was someone else that showed up. It was possible she drifted into sleep at the exact right moment, causing her to miss the sounds of someone opening the building door.

My focus drifted to the shopping bags on the passenger seat. I banged the steering wheel with my fist.

They say when you're truly upset about something, you tend to fixate on the minutiae as a distraction. So I shouldn't have been shocked that the thing nagging me the most as I regarded my bags was that I'd forgotten to get myself a damn pretzel.

CHAPTER 21

I could hardly believe I made it through the week without getting into my car and hightailing it to Mexico where no one could find me. As I sat in front of my vanity mirror Friday morning applying my mascara, I imagined what it would be like to run away from it all. I could lounge on a beach with some adult beverages that only come in pineapples, read the day away while I work on my tan, and maybe take a relaxing walk along the shoreline at sunset. Sounds nice, doesn't it?

Instead, I was getting ready to fake an interview, lying to most of my family about what I was doing, and if I didn't get a handle on my stress, I was sure to start growing gray hair at a rate that could be considered a competitive sport. And let's face it, that would be a huge disservice to the amount of money I spent on this mermaid ombré hair.

The financial group that Gavin had worked for was located in Westlake near Crocker Park. I bargained with myself that if I stayed the course and didn't run away to Cancun,

I could quickly stop in the Barnes & Noble that was at the shopping center after my fake interview.

When I arrived at Border and Main Financial, I took a couple of deep breaths before getting out of my car. My main concern was that I might get caught somehow. I didn't know how that would happen, but visions of being thrown out by security guards danced in my head.

The building itself was impressive with its mirrored glass and lush landscaping. The property was pushed back from the street, so it took you away from the hustle and bustle of Crocker Road.

I found the receptionist tucked away in a little alcove area, her eyes fixed intently on the computer monitor in front of her. The only sound in the waiting area was the clacking of her nails against the keyboard as she typed in a flurry. As I stepped up to her counter, I wondered if my typing skills had worsened since I'd stopped working in an office environment.

While I waited for her to acknowledge my presence, it occurred to me that I had an advantage talking to this woman over anyone else in the building. After all, receptionists were the bartenders of the corporate world. I knew from my former job that a lot of people often took their problems to the receptionist. Having no allegiance to any specific department, they were the neutral party who knew all the inner workings of the office and had a sort of bird's-eye view of the daily happenings. A burst of confidence rushed through me as I formulated my plan of action.

The petite woman with chestnut brown hair so perfect it looked like a wig smiled up at me. Her full lips were covered in a sparkly gloss, and they struggled to separate as she opened her mouth. "Good morning, sorry about that. If I stop myself mid-sentence, I have no idea what I'm typing anymore. How can I help you?"

"Morning, my name is Lana. I'm here for an interview."

Her eyes lit up with amusement. "Ah, I see, you're here for my job. Welcome, welcome."

An awkward laugh escaped. "Not that it's my business, but my guess is that you're leaving on good terms?"

She leaned back in her seat, settling her hands in her lap. "Yes, I've started my own business and juggling the two has recently become too much to handle. So it's time for me to move on to the next chapter in my life. The company is great, and if you get the job, you'll love it here."

"Oh, that's good to hear. It helps to hear it from one of the employees."

"Do you want any coffee or water while you wait?"

"No, thank you."

"Well, my name is Carla. If you get the job, I'll be the one to show you the ropes. It's pretty standard administrative stuff. Have you been a receptionist before?"

"No, but I've worked in an office before, so I have a bit of that background already."

"Why are you leaving your current job?"

"What?" The question caught me off guard and I scolded myself. In all my preparations, it had never dawned on me that—duh—someone was going to ask me this question.

"Your job now. You are employed right now, aren't you?"

"Oh yes, well, it's kind of . . . complicated. I work for my parents."

Carla held up a well-manicured hand. "Ah, say no more. I get that. Working for family is one of the most difficult things to do."

"You can say that again."

There was a glass door off to the right of the reception area, and a tall man with salt-and-pepper hair and horn-rimmed glasses stepped out. "Are you Lana Lee?" He adjusted his glasses as he read from what I was guessing to be my résumé.

"Yes, that's me."

"Nice to meet you. I'm Randall . . . well, I go by Randy around here." He extended his hand.

I returned the gesture, giving him a firm shake. "Nice to meet you."

"Please, follow me this way."

Carla whispered, "Good luck," and gave me a thumbs-up.

I smiled and mouthed *thank you* before turning to follow behind the interviewer.

He took me into a small conference room with a round table and four chairs. I sat opposite him, my heart pounding as if I'd run a 5K moments before.

"You look a little nervous," he said with a smirk.

One thing you should never do to someone who is nervous? Point it out to them. My heart started to beat faster.

I attempted to smile graciously. "I am. It's been a while since I've been on an interview."

"Nothing to be nervous about here." He tapped the papers in his hands against the table, straightening them out. "We're pretty laid back, and the interview will be pretty straightforward."

"Okay, I'm ready." I did my best to appear as if he'd re-assured me and I was starting to relax. In truth, a pit was forming in my gut. I wanted to run out of the room scream-ing. A sandy beach at sunset flashed through my brain. *Fo-cus, Lana*.

"We deal with a lot of sensitive financial information here. Things may pass through your desk at times for filing purposes, or we may ask you to prepare letters to send out to our clients. We *do* handle some high-profile accounts. Are you able to keep things of this nature private?"

It seemed like a stupid question, because who was going to say no to that, but maybe they were obligated to ask. Of course, I said, "Yes."

He checked a box on the form he had placed on top of my resume. "Splendid."

"Can I ask if you have tier-based employment?"

Randy studied me over the rim of his glasses. "In regard to?"

"I was wondering to myself if everyone handled high-profile accounts or if that was designated to specific em-ployees?" I batted my eyelashes.

"Why yes, we do have tier-based employment in those terms. These sorts of things need to be handled by some-one with the expertise to accept the challenges that could come with an A-list client."

"So if someone leaves, would their clients automatically go to a specific person?"

He hesitated. "Not necessarily." Seemingly perplexed by my line of questioning, he removed his glasses and bit on the arm. "I have to ask, Miss Lee, are you certain you're interested in the receptionist position? Or are you using it as a segue to get a more . . . how do I put this . . . ? A more established position?"

I squirmed in my seat. "No, no, nothing like that. Mere curiosity is all. I'm very much interested in being a receptionist."

He put his glasses back on. "Okay, next let me ask you about your experience in the financial industry. Do you have much knowledge in that area? From your resume, it doesn't appear so. It says that you were a reporting analyst for a little while. Aside from that, you've worked at some place called Ho-Lee Noodle House?"

I nodded. "Yes, that's correct. It's my family's restaurant."

For the first time since sitting down, he put the papers down on the table. He leaned back in his seat and settled his hands on the armrest. "I see. And are there plans for you to take over this business?"

"Not at this time," was all I said. At this point, the less I commented, the better. I was liable to talk myself into a gibberish rant if I tried explaining anything else.

"Okay, well, I will tell you that we are searching for someone who plans on sticking around. Our company is largely based on loyal employees who have the business's best interests at heart. And that sentiment goes right down to the janitorial services."

Even though I understood what he was saying, there was something about the way he said it that I didn't like. I caught myself thinking that I might decline this job, and then remembered it wasn't mine for the taking to begin with. "I totally understand. I am definitely a loyal person."

"Great. That's what we love to hear. Now tell me a bit

more about yourself and why you think you're right for the job."

My eyes traveled to the clock above his head. We'd only been sitting together for ten minutes and it had felt like ten years. I put on my customer-service smile and did what sleuthing has taught me to do best—stretch the truth.

The interview had trudged along for forty minutes while I yammered on about how I was a quick learner and a self-starter and had exceptional phone skills. At some point, he'd stopped me and asked about my words per minute. I didn't know, so I said somewhere in the sixties. That seemed to satisfy him because he didn't question it or make much comment.

When the grilling session had ended, I noticed that my hairline was beginning to sweat, and I couldn't wait to get out of the small, stuffy room. We shook hands and he promised that he'd be in touch within the next couple of days after they interviewed two more possibilities. My ego was a bit dampened by that. Apparently, even though it wasn't a job I was actually trying to get, I still wanted to be the one to get it. I made a mental note that if I ever went back to therapy, I'd have to bring that up.

Carla was still at her desk typing away furiously on her keyboard. Her eyes flicked upward as I walked by. Her hands hovered over the keys. "So . . . how did it go?"

I leaned against her counter in a conversational manner. "I think it went all right. Hard to say. Randy doesn't make many facial expressions, does he?"

The receptionist burst into laughter. "You hit the nail on the head. Randy is a very even-keel sort of guy. He likes to observe people's actions and responses. But don't worry, I'll put in a good word for you."

I felt kind of bad after that because I wasn't going to accept the job even if they did decide to pick me. But I had to keep up appearances if I wanted her to confide in me. Carla seemed nice, and I hoped that this whole thing would be worth taking advantage of that kindess. "Thanks, I really appreciate that." My eyes drifted to the entrance as if I were planning to leave. I opened my mouth to say something then pretended to hold back.

Carla picked up on my suggestive body language immediately. She checked the closed door behind her that separated the alcove from the rest of the office. "Call me crazy, but I get the feeling that you want to ask me something." She pushed aside the keyboard and rested both elbows on her desk. "Come on, don't be shy."

"Well, it's just that . . . I don't know, I feel kind of weird asking this . . . but that guy that . . . well, he died under suspicious circumstances. Gavin something or other."

"Ah, yes, Gavin Oliver," she replied, nodding as if everything made sense now. "Rest his soul. He was an interesting man. But I'm not sure why you're asking about him."

I squirmed, shifting from leg to leg. "I had this crazy idea on my drive here this morning. You don't suppose that it had anything to do with his job, do you? Like have the cops been around investigating anyone? I'd hate to leave my parent's restaurant and find myself working with a murderer." It was a farfetched notion, but I was hoping I could appeal to the speculatory side of her. Some of the best women I know speculate; our intuition calls for it.

She leaned forward; her voice hushed. "Well, there was

this super-handsome detective poking around. He asked to talk to some of Gavin's coworkers, and I overheard he wanted to know if anyone would benefit from Gavin being out of the picture."

My nostrils flared involuntarily as I digested the words "super-handsome detective." That was *my* super-handsome detective, thank you very much. But I urged myself to not be petty, and I put on my big-girl panties. This wasn't the time to get unnecessarily jealous. "Oh really? And is there anyone who would benefit from Gavin being gone?"

Carla snorted. "Um, hello, yes. Most everyone he works with benefits from him being gone. Gavin was a power player. He had all the best clients, and really well-to-do businessmen in the city relied on Gavin for his financial expertise."

It was a hard thing to imagine, having met Gavin in person. But that was an isolated event, and I truly didn't know anything about his character. "Randy mentioned that Gavin's clients would be distributed among established employees. So none of Gavin's clients would go to anyone new?"

"Oh no, you'll learn that if you get the job. His clients are being split up among the more veteran advisors. The newbies would get either low-end clients that wouldn't harm the company if they decided to leave or new clients they could start a fresh relationship with."

"Ah okay, that makes sense. So who's the most veteran advisor that got Gavin's biggest-name clients? He's got to be the guy to look out for around here."

"That would be Daniel Hill. From what I heard around the office, Daniel will be getting close to seventy-five perfect of Gavin's portfolio."

My stomach clenched. "Daniel Hill? He doesn't happen to be a really tall guy with blond hair, does he?"

Carla's eyes widened. "Wow, you guessed it. Do you know him?"

Goose bumps formed on my arms and legs. "Yeah, you could say something like that."

CHAPTER 22

I was hyped. This could be the break in the case that we needed. Not only was Dan lacking the customary sadness that would come with the loss of a bandmate and friend, but he'd fought over a woman with him shortly before Gavin's untimely demise and *now*, I also knew he had something to gain financially by cutting Gavin out of the picture.

In a rush, I'd excused myself from Carla, creating a fib about not realizing the time and being late for my shift. In reality, I had until about eleven o'clock because I'd switched shifts with Nancy. Not that I was happy about working until nine on a Friday night, but sometimes, you had to take one for the team.

It was only five after ten, and if I played my cards right, I could sneak into the bookstore for about fifteen minutes. I called Megan on my way to Crocker Park. She would be half asleep, but I had to tell her my thoughts.

With a frog in her throat, she answered the phone. "Hello?"

"Megan. You are never going to guess what happened!"

She yawned. "It better be something good, because you're interrupting my beauty sleep."

"Dan the drummer is Gavin's coworker, and he got a huge chunk of Gavin's clients. Between that and the Brandi thing, I think this is our guy. It has to be. He snuck over to Gavin's apartment, probably not expecting a woman to be there. He would know to be careful with the door since he went over there all the time. No one would be the wiser. I'm telling you this is it."

"Calm down, Lana. I haven't heard you this hyper since that one time you drank an entire pot of coffee in under two hours. Where are you now?" She was beginning to sound more awake.

"I'm heading to Barnes & Noble for a quick stroll through the stacks. I need to clear my mind, sniff some paper."

"Of course."

"Don't you agree? All the pieces are starting to add up." I inhaled deeply. "Now we have to get some concrete evidence on his whereabouts that night. You know, see if we can place him at the scene of the crime somehow."

"Lana, he's a pretty big guy. Don't you think he'd make some noise and that neighbor chick Pamela would hear the stomping? I doubt we have a twinkle toes on our hands. He seemed pretty clunky to me."

"Maybe. I don't know. I still think she fell asleep and didn't fully comprehend what was going on above her. Then she woke up after the fact, not realizing that a fight had taken place. Plus, if she was in her bedroom, she may not have heard things as clearly since it all went down in the living room."

"Okay, true. But if this guy was really someone to consider, wouldn't you think Adam would have this information and be working that angle?"

I groaned. "We have no idea what Adam is thinking or who he is looking into. You know he keeps all his work stuff close to his chest. I'd be the last one he'd tell about a possible lead."

"Either way, I think we should take a day to think on it. I can't shake that somehow Brandi is involved. And we haven't sorted out what the deal is between her and Rina. There are still too many loose ends."

I huffed into the phone. "Are you kidding me? You're starting to sound like me. How have the roles reversed?"

"Full moon?"

"Ugh, whatever. I have a good theory."

"Hey, I agree with you. The scenario has a lot of potential. But isn't it you that's always going on about how we have to eliminate all other possibilities?"

"I guess."

"Okay, so let's do that. I'm in the process of stalking Brandi's movements via her social media. I'm hoping she has some nights out planned for the weekend. Wherever she goes, we'll be there."

"All right. Don't forget I have to work until nine tonight."

"I'll be working tonight too. Let's keep our fingers crossed that Brandi chooses tomorrow evening to paint the town red. In the meantime, take some deep breaths, chill on the coffee, and go sniff some books. I'll text you later."

In the time we were wrapping up the call, I had parked at a metered spot a few storefronts away from the bookstore. Even after Megan's less-than-thrilled reaction, I felt good about the information I'd learned today and I wasn't going to let anyone rain on my parade.

I put a few quarters into the meter and checked the time on my cell phone. I needed to get to the bookstore, pronto. After all, those pages weren't going to sniff themselves.

Asia Village was in full swing when I arrived. It wasn't often that I showed up to work this late, so I wasn't used to seeing the parking lot packed with cars and shoppers already zipping around.

Nancy was sitting at the hostess booth and greeted me with a warm smile as I walked in. "Good morning, Lana. How was your doctor's appointment today?"

There were a few tables occupied and everyone had plates in front of them. They appeared content and enjoying themselves over an early lunch.

"Everything checked out good." I avoided eye contact with her as I said it. Lying to loved ones never provided me any enjoyment, but no one questioned or denied a doctor's appointment as a quick reason to switch a shift. I can't tell you how many times I'd been to the "doctor" in the past year. The upsetting part is that I probably was due for a checkup at this point.

"Nothing special happened. The Matrons missed you this morning and asked if you were sick. I let them know you had gone to have a checkup. Also, your sister was here looking for you."

I doubted the Matrons bought that story. Knowing me and my antics better than most, they probably knew that I was up to something. In a way, I was relieved it was Friday, hoping that by Monday they would forget to question me.

I was curious about Anna May though. That was two times in one week that my sister had stopped by on her way to work. "Did Anna May say what she wanted?"

Nancy shook her head. "No, she said she would try and stop by again later."

I double-checked my phone for missed calls, but there were none. I wondered to myself why she'd come in to the restaurant but not call me. "I'll be back; I'm going to put my things in the office."

"Lana, do you think your doctor is a handsome man?"

I stopped in mid-step. "My doctor is a woman, why do you ask?"

She chuckled to herself. "Because you are so dressed up today. I am thinking maybe you like your doctor."

Blushing, I said, "Oh no, nothing like that. I haven't done laundry all week and didn't have much to wear. I figured, why not dress up?" I could have smacked myself for forgetting my outfit. That little time at the bookstore could have been used to run home and change.

Thankfully Nancy bought my laundry lie. It was a well-known fact that I could be quite irresponsible when it came to adult activities. That included keeping up with laundry. "Lana, it is very important for a woman your age to take care of herself and to keep a nice house. You do not want your boyfriend to think you would not make a good wife."

If it was any one of my mother's other friends giving me this advice, I might force a smile and agree to spare the argument. But since it was Nancy, I said, "Any husband of mine is going to have to do his own laundry."

Nancy threw her head back and laughed. She clasped her hands together. "Oh Lana, you have such a strong mind. Much like Kimmy. I tell Peter all the time, he will be very busy if he marries her."

We shared a laugh before I went to drop off my purse and coat. I waved hello to Peter as I passed through. I checked my voice mail to see if I had any missed calls on the work line, maybe even something from Anna May, but again there was nothing. I assumed it wasn't an emergency and decided not to worry about it for the time being. She knew where to find me.

While Nancy took her lunch break, I got into the swing of things, introducing myself to the existing tables, offering to get them anything they needed. The time moved quickly as customers came in and out through the early afternoon.

After lunch was over, and I'd snuck a teriyaki stick in between serving tables, Kimmy stopped by. She poked her head through the kitchen doors. Peter had his back to both of us, so he didn't know she was there. "Nancy told me I could come back here." Her loose ponytail wobbled as she slithered into the kitchen.

Peter was generally a calm person and nothing much seemed to startle him, but I swear I saw his hand jerk up from the grill when he heard Kimmy's voice. "Whoa, hey."

She rolled her eyes. "Don't worry, I'm here to see Lana."

With a shrug of his shoulders, he turned back to focus on the teriyaki skewers that were still browning.

"Come on," I said, waving her over. "Let's go into my office."

Once the door was shut, I asked, "What the heck was that about?"

Kimmy blew a raspberry. "Oh, it's no big. Mr. Cranky Pants and I got into an argument because he fell asleep during the movie we were watching last night and have been trying to watch since Monday. It's the third time this week."

"Sounds like you guys need to pick a different movie."

She pursed her lips. "Yeah, well, I'm sick of this. He is so tired all the time and I'm starting to feel neglected. Can you give him some days off?"

"I would, but he asked me if he could work more because he has something he wants to buy."

Kimmy shimmied to the edge of her seat. "Do you think it's something for me?"

"He didn't mention anything to me. You know he is a man of few words."

She crossed her arms over her chest and tilted her head back. "Well on the off chance it's for me, then I suppose I can cut him some slack."

"Is that why you came by?"

She unfolded her arms and crossed her legs. Kimmy was always a little high-strung but today she seemed a little extra amped up. Between the two of us, I was beginning to think that maybe Megan was right. It was a full moon. "Actually, no. I came by to talk to you about the case. I tried to go and talk with Rina, and she totally blew me off. Like, can you believe it? Me."

I rolled my eyes. "Join the club, sister."

"Whatever is going on with her is . . . well I don't even know. But I'm thinking if we want our girl back to normal, we've got to clear her name and get this whole nasty business with Gavin squared away. She's going to push away everyone that cares about her."

I decided to tell Kimmy about the information I'd learned earlier on my fake interview.

"Aw man, you got to go undercover for an interview? I want to do that."

"You're missing the point."

"I know, I know. Okay, sorry. I can't say I'm not entirely surprised. The guy was kind of slimy and clearly he could care less that Gavin was no longer among the living." She flopped backward in the chair. "Man, what a jerk, huh? Imagine that being your best friend."

I rested my forehead in my hand. "I'd rather not."

"What now then? We gotta corner this guy and get him to say something incriminating. Good thing I got his phone number." More quietly, she said, "Do you think I should go on an undercover date?"

"Definitely not. If he is the one who did it, you don't want to be alone with him. Trust me." I gave my friend a cautious glance. I knew from previous experience it was not the best idea to put yourself in the lion's den.

"Okay, well point me in a direction here, Lee. Give me something to do."

"Lay low for a little bit. Megan is working on getting us a casual run-in with that Brandi woman we threw out of here.

We need to figure out what her connection is with Rina before we go chasing any other leads."

Kimmy rose from her seat, pounding her fist into her other palm. "Right. Good plan. I'll get my stilettos ready."

CHAPTER 23

Five o'clock rolled around at an alarming speed for a Friday. Normally the day dragged on and when I hightailed my way out of the restaurant ready to start the weekend, I'd often felt like I'd lived eight lifetimes since nine that morning.

Nancy and Peter said their goodbyes as they headed out, and though I wished that I was going with them, I was hopeful that the rest of the evening would go just as fast. Lou, our evening chef, took over the kitchen, and Vanessa Wen came bouncing in to handle the hostess area and wait a majority of the tables. Unless there was a dinner rush, I planned to hide away in my office and maybe get some phone time in with Adam. We'd barely talked all week and I was beginning to miss him terribly.

At six thirty, I started to get hungry again, and still being on a shrimp kick, asked Lou if he would grill me up some shrimp teriyaki to go with a bowl of white rice.

Lou was a friend of my mother's from quite a ways back.

They met many years ago when Thistledown was only a racetrack versus the racino it was known as today. Obviously, being two of the few Asians in the area, they had gravitated toward one another during a race where they'd bet on the same winning horse.

Lou was a nice enough man. He used too much hair product and his goofy demeanor bordered on toxic positivity, but he was growing on me as time went on. I never liked to ask people their age because it felt rude and was none of my business, but I guessed him to be somewhere in his late forties, early fifties. He reminded me of Chow Yun-Fat with his apple cheeks and laugh lines. As far I knew he'd always been single and didn't have any children. If he'd ever been married, he never spoke of it.

To be honest, I was surprised that my matchmaker of a mother and her friends never tried setting him up with someone. If there was anybody who wanted to see everyone paired up, it was Betty Lee and my gang of "aunties."

I observed Lou as he grilled my shrimp and vegetables. I emphasized that I wanted extra Chinese water spinach and to take it easy on the ginger. My stomach growled audibly as I watched the shrimp turn a nice shade of pink, and I wondered if I should have some noodles instead. Before I could change my mind, I helped myself to a giant bowl of jasmine rice out of the rice cooker.

Lou finished sautéing my food and with a flourish of his metal spatula, toppling the steaming shrimp and vegetables over my rice. I started to salivate. "Thank you. I'll be in my office if anyone needs me."

Lou gave me his signature salute with his spatula. "Anytime, boss. Enjoy your dinner."

I couldn't get to my office fast enough. Clearing off my desk, I made some room for my bowl and dug around in my purse for my cell phone. Maybe I'd take a few bites before calling Adam.

With my chopsticks, I plucked out a crisp snap pea that had been grilled to perfection. I had to say that though I favored Peter's style of cooking, Lou's was beginning to catch up, and I tacked on points for his growing ability to add the perfect amount of teriyaki sauce to this classic dish. He knew I was a sauce enthusiast, and I always asked for an extra ladle's worth. But today, I hadn't needed to mention it.

I was appreciating a finely tenderized piece of shrimp when my office door swung over so hard that it smacked into the guest chair, threatening to tip it over. It teetered on its metal leg before settling back into place.

My sister was standing in front of me, her arm stretched out still, fire in her eyes. If she didn't calm down, smoke might start drifting from her ears. "Lane Lee. What. The. Hell."

A shrimp tail was sticking out of my mouth. I quickly inhaled it and covered my mouth with my hand. "Excuse me?"

"What the hell were you thinking by starting another rumor about me? It got back to Mom and she asked me why I'm hiding my new boyfriend from her. She wants to meet this new guy right away."

I placed my chopsticks on the rim of the bowl. "Why didn't you tell her the truth? I thought we agreed it was probably her that couldn't keep her mouth shut."

Anna May closed the door, gently this time, and sat down

on the edge of the visitor's chair. "Because I had already convinced Mom that Henry and I were never actually dating."

I almost choked on my shrimp. "And she believed you? That makes no sense. You've said those words to her before. That you two were dating and not to tell anyone."

Anna May covered her eyes with her hands. "I made up a story about how she misunderstood me and that we were only thinking about dating but then I found out he was still married so I told him no. She believes that we were friends and nothing else. We've never kissed in front of them or anything. We don't even hold hands."

I cocked my head at her. "That is the lamest thing I've ever heard. Who taught you how to lie?"

My sister scowled at me. "Sorry, I guess I should have learned from the master."

"Don't even." I held up a finger. "Today is not the day, big sister. I've got my own problems to contend with."

"Well, here's another one for you. You need to fix this. Mom knows you're the one who told the Matrons, and so she thinks you know something she doesn't."

"Why hasn't she asked me then?"

"Because she thinks you were confiding in the Matrons and doesn't want to put them on blast. How am I supposed to know? This is your world, not mine."

"You know, I've said it before, if you didn't act so high and mighty all the time, you wouldn't have these problems."

Her mouth clenched.

"Why can't you tell Mom it's not true? I misspoke. The end."

"Don't you think I tried that first? She doesn't believe me."

"Ugh, well geez, I'm sorry. How was I supposed to know that it would turn into this? I was only trying to help."

Anna May stood abruptly. "I have to go. Henry is waiting for me. We have some things to discuss. I'm telling him today that if he doesn't speed things up with his divorce, then I am jumping ship. I am no man's side piece."

"I'm surprised you know that phrase."

"Cute, Lana. Real cute." She whipped open the door. "Fix this. Tell someone, somewhere that you got it wrong. I am a free agent. There are no secret boyfriends and I'm not involved in any affairs."

Before I could respond, she slammed the door, rattling the wall so hard that my college diploma fell off the wall.

Despite the interruption from Anna May, I was able to get a little bit of phone time in with Adam before returning to the dining area. We planned to meet at the Zodiac when I got off work. The news perked me up because the last time I'd seen him face-to-face was Sunday.

Vanessa needed a break so she could have some dinner. That was a nice perk of the job—free meals. Every employee at Ho-Lee Noodle House ate well.

I manned the hostess station while she was gone. The restaurant was practically empty except for a middle-aged couple that had strolled in a little before Vanessa went on break. Since there weren't any other customers, they'd already gotten their food and were halfway through their meal.

Once I'd checked on their tea and made sure they had all that they needed, I poked my head out into the plaza to see what was going on. Every once in a while, we had a slow

Friday night—which is why we'd chosen it as our speed dat-ing night that week. But this was a little ridiculous. Where the heck was everyone?

Asia Village was mostly quiet. I saw a few shoppers sprin-kled throughout the plaza, but the only place that seemed to have any activity was the Bamboo Lounge. I couldn't see into the lounge because their storefront was tinted glass, but I heard the commotion when the doors opened as someone exited.

My only customers were ready for their bill, and I cashed them out, wishing them a wonderful weekend. When they headed out into the plaza, I noticed they went left, and I sprinted for the door to watch where they were going. Sure enough, I saw them opening the door to the Bamboo Lounge.

Man, was Penny taking all our customers tonight or what? Something had to be going on over there.

The rest of the night was quiet, and so with nothing else to do, Vanessa and I cleaned up the dining area together. I let her go half an hour early and told Lou he could start cleaning the kitchen since it seemed we weren't going to have any more customers.

When Lou was finished, I sent him on his way and locked up the restaurant, deciding to head over to the Bam-boo Lounge to see what all the commotion was about. When I opened the door, I was blasted with off-key sing-ing. A young woman was on stage attempting to sing the Dolly Parton classic, *I Will Always Love You*, à la Whitney Houston.

My shoulders jerked with the epic miss of each high note as I slunk over to the bar where I'd spotted Penny Cho.

She gave me a wink as I leaned against the counter.

"Okay, when did you add American music to the playlist, and what the heck are you giving away tonight?"

Penny beamed. "Isn't it great? Well, not this," she laughed. "Someone needs to tell this woman she's tone deaf. But I added some American stuff this past week and tonight is my first singing competition."

"Singing competition?" I asked. "How come I haven't heard about this?"

"Well, Miss Busy Pants, if you came to the board meetings, you would know. Plus, I put out flyers. Are you living in another dimension?"

"Apparently. I had no idea. I was trying to find out where all my customers were tonight. This is the slowest Friday night I've seen in a long time."

"I would have brought it up when you came in on Tuesday, but with Rina being around, well—"

"What do you mean?"

Penny ran a hand through her hair. "I figured it was some kind of intervention."

"Am I that obvious?"

She smirked. "Kinda, yeah. I'm not disagreeing with it; that girl needs help. Something is definitely up with her."

"Why do you say that?"

Penny glanced over her shoulder as if she were worried someone might overhear us. Then she leaned over the bar, gesturing for me to come closer. "Well, you know I'm here later than everyone else since we have extended hours."

"Yeah . . . and?"

"I was locking up the doors around eleven or so, and I happened to see Rina the night of the speed dating event. Some woman met her outside her shop, handed her something, the two women yelled at each other, Rina shoved her a little bit, and then the woman stormed off."

The hairs on my neck stood up. "What did this woman look like?"

"Tall, long dark hair, short skirt, super-long legs . . . busty. And that's me putting it lightly."

Dread washed over me. That described Brandi Fenton. But what were they doing at the plaza meeting in secret? And how? I tried to flesh out the scenario in my head, but I couldn't. Rina and Gavin had left earlier in the night. That meant that Rina would have had to come back to the plaza hours after they'd already left. And where had Gavin been?

"Lana, are you listening to me?"

"Huh? Sorry. What did you say?"

"I said that I was beginning to think maybe she's into something weird, like is she taking drugs or something? I assumed that's why you and Kimmy brought her here, and then when I saw her storm out . . ."

I almost burst into laughter, but I held it in. "No, nothing like that."

"That's a relief. So then what's going on with her?"

My head was elsewhere, and I remembered I needed to get to the Zodiac.

Penny watched me intently, waiting for answer.

I shrugged. "I don't know. That's what I'm trying to figure out."

CHAPTER 24

I'd hurriedly said goodbye to Penny and left her in a state of bewilderment. I didn't have a lot of time to worry about what was running through her mind because I was too pre-occupied with what was going on in my own.

When I pulled into the parking lot of the Zodiac ten minutes later, I scouted the darkened area for Adam's car. I didn't see it. "Good," I whispered to myself. That meant I had some time to talk to Megan about this new discovery before he arrived.

The bar was packed with people and I felt out of place, still in my dress clothes. But hey, it wouldn't be the first time I'd walked into this place wearing something that didn't match the environment.

I found Megan behind the bar moving swiftly around the bartenders as they rushed to get everyone served. I stepped up to my usual spot and signaled her. It took her a minute to notice me, but once she did, she glided over and turned her ear in my direction. "What's up?"

"I need to talk to you. It's important."

"Okay, give me a minute. Meet me in the bathroom."

I gave her a thumbs-up and headed for the ladies' restroom.

A blonde and a brunette were in front of the mirrors, giggling and reapplying lipstick. I could feel their carefree attitudes wash over me, and I envied them. Just a simple girls' night out. The recent dynamics of my outings weren't so laissez-faire.

Megan barreled into the bathroom, startling the other women. The blonde nudged the brunette and they scurried out, perhaps sensing some tension. Megan smiled politely to them as they exited.

"What's up?" Megan asked, her tone hyper. "I need to get back out there. No clue what the heck is going on tonight, but we are slammed."

"That is the exact opposite of my night."

"Is something wrong?" She stood in front of the mirror and began readjusting her ponytail.

I started to tell her what Penny had told me about seeing Rina.

She held a bobby pin in between her lips and attempted to respond without dropping it. "This is coming off worse by the minute. Don't you think? This makes it two times that she met up with Brandi."

"I know. And the scenarios I've come up with aren't good."

"Like what?" Megan took the bobby pin from her mouth and secured the loose hairs below her ponytail.

"What if—and this is a big if—but what if this whole thing was staged somehow?"

Megan turned to face me, leaning against the sink. "Like

the whole idea they knew each other already and plotted to kill this guy?"

"I know, it sounds crazy and total conspiracy driven, but Brandi's reaction to seeing Gavin with another woman was a bit dramatic."

"I thought you wanted to stay in line with Rina being innocent."

"I did." I shook my head. "I do. It's . . . I don't know how to explain this."

"Do you think it's possible that Rina was meeting someone else, and the description just so happens to match Brandi's? Penny could have seen it wrong. I mean, what about Rina even says she'd be someone interested in drugs. It's way off base."

"I agree. I almost laughed in her face. Not a bone in my body thinks the interaction had anything to do with drugs. I'm worried it's something to do with Gavin."

"I think all we can do at this point is stick to our plan. I hadn't gotten a chance to tell you yet, but after combing through Brandi's social media—and man is that girl stuck on herself—I noticed that she always heads down to the Flats on Saturday nights. She rotates between Punch Bowl Social, The Big Bang Dueling Piano Bar, or Shooters."

"So are we going to have to hit up all three?"

"I'm thinking we wait a little while into the evening, say ten-ish, and we'll see if she posts her location. If she does, then we'll head there. If by eleven we don't see anything, we're going to have to take a chance and stop in each one."

"I hope that she actually goes out tomorrow night. If she decides to randomly stay home, then this will all be for nothing."

"Girlfriend, you and me both. Now I have to get back out there. Are you staying for a bit?"

"Yeah, Adam is meeting me here."

"Cool, I'll see you out there."

Alone in the bathroom, I did an assessment of my own appearance, touching up my makeup and smoothing my hair down. More than anything, I wanted to discuss all of this with Adam. As a detective, he gave me some valuable perspective into things that I might be viewing completely out of whack. But, especially with this being his case, there wasn't anything he could say. Besides, he'd told me to keep my sleuthing under wraps.

Satisfied with my touch-ups, I headed back out to the bar, and the two women who'd been in the bathroom earlier were the first people I saw when I stepped out. They were holding billiard sticks and laughing hysterically, both buckled over and clutching their stomachs. It made me consider that maybe I needed to take a page from their script and try to have some fun tonight.

Five minutes later, Adam showed up and I was relieved to see he was also dressed up. Granted, he had removed his tie, undone the top two buttons, and rolled up the sleeves, but at least I didn't have to feel so mismatched.

He kissed me on the cheek and massaged my shoulders. "You look like you had a rough day."

"Word on the street is that I'm pretty transparent these days," I said, thinking about Penny's comment earlier that night.

"It's written all over your face."

He took the empty stool to my left and kept a protective hand on my thigh. "I know you're probably stressed about Rina's situation. But is anything else going on?"

While we waited for his beer, I told him about the situation with my sister.

He rubbed the side of his neck. "This may not be a popular opinion, but your sister probably shouldn't have gotten involved with him. I see this stuff happen at the station all the time. These guys have troubled marriages, some from the job, and some from other situations. And instead of nipping it in the bud, they drag things out."

"Do you think it's because there's still hope that things will work out?" I hadn't said so to Anna May, but I feared that was the real reason Henry hadn't moved forward with terminating his marriage.

"Sometimes. But I also think sometimes it benefits both parties not to make any move. Insurance is involved, pensions, 401Ks, kids. It gets messy."

"What do you think about Henry's situation?"

Megan returned with Adam's beer, slid it across the bar, and skuttled off.

He took a long sip before answering. "From what I can see, he's a solid guy. I think he genuinely cares for your sister. But if what he's saying is true and he's stalling because he's worried about what his soon-to-be ex-wife will do, well then Anna May has a bumpy ride ahead of her. She's going to need to think long and hard about if she wants to go through that with him. These things can take two or more years depending on assets and if both parties can come to an agreement."

I let out a deep breath. "I hope she's thought about those things. We don't talk like that . . . the whole girl-gab thing. I wish we did sometimes."

He squeezed my leg. "You have Megan for that. And don't forget Kimmy."

"I know."

"So is that the big kerfuffle? Or is there more?"

My foot tapped on the metal rest and I wondered if I should tell him about what Penny saw after all.

He sensed that I was holding back, set down his beer bottle, and leaned in closer. "You can tell me anything. You know that."

"Even if it's about Rina?"

"You can tell me, but I may not be able to respond depending on what you're about to say."

"It's hearsay," I replied.

"Okay . . ."

"What if I told you that Brandi Fenton, Gavin's ex-girlfriend or whatever she was to him, might have an association with Rina? Would you think anything strange about that?"

He seemed to stiffen. "Considering how things played out that evening, I would give it some attention, yes. Especially if one or more parties claimed to have no previous affiliation."

The look he gave me was pointed, and my stomach sank. Without saying it directly, he was telling that either Brandi, Rina, or both had already claimed they didn't know each other.

Adam sipped his beer and we sat in silence for a few minutes.

I could sense him watching me out the corner of my eye. "Are there any other hypotheticals you want to run past me?" he asked.

I was afraid to say more. Maybe I didn't want to know. It was already going to be hard enough to face Rina after everything I'd compiled up to this point. I thought over my theories about Dan the drummer and how certain I'd been only a day before that he was somehow behind this whole thing. Was I really willing to drop that notion and replace it with this one? But what was Rina hiding, and why had she been meeting with Brandi, at least once when I'd seen them with my own eyes? And why did it need to be a secret? Was she worried that if she confided in me I would run and blab to Adam? Was there perhaps something else she was hiding that she was afraid would come out as a result of this? If so, then what could that possibly be? I felt myself becoming more and more agitated as each question produced yet another.

Adam nudged me with his shoulder. "Hey, space cadet, why don't we get some cheesy fries and forget about all this nonsense? Cheesy fries always cheer you up."

"In that case, maybe order two plates."

CHAPTER 25

By the time I woke up Saturday morning, Adam had already left. I reached for his pillow and hugged it close to my body. It smelled like his cologne. As I tried to lose myself in the hints of sandalwood that he'd left behind, I felt Kikko's fur bristle against my leg. I heard her snort and there was a ruffling of blankets. Next came the paw pressing awkwardly on my intestines as she navigated herself toward my head. A second later, I felt her snuffle in my ear and lick my cheek. My ploy to pretend like I was still sleeping hadn't worked.

When I opened my eye, I saw her bulging eyes staring back at me. She pawed at my face. "Okay, okay. Tinkle time. I got the message."

In sweatpants and slip-on boots, and with a hoodie pulled over my head and falling over my eyes, I trudged outside into the cold morning air. Kikko's buffalo-plaid winter coat shimmied as she wiggled her body back and forth along the same foot of grass.

I watched a woman scraping frost off her car windows.

Winter was around the corner. The thought of it made me groan so loud that Kikko paused to give me what I interpreted as a dirty look. I had broken her concentration.

Back inside, I prepped my morning coffee, mindful of the noise I was making so as not to disturb my sleeping roommate. I'd heard her come in the night before at close to four in the morning.

I sat at the kitchen table in a daze, waiting for my coffee to cool down, and thought about what I was going to do about Anna May. In the grand scheme of things, her dating issues were not catastrophic. But it was weighing on me, and perhaps I needed a distraction from the other issues I was facing.

I'd never gotten the chance to visit Modern Scroll throughout the week as I'd hoped. And if I was being honest with myself, I was feeling a little bit of guilt for visiting Barnes & Noble instead of supporting my friend, Cindy Kwan's business. I know that I myself would feel slighted if she chose to head out to P.F. Chang's instead of supporting Ho-Lee Noodle House. That's not to say I expected everyone to eat at my family's restaurant one hundred percent of the time, but it was nice to know that the ones around you made the effort.

It also seemed like the best place to drop a rumor. I'd considered doing my dirty work at Asian Accents, the plaza's salon—aka Rumor Headquarters—but I feared running into the Mahjong Matrons and getting myself into another bind.

With the cogs in my brain starting to turn, I got dressed, left a note for Megan in case she woke up before I got back, and made my way to Asia Village. It was time to plant a new seed.

* * *

I nabbed a parking spot close to the entrance and scurried inside. The brisk winds of November were picking up, and I dreaded my night out in advance. The wind downtown could become quite strong in the winter months. This was my favorite time to hibernate, and I would be much more content nestled under a chenille throw blanket sipping coffee with a good book in my hands. Or you know, on a beach in Mexico with my pineapple drink. Either way, I wasn't too excited about the coming evening, especially since we potentially had to barhop.

Inside the plaza, my focus was directed on Ho-Lee Noodle House since I didn't want to run into anyone from the restaurant. Anna May was supposed to be there right now helping out Nancy, and I didn't want to have words with my older sister.

Eyes on my family's restaurant, I turned around and bumped into someone who was standing behind me. When I looked to see who I would direct my apology to, I realized it was my mother. And my grandmother was standing behind her, craning her neck to observe Wild Sage. She and Mr. Zhang had a cute little romance together. Most of their interactions involved doing laps around the plaza and an occasional game of mahjong. It ruffled my mother's feathers when I referred to him as my grandmother's boyfriend. I didn't have a lot of proof that they were anything more than friends—and frankly, I didn't want any; it was my grandmother, after all. But I did enjoy seeing her share company with a respectable man like Mr. Zhang.

While I was observing my grandmother, my mother

smiled with amusement at catching me off guard. "I am always telling you to watch where you are going."

"Sorry, Mom, I thought I saw someone—"

"You are not fooling me. You do not want to work today, and you know if Anna May sees you then she will ask you to help."

"You know me so well." If that's what she thought, then I was more than okay with that.

"I haven't talked to Anna May since last Sunday. Have you?" I was trying to bait my mother into saying something about the rumors that were spreading throughout the plaza.

But all she said was, "I called her one time. That is all. Nothing for you to think about."

I raised an eyebrow at my mother. "What do you mean?"

"Nothing, nothing. Where are you going?"

"Oh, right, the bookstore. Going to see Cindy."

"Okay, you can go. A-ma wants to visit Mr. Zhang before we go home. We came to buy some food to cook dinner tonight." She held up a brown bag with a handle from the plaza's grocery store. "Do you want to come eat dinner with us later? A-ma is cooking Taiwanese special."

By that, I knew my mother meant my grandmother was making lu rou fan, which in American terms is braised pork over rice. It was one of the island's favorite comfort dishes and happened to be one of my favorites as well. My grandmother knew I wasn't a fan of pork belly—which could be listed among my oddities as an Asian person—but she was well aware that I loved the sauce it produced and the hard-boiled eggs that soaked in all the flavors of star anise, cinnamon, and cloves. The sauce had a touch of sweetened tang to it, and I loved spooning it over my rice.

"I have plans tonight, Mom. Otherwise, I would. It's been a long time since I've had A-ma's cooking."

"Okay, if you change your mind, come over."

My grandmother smiled at me from behind my mother and I said goodbye to them as they made their way over to Wild Sage. Thankfully in that time, Anna May hadn't wandered out of the restaurant to find us all standing around.

I made a beeline for the bookshop so I wouldn't be stopped again. I noticed that Rina was lounging by the entrance of her store, focused on her nail or maybe something on her finger. I shifted myself closer to the wall of the bookshop, hoping she wouldn't see me. And then it occurred to me that I didn't know why I was trying to avoid her. Clearly, the new information from Penny was clouding my judgment. I couldn't explain to myself why Penny's information had made me feel so wary after already seeing Rina meet up with Brandi at the Islander, but strangely it did. Maybe because it meant it wasn't a one-off—there was some kind of relationship there.

Pulling on the handle of Modern Scroll's door, I slipped inside and breathed, relieved at having not been discovered, catching a few weird glances from people lingering around the doors. I forced a smiled and zipped over to the mystery section.

Even though I had really come to plant fresh gossip with Cindy, it wasn't going to hurt anything if I took a few minutes to peruse the shelves of my favorite genre. An added bonus, it would appear more natural versus me just coming in to flap my gums. I wasn't known for spreading information. If anything, I was usually the one hiding something.

I slid my index finger across the spines of the alphabetized paperbacks and plucked a Diane Kelly novel from the shelf. I had plowed through her Tara Holloway novels and was excited to find a newer series about flipping houses. I tucked it under my arm and kept skimming.

After I selected a few more books, I felt satisfied with my choices and headed up to the cash register to stand in line. Two customers were in front of me and the woman at the counter was especially chatty, so I had time to check my cell phone.

There was a text from Kimmy that said she'd spotted me while I was talking to my mother and for me to stop by China Cinema and Song before I headed out. I would have been a little surprised that she hadn't yelled for me or chased me down, but I knew oftentimes she tried to avoid interaction with my mother. My mother was a lot stricter than hers and it wasn't unusual for my mom to give her a lecture about her boisterous behavior.

It was finally my turn to check out and Cindy Kwan smiled with enthusiasm when she realized I was her next customer. "Lana Lee! I feel like I haven't seen you in ages. Here I was worried you'd given in to the box stores and left me hanging."

I let out a nervous laugh. "I would never."

She gazed over my selections. "You and these murder mysteries. Do you ever read anything else? When's the last time you read a love story?"

"You know I need the intrigue."

"Next time you're here, I'll set you up with some romantic suspense novels. I know the perfect ones." She slid my books closer to her and flipped them over to scan the bar codes.

"I think I have all the romantic suspense I handle." I added an exaggerated sigh.

Cindy set my Diane Kelly book down and adjusted her glasses. "Oh? In a good way or a bad way? I hope you're not having any problems with Adam . . ."

She was *almost* too easy a target to plant my fake information. And I *almost* felt guilty. Keyword: almost.

"No, nothing like that," I replied. "Adam and I are fine. It's this thing with my sister."

Cindy nodded with understanding. "Oh, yup. I heard it too. Dating a married man is not a good look around here. Then this obvious cover-up story comes floating around from the Matrons that she's seeing some mystery man? Yeah right. Then where has he been?"

My throat felt tight. It hadn't occurred to me that people might think the second rumor was a cover-up for the first. Here I was teasing my sister about her lying skills, when mine were clearly faltering more than I was aware of. "But she hasn't been dating a married man. I'd know something like that. I'm her sister."

The bookshop owner crinkled her nose, which caused her to readjust her glasses again. "So what's the real story then? I promise I won't tell."

This was the second time in as many days where I had to hold back laughing in someone's face. "The truth is, she's dating a considerably older man. And I think she's nervous to bring him around because she doesn't know if things are going to work out with him."

Cindy leaned in closer. "Really. How old?"

My brain was grabbing at straws. "Maybe twenty-five years older." After it came out of my mouth, I winced. Was this the best route to take the rumor? It would get back to my mother after all, and I started to worry if I was, once again, making things worse.

"Interesting. I wouldn't have pegged your sister as the type."

I started to get mad about the insinuation. "And what is that supposed to mean?"

Cindy appeared taken aback and held her hands up in defense. "Chill, Lana. I didn't mean anything bad by that. I only meant that I didn't think she'd date a man so much her senior because I know she wants to have a couple of kids. Usually men that age don't want to start from scratch."

"Oh. Right. Yeah . . . sorry."

"Geez, Lana. I heard there's a Zen store that might be opening up here in the next few months. Maybe you need to swing through and get yourself some calming stones or balance your chi. Something. You're so tense all the time."

Cindy's comment made me feel defensive all over again. I was as calm as I could be considering everything going on, but there wasn't any point in explaining to her what the real cause for my upset was.

"How come I haven't heard about this new shop that might be opening up?"

"You've missed like three board meetings."

"You're not the first one to comment on that. Things have been busy. What else have I missed?"

Cindy placed my books into a paper bag "Not too much. You know with Yi's Tea and Bakery still closed up it's been a point of contention for everyone. We want to know what the heck is going on. The rent is still being paid on it, so Ian hasn't put any pressure on Shirley Yi to do anything right away."

"How the heck does she have the money to keep it running without bringing in any cash?"

Cindy gave me my total and said, "Beats me. But hey, with that family, I'd rather not know."

I paid with my credit card and glanced behind me. The guy waiting in line was mean mugging me for taking so long. With a polite smile, I turned back around.

Cindy handed me the receipt and slid my bag across the counter. "It was good to see you, Lana. Don't be such a stranger. You have to remember that making time for the things you love is important."

"I'll keep that in mind," I said, taking my bag. "And don't forget, mum's the word on the Anna May drama. She'd kill me if she knew I'd told you."

"Don't worry, Lana. Your secrets are always safe with me."

CHAPTER 26

On my way over to China Cinema and Song, I thought about what I'd done by leaving this gossip bait for Cindy. It wasn't my best work, but if I could get this stigma away from my sister about her being involved with a married man, then maybe she would forgive me for causing an interrogation by my mother.

In hindsight, I realized I shouldn't have tried "helping out" to begin with. But it had seemed like a good idea at the time. Another mental note to add to the list of how to be a better person: *Do not insert yourself into family matters that have nothing to do with you.*

Kimmy was bouncing on the balls of her feet as I entered the entertainment shop. "Are you ready for our next encounter tonight?"

"Huh?"

"Megan texted me last night and told me about how we're going to track down Brandi."

I'm sure at this point, my facial expression betrayed me. I couldn't hide the shock. "Megan actually texted you?"

"I know, right?" Kimmy said. "Pigs were flying over my head as the text came in. But hey, if she's willing to play nice, then so will I. It's all in the name of justice, after all."

"Uh-huh."

She tilted her head and gave me a once-over. "What's your problem? I thought you would be excited that your two bestest pals were playing nice with each other for once."

I shook my head and exhaled. "It's this thing with Anna May. She's mad at me for trying to help with something and now I'm trying to fix that."

"Oh, right, because your sister is dating that married guy. I've heard it all over the plaza. And I also heard that Donna Feng is absolutely disgusted with her."

"How'd you here that?"

"The Matrons, of course. I was in the salon earlier getting my nails done." She held up her hands and wiggled her fluorescent pink nails. "They were saying something about how the story is all wrong and Anna May is dating some other guy that no one knows about. As if anyone would buy that story."

I cringed. "None of it is true or what anyone thinks. It's . . . well, the truth isn't very believable either."

The phone behind the sales counter rang. Kimmy spun on her heel to answer it. "We can talk about it more later tonight and you can give me the actual scoop."

I didn't get the chance to tell her that conversation wouldn't be happening, because she'd already picked up the phone. Instead, I made a quick exit from the plaza and headed home. My main goal had been to come away from Asia Village feeling a sense of accomplishment for at least one thing going on in my life. But as I drove home, I felt that I'd come up short.

From an outside perspective, watching Megan and I get ready for the evening would appear just like any other Saturday night in the life of a twenty-something. But behind the façade of normalcy, so much more was going on.

We were plotting and scheming.

Tracking down Brandi had been a long time coming. It was our one shot to confront her and we couldn't blow it. Of course, the usual doubts surfaced in my mind as I thought about the odds of finding her, the likelihood of having a useful conversation with her, and whether or not it would produce results that actually meant something.

I didn't know which way was up or which was down. Was Rina involved somehow? Had she and Brandi been secretly working together to take down Gavin for his treatment of women as playthings? And if so, why? I didn't know Brandi, so her motives could range from petty to severe. But what on earth was Rina's objective?

I'd also taken into consideration the age-old adage that "things aren't always as they seem." Hell, it applied to the situation with my sister. So why couldn't it also apply in this circumstance?

And what role did Dan the drummer play? He had the most to gain financially from Gavin's death, it seemed. On top of that, he'd already had existing bad blood with him that conveniently tied back to Brandi.

What was I missing? It felt like an image hiding in my peripheral, slightly out of view. You know it's there, but you can't quite get it in focus.

Megan was putting the finishing touches on her hair, reinforcing her updo with a max-hold hairspray to combat the wind. "I think we should Uber tonight, don't you? It'll be easier than driving to the other side of the Flats. Then we don't have to worry about a designated driver."

I plucked a stray eyebrow that had no business being so low on my eyelid. "Agreed. Better not to deal with it or the parking fees."

"What do you think will happen tonight?" She asked, leaning against the sink. "Do you think that we're finally going to get some answers?"

"I sure hope so. I can't take much more of this. I want this over with so we can get back to normal life. The holidays are going to be here before we know it, and I'd like to enjoy them."

Megan pushed off the sink and turned to leave the bathroom. "I'm going to call a car. I'll text Kimmy and let her know we're heading her way."

Giving myself a final glance in the mirror and feeling satisfied with my appearance, I shut off the flat iron and followed Megan. I'd gone with a sequined mini-skirt and black tights that would pair well with suede knee-high boots I'd recently purchased from Aldo.

I sat down on the couch to put them on. "Adam hasn't said much about anything, obviously. But I wonder how this whole thing is going for him."

Megan was busy requesting a pickup, so she only nodded in response.

I fiddled with the zipper on my boot. "I'm starting to get nervous. What if we can't help this time? What if this is all for nothing?"

Megan tapped the screen of her phone, tossed it into her purse, and met my eyes straight on. "Lana Lee, don't even talk like that. We are in the business of impossible odds. This is right up our alley. Don't you worry about a thing."

CHAPTER 27

The Flats of downtown Cleveland have a long history. The East and West Banks surround the Cuyahoga River and were the settling points for immigrants back in the day. And when I say back in the day, I mean the late 1700s.

Later down the line, it became a hub for industrial businesses, and then added nightlife, and eventually residential prospects. Though at times the area had a bad reputation, it continued to resurge and renew itself.

The heyday of the Flats as a place for nightlife was before I'd come onto the scene. I'd heard stories of its former glory and the chaotic fun that took place on the weekends. With a lull in popularity since that time, the area was once again becoming a hot spot and attracting a fresh generation ready to leave their mark.

Tonight's escapades would begin on the East Bank where both Punch Bowl Social and the Big Bang Dueling Piano Bar were located. Megan and I had concluded earlier in the evening that it would be better to start off where we could kill two birds with one stone. If we came up empty at one of the bars, we'd only have to walk around the corner to get to the other.

Kimmy was in charge of keeping an eye on Brandi's social media to see if she posted her location or if we could gather what her intended plan was for the evening. All of us had our fingers crossed that she'd make it easy on us to find her.

The Uber driver dropped the three of us off in front of Punch Bowl Social and we hurried to wait in line, all three of us pulling out our IDs for the doorman.

Once inside, the heat that radiated off of the packed-in bodies had me struggling to get out of my leather bomber jacket. It was my "cute" warm coat and usually what I toted around with me for just these occasions.

Megan ordered some drinks while Kimmy and I scoped out the surrounding area. Women were clustered in groups—probably complaining about their footwear—and men were huddled around checking them out. There is no more awkward moment than being a fly on a wall and watching two guys approach a group of women and get dismissed. Say what you will, but I have to hand it to the menfolk. Rejection isn't easy.

Once we had our drinks, we casually perused the first floor of the spacious bar. The place was big. It had two floors and a rooftop patio that came in handy during the spring and summer months.

On the first floor you could enjoy bowling, shuffleboard, and pinball. I even heard there's some karaoke that takes place. But we all know my sentiments on singing in public.

I personally abstain for the safety of others, and keep all my vocal renditions limited to the shower and the privacy of my car.

"Let's check upstairs," I suggested.

The three of us made our way to the stairwell and headed up to the next floor. It wasn't quite as packed, but it was even hotter than downstairs.

"I don't see her anywhere," Kimmy shouted in my ear. "How long do you think we should stick around? I'm kind of antsy."

Megan leaned in close to be heard. "Let's finish our drinks and then we'll head over to Big Bang. Has she posted anything?"

Kimmy pulled out her cell phone and after a minute of searching, replied, "Nothing."

We finished our drinks, set the glasses on the bar top, and marched out like penguins to investigate the next bar.

The Big Bang was a smaller venue than Punch Bowl so there was less ground to cover. Even though we could have been in and out in five minutes, Megan suggested we have a drink anyhow.

I chewed on my straw, my eyes scanning the crowd and feeling disappointment overtake me. We'd huddled at a high-top table off to the side of one of the pianos and had a good viewpoint of the entrance, just in case Brandi should walk in.

After fifteen minutes of nothing exciting happening, Kimmy slammed her glass down on the table in triumph and smiled wide. "We have pay dirt, ladies. She is at Punch Bowl, but she's on the roof."

Kimmy turned her phone so Megan and I could see a photo of Brandi leaning casually over the side of the roof as if she were taking in the city skyline.

"Let's head back before she leaves," I said, abandoning my drink.

I felt myself rushing. My steps were hurried as we returned the way we came, and I could feel my heart pounding in my chest. When we passed the doorman, I headed in the direction of the stairwell. But Megan grabbed my arm before I could go any farther.

"Chill out, Lana. We can't act like we came here to interrogate her. Let's get a drink down here and make our way upstairs. It will look more natural."

"You're right," I said, taking a deep breath.

"Kimmy, watch the stairs, would ya?" Megan asked.

Kimmy gave her a thumbs-up and turned her back to us.

Megan wrapped an arm around my shoulders and shimmied us closer to the bar to wait for the bartender. "You've got to pull it together. You're letting your emotions get the best of you."

"I know. I just want results, you know? I feel like we're throwing spaghetti at a wall to see what sticks."

Megan shrugged. "We kind of are. There is no rule book for this sort of thing."

"This could exonerate Rina . . ." I replied.

"It might. It might not. We have to do our due diligence and hope for the best."

The bartender came around and Megan recited the drinks we wanted. A few minutes later, we got our drinks and paid our tab.

As we were moving away from the bar, a drunk woman knocked into me, almost causing me to spill my drink. "Ohmigod! I'm so sorry, I was looking at that guy. That guy over there . . . he's like seven thousand feet tall." The woman pointed in the opposite direction of where we were standing. When I turned to look, there was no sign of who she was referring to.

I smiled obligingly at her and told her not to worry about it. Her eyes began to cross as I spoke to her, so I wasn't sure she'd even heard a word I'd said.

Megan nudged my hand, distracting me from my encounter with the drunk woman. "Take a sip. Calm yourself. Get that agitation off your face, and remember why we're here. Or rather, that we're here to look like we're having a good time."

I sipped my drink and rolled my shoulders, and the whiskey warmed my throat. I knew Megan was right. I was so worried about blowing our cover that I was going to be the one that blew our cover.

We made our way back up the stairs for the second time that night and walked the length of the bar to reach the roof-access staircase. The wind was a bit stronger up there, and I was thankful to see some heat lamps sprinkled around the open area.

Near the front of the building, we spotted Brandi in a rather revealing black dress. She wore a tight, red leather jacket over it, but her legs weren't covered, and I wondered how cold she was.

Her company included a woman with an equally short dress but in blue, and a tall man with an untucked dress shirt and jeans. He had his arm around the blue-dress woman and

I assumed that Brandi was playing the role of third wheel tonight.

Megan pulled Kimmy and I in close so we could talk without being heard. "Let's make our way over in that direction. Let a couple minutes go by, and then Kimmy, I want you to say you recognize her from somewhere. See if she bites."

Kimmy patted at Megan's arm. "Don't worry, girlfriend. I got this. My acting skills are on point."

Megan sucked in her lips but didn't say anything. I was only half-listening, as my attention was focused on what Brandi was doing. She appeared to be telling some type of humorous story. The couple laughed as Brandi gestured dramatically with her hands. She didn't seem to be upset or have anything hanging over her head.

I tried my best not to stare and made it a point to let my eyes travel around the rooftop as if I were observing my surroundings.

For the moment, Brandi didn't seem to notice us moving in her direction. Megan was rambling on about something she'd seen in the news, and I knew well enough that it was her way of making things look natural. Megan wasn't the type to talk about that sort of stuff. And frankly, neither was I.

Kimmy played along well and interacted with the conversation. I threw in a nod and a smile at what I felt were appropriate times, but I couldn't tell you what was actually being said.

A few minutes had passed, and as Brandi was still acting out the story she was telling, I wondered if she loved to hear herself talk.

Megan signaled to Kimmy, and Kimmy acknowledged the gesture with a wink. Before I could fully process what was happening, Kimmy was sauntering over to Brandi. I was impressed with the expression on her face, which resembled how you'd react to seeing an old friend from your distant past.

"Hey, don't I know you?" Kimmy said. "You're so familiar to me, but I can't place you. It's driving me nuts."

Brandi shifted her weight from one heeled foot to the other, a hand settling on her hip that was jutting out from her stance. She gave Kimmy a once-over. "No, sorry. You have me confused with someone else." She didn't hesitate to turn back around, completely disregarding Kimmy's presence.

But my friend was not that easily discouraged. "No, I swear I know you from somewhere. I never forget a face."

Brandi whipped back around, her hair fanning out around her like a Pantene commercial. "Doubtful. You don't look like the crowd I'd hang out with it." She started to turn back around, but Kimmy grabbed her forearm.

She has a hot temper and it runs fast and deep. "Whoa there, Miss Thang. What is that supposed to mean?"

Brandi jerked her arm back and thrust an accusatory finger in Kimmy's face. "First of all, don't put your hands on me. And second of all, I meant I don't hang out with low-class trash."

Kimmy arched her back and raised her chin. "Oh no, honey. I'm not low-class trash. It's not me traipsing around in that dollar-store dress and pleather jacket."

The blue-dress woman and her boyfriend took a step back, seeming totally embarrassed, their eyes wide and mouths agape. I got the sense they wanted to distance themselves from the impending catfight.

Brandi rolled her neck and closed her eyes for a beat. When she opened them, fire beams could have blasted out from each pupil. "This dress is designer, and this jacket is worth more than you make in a month."

"Oh, I didn't realize being a hooker brought in that much here in Cleveland."

Megan and I both cringed.

Brandi hadn't taken the comment well either. She stepped forward, her nose inches away from Kimmy's.

I groaned. "I can't watch this anymore. What a nightmare." I took a step forward to break up the two women, but before I could reach them, a bouncer came rushing over.

He was tall and muscular, and the frown on his face held a hint of anger behind it. "Ladies, am I going to have to throw one of you out?"

Neither woman responded and continued to stare each other down.

The bouncer turned his attention to Brandi. "I thought you weren't going to start trouble tonight."

She folded her arms over her chest. "It wasn't on my list of things to do, but then this two-bit hussy decided to get in my way."

Kimmy snorted. "Two-bit hussy? You're really grabbin' from back in the day, aren't you?"

Brandi opened her mouth to reply, but the bouncer held up his hand. "Come on, miss," he said to Kimmy. "I know those drinks aren't cheap, and I'd hate to remove you. Why don't you head downstairs, or I'll have to make you waste your money."

"Fine," she replied, indignant. Kimmy gave Brandi one more death stare, and as she turned, she sneered. "Heathen."

"What did you say?" Brandi shouted.

The bouncer stepped in front of Brandi so she was completely out of sight.

I grabbed Kimmy's arm. "Way to go, hothead. You blew our chance."

"Don't even start with me, Lana. She shouldn't have called me trash. Thanks for neither of you having my back, by the way."

"The point was not to start a bar fight," I replied through gritted teeth.

Megan put a hand on both our shoulders. "Girls, let's go downstairs before we draw any more attention to ourselves. People are beginning to stare."

I turned without saying anything else. I had no words. I stormed to the stairs, people glancing in our direction as we passed. As I began to descend the staircase, a clammy hand touched my wrist, "Lana, is that you?"

When I turned to see who it was, I was surprised to see Gavin's neighbor, Pamela.

Have I ever mentioned how this city is too small for its own good?

CHAPTER 28

Pamela followed us downstairs, and once we were out of the walkway, I introduced Kimmy to Gavin's neighbor. Megan and Pamela, having already met, said hello and Megan added a "Nice to see you again."

Pamela jerked her head in the direction of the stairs. "I caught the tail end of that. What the heck was going on up there?"

"Long story," I replied. "Funny bumping into you here. Girls' night?" I glanced around, wondering who she had come with.

"Um, just stopped through. I met with a friend at Margaritaville across the street and didn't feel like going home yet. Thought I'd pop in here and have a drink."

It seemed a little odd for a woman to come to a place like this by herself, but these were modern times, and who was I to judge? Especially if you were a single woman with a group of friends who were all in some form of a relationship. Sometimes you had to take matters into your own hands and be your own wingman, that is, if Pamela was really here scouting for guys. I couldn't help assuming she wasn't. "Well, you're welcome to join us," I said.

"Thanks. Also, I don't mean to pry, but are you aware of who that woman was that your friend here was arguing with?"

Kimmy inserted herself between the two of us. "Yeah, we know who she is."

Pamela was caught off guard by Kimmy's directness and took a step back. "If I were you guys, I'd stay away from her. Trouble seems to follow her wherever she goes."

"You know her then?" Megan asked. "Have you seen her before at Gavin's?"

Pamela nodded. Her hair was tucked behind her ears, and I had a full view of how pink her cheeks were. I couldn't tell if it was from nerves, the alcohol, or the increasing level of heat that filled the building. "They were hot and heavy for several months, and I bumped into her in the hallway a few times while I was getting my mail. She was never nice to me, I don't even know her name."

"Go figure," Kimmy replied.

"I held the door for her a time or two and she acted as if it were my job. Didn't even say thank you."

Megan shook her head. "I loathe people like that. Aside from that, is there anything you can tell us about her? I know Lana already told you the truth about who we are. Maybe you can lend us a hand or steer us in the right direction. You must know something."

Pamela's eyes darted toward the exit. "Uh-oh, I just remembered something. I think I left my cell phone at Margaritaville, and they're closed. I'm going to head back and see if there's anyone inside that might be able to help. Will you guys watch my drink? I'll be right back."

"Sure," I replied, holding out my hand to take her glass. "Do you want me to come with you?"

She handed me the sweaty glass. "No, that's okay. It won't take me long. Be right back."

The three of us watched her as she made a mad dash to the exit. Through the window we saw her heading in the direction of Margaritaville, bracing against the wind.

Kimmy raised an eyebrow. "Well, she's a weird little gal, isn't she? Kinda skittish."

The group of men that had occupied the table next to us were now gone, so we shimmied over to claim it for ourselves.

I set Pamela's glass down and wiped the condensation from my hand. "She's like that. The two times I've met her, she's seemed as though she'd rather be anywhere but where she is."

Kimmy burst into a fit of laughter, her drink sloshing over the sides of the glass and spilling onto her hand.

Megan and I exchanged a weary glance. I didn't know if Kimmy had seen something funny or was to the point of hysterical intoxication. I was hoping for the former because I was not trying to hold anybody's hair back.

Megan handed Kimmy some napkins from the dispenser on the table. "What the heck are you cackling about?

Kimmy accepted the napkins, wiped her hands, and brought her laughter down to a chuckle. "I had this thought. All this time we're searching high and low for Gavin's killer, and wouldn't it be funny if it was that petite gal this whole time? And then I thought how absurd that thought is and I couldn't hold back anymore. That girl couldn't push over a Wet Floor sign."

Megan and I joined in the laughter, but not to the extent of Kimmy's boisterous outburst. The thought amused the three of us until we realized a half hour had passed and Pamela had not returned.

Then we all started to think that maybe Kimmy was on to something.

That night Kimmy crashed on our couch while we waited for a late pizza delivery. Megan and I camped out at the dining room table as our friend snored away in the other room.

"Tonight was a giant bust," Megan said, picking a piece of pepperoni off her slice of pizza. "What are we going to do?"

"No clue. I don't want to admit it, but I feel hopeless," I replied.

"I think it's time to confront Rina again. You need to tell her that you saw her with Brandi and that we deserve an explanation."

I laid my head on the table, staring at the pizza waiting for me on my plate. "I don't wanna."

"Well, buck up, girlfriend. You can't dodge her forever. Not if you want to help her."

"Okay, fine. I'll try to track her down tomorrow after dim sum with my family. Are you happy?"

"Yes, now eat your pizza."

CHAPTER 29

The next morning, I ventured out to dim sum without Adam. He was busy with detective stuff and had mentioned via text he probably wouldn't see me until Monday evening. Part of me felt a sense of relief because I didn't want to share with him what I had been up to the night before or how it seemed like I was digging a deeper and deeper hole.

I kept quiet through most of the meal with my family. My sister wasn't speaking to me, and my mother was too busy ignoring that anything was wrong to pay us any mind. My grandmother was content with her plate, and seeing as my dad was a man of few words to begin with, nothing was very different in that department.

At one point my mother asked me how my ideas for updating the restaurant were going, and I gave a half-hearted answer. I still hadn't given it much thought since she asked me last. It had become my back burner project and in a way I wished it had never come up.

Once dim sum was over, I rushed through goodbyes, skimming the briefest over my sister, and hopped into my car with the intention of tracking down Rina. Since her shop wasn't open on Sundays, I headed straight for her condo.

My biggest worry was that she wasn't going to answer the door. Or if she did, that she would immediately slam it in my face.

When I reached her floor, I used the knocker and lightly tapped on the brass rest.

A few moments later, the door opened and Rina stared back at me. Her face betrayed shock, and she quickly composed herself, pursing her lips and brushing loose strands of hair away from her face as if to say, *I've got nothing to hide.*

"It's time we talk," I said, keeping my voice neutral.

"I agree," she replied, matching my tone. "However, I have company."

My eyes traveled past Rina to her living room where I saw none other than Brandi herself. She regarded me with a sneer of disapproval, folding her arms over her chest and turning her head away as if acknowledging me was below her pay grade.

"I don't mind saying what I have to say in front of Brandi. You know why I'm here. If you're okay with it, then so am I."

"Come in." She stepped to the side.

Okay, this was good. Albeit different than I had anticipated, but this was further than I thought we'd get.

"Do you want something to drink?" she offered.

"No, I'm all right, thanks."

I chose to sit on the love seat, and Rina sat next to Brandi across from me on the couch. Her appearance today was definitely different than how I've seen her in past run-ins. I'd only seen Brandi a total of two times in my life and both times she was dressed to the nines—and a little on the promiscuous side. This afternoon, she was dressed in a long-sleeved black-and-white blouse with skinny jeans paired with black loafers.

"You wanted to talk, so talk," Rina began.

It still shocked me to see Rina act the way she'd been for the past week. This cold, blunt person that sat before me was out of character compared to the warm and vibrant woman that I thought I knew. Then again, people deal with grief and tragedy in a plethora of ways. Even still, I had a little niggle of concern that her new attitude might have something to do with the woman sitting next to her on the couch.

"I'm just going to come right out and say it." I edged myself forward on the cushioned seat. "I saw you and Brandi meet up at the Islander last Monday."

This got Brandi's attention, and for the first time since I sat down, she actually looked at me. But whatever she was thinking, she didn't relay. Rina made no comment either and allowed me to continue.

"I want you to stop keeping secrets from me and tell me what the hell is going on. I'm trying to help you, Rina. Can't you see that?" It felt a little weird to be saying this in front of Brandi, considering I thought she might have something to do with Gavin's death, but at this stage in the game, time was not a luxury I could afford. Whatever needed to be discussed needed to happen now, regardless of who else was in the room.

Rina appeared incredulous for a split-second, and I assumed it took a moment for her to process the news of my following her and what that meant. Then her lower lip quivered and her hands flew up to her face as she let out a painful wail.

Brandi clucked her tongue and glared at me. In a lithe movement, Brandi draped an arm protectively around Rina's shoulders.

"Oh my god," I said, springing up from the love seat. I shuffled over and knelt beside her, placing my hand on her knee. I gave her a gentle squeeze. "I'm so sorry, I didn't mean to make you cry."

Her body jerked involuntarily from crying, and I gave her knee another squeeze. "It's not that, Lana. I'm sorry I've been such a jerk. And I don't know what to do. Brandi is the only one who understands what I've been going through."

My eyes darted over to Brandi who was beaming with a sense of satisfaction at this statement. "What do you mean, Brandi is the only one who understands?" I felt my body turning cold. Was the thing I'd been fearing this whole time true? Did Brandi hold the key to compassion because they had been in this together from the beginning?

"Can you get me some tissues?" Rina said between sobs.

"Sure, sure." I hurried to the bathroom, grabbed the box off the back of the toilet, and handed it over to her before returning to my spot on the love seat. "I don't want to rush you along, but you have to help me out here. Why do you feel that only Brandi can relate to you?" I turned to Brandi and said, "No offense."

She shrugged her shoulders. "Whatever."

Rina plucked a tissue from the box and blew her nose. Her face had reddened quickly, and I scolded myself for being the cause of upset. Perhaps I had been a little too insensitive of Rina's situation. She dabbed at her eyes. "Brandi warned me that he was trouble. She told me not to get involved with Gavin because he had a lot of enemies."

Brandi nodded. "The man was a plague among women. I'm sorry that he died, but he wasn't a good man."

Ignoring Brandi's commentary, I asked, "That's why you were meeting with her that day?"

"No, she found me after Gavin and I had already left Asia Village. I was a mess that night between having a drink thrown at me and then going to a sweaty bar. Instead of making Gavin come downtown with me, we went back to Asia Village. I always keep a spare set of clothes in my office for emergencies. He waited for me in the car while I ran in." She paused to take a breath.

"Okay, so you guys went from Asia Village to Lakewood, then came back here before going to his place?" This tracked with the timing of what Penny had told me the other day.

"Yeah, he lives right around the corner from here, so it seemed like the best option. When I was locking up, Brandi caught up with me."

Brandi chuckled at the memory. "I was lit up like a Christmas tree that night. I remember stumbling over and telling her I wanted to save her life."

"Save her life? That's a bit dramatic, don't you think?"

Brandi scowled. "It might have been dramatic, but it's what I felt. I didn't want Rina to go through what I went through with that good-for-nothing jerk. He was just going to use her until he got bored, and then break her heart without a second thought. Rina doesn't need that sort of thing in her life. No one does. Would you want to see another woman go through that?"

It felt rhetorical, so I didn't respond.

Rina grabbed for another tissue. "Brandi meant well, Lana."

After seeing her interaction with Kimmy, it was hard for me to grasp this other, more compassionate side of Brandi that Rina seemed familiar with.

Brandi nodded. "Damn straight I meant well. Us girls have to stick together. The dating scene can be a vicious place. No sense in fighting amongst ourselves. That way leads nowhere quick."

Rina let out a staggered snuffle. "Anyways, back to how we became friends . . . that night she gave me her phone number and told me to call her when I realized she was right about Gavin."

"And that's when you guys met at the Islander?"

"Yeah, but by then I was reaching out to her because of what had happened to him." She paused and sniffed again. "I really thought he was a good guy, Lana. I mean sure, maybe Brandi had some valid points, but I wanted to find out for myself. I never got the chance to know him, but he treated me nothing short of a princess that night."

Brandi rolled her eyes. "Typical Gavin. That's what he always did, baby girl. I know it felt nice, but it wasn't real."

I bit my tongue. I didn't like that this woman was calling my friend "baby girl." Maybe I was being overprotective, but I didn't like her practically coming out of nowhere and acting like she was Rina's bestest friend on the planet.

Brandi continued. "That's what he did to me. And that's what he did to all of us women. He used us as playthings. Sure, he was nice and acted like a gentleman. My god, I've never had a guy open every single door for me, pull out every chair. And the compliments. He had thousands of them. I was his 'queen,' as he liked to call me. But then once he had you, he knew it. He gave you what a lot of men won't, and then before you knew what happened, he dumped you flat on your ass. Wouldn't return a call, text . . . he basically acted like he didn't know you. You started to feel a little insane . . . like did you imagine all the kindness he extended? Was any of it real?" Brandi's eye twitched as she finished her rant.

Though I wasn't her biggest fan, I did feel for her. I'd known men of this nature myself. Sadly, it wasn't as rare as it should be.

Trying to return my focus to Rina, I said, "But he got you to go home with him on the first night. Didn't you think anything about that and what his true intentions might be?"

"It was actually my suggestion, Lana. And please don't judge me for it. I've been so lonely." She spread out her arms. "Look at this place and imagine being here night after night, with no one. This city is still new to me. I feel out of place. And I can't depend on you and Kimmy all the time."

"Of course you can. That's what we're here for." My eyes dropped down to my shoes. "I'm sorry that I let you feel that alone. My head's been so far up my . . . well you know."

"It's not your responsibility, Lana." A few tears trickled out and I thought she might have another crying spell. But she inhaled deeply and wiped at her cheeks. "That's why I decided to do the speed dating after all. It felt so out of my character and I thought it might be exactly what I needed. That morning I went out and bought a flashy dress, something that I wouldn't normally buy. I thought that I could be the new-and-improved Rina. And well, we saw how that turned out."

Brandi interjected. "You don't have to change anything about yourself. Never think that. You're gorgeous just the way you are. You also don't have to worry about being alone anymore; you have me now too."

Rina smiled at Brandi. "Thank you." She turned back to me and said, "Anyhow, back to what we were saying before I went on a tangent: I thought maybe if I talked with Brandi, I could find something out about what happened. If she knew anything that could help. But she didn't."

Brandi removed her arm from around Rina and leaned forward, looking me in the eye. "The guy had a lot of enemies. But I don't know anybody who would take it this far."

"Well clearly someone did." I flopped backward on the couch. "As frustrating as all of this is, I have to say, Rina, I'm impressed that you would try and dig for answers. I know it's not your thing."

"Well, usually it doesn't involve me," she replied. "And I'm sorry I didn't tell you. That day when you and Megan came over, I could feel that you guys didn't quite believe me. And I didn't know how to explain about Brandi confronting me at the plaza. I know you didn't get a good first impression of her, but she is a really nice person." She paused to look at her new friend. "I didn't want you guys to hound her with questions. This has affected her more than you realize. She had a lot of feelings for him before she decided to finally break things off with him."

"You're right, I do find that hard to believe. Especially considering my second impression." My eyes slid in Brandi's direction.

"What do you mean?" Rina asked.

Brandi held up a hand. "She's talking about when I laid

into her friend at Punch Bowl Social. It wasn't my finest moment, but I felt attacked. . . . I knew who you guys were and what you were trying to do. I'm not stupid."

Rina glanced between the two of us, obviously confused. I went quickly through the story of events that took place at Punch Bowl, worried that Brandi would cut me off and deliver her own recounting of what happened, but to my surprise, she did not.

Rina shook her head and turned to acknowledge Brandi. "That must have been awful to think you were being ganged up on."

Rina's comment gave me pause. I wasn't sure if it was my less-than-stellar confrontations with Brandi, but I couldn't see her as some poor, helpless victim who was getting "ganged up on." I felt that, perhaps, Rina was a little blind to Brandi's true nature. Although, who knows, maybe it was me that wasn't seeing things clearly.

I asked myself if I could find it in my heart to see Brandi through a different lens. I concluded that at this particular moment in time, I couldn't. Something like that would take time. But I didn't want to sway Rina's judgement. She had to make that call on her own.

If I wanted to get to the bottom of this murder, I couldn't allow my thoughts to be clouded by sympathy that might not be warranted in the long run.

I felt the conversation—and my stamina for this whole conversation—winding down. But I still had questions. Bluntly, I said, "There's still something I don't understand. Why the urgency to keep the shop open? Kimmy told us that you were concerned about money."

Rina nodded. "Things are tight. Business hasn't been

the best over the summer and this condo isn't exactly the cheapest thing I've ever bought. With how much legal fees are, I didn't see a way I could sustain my lifestyle and pay an attorney. If things keep going at this rate, I'll have to sell this condo, and I really don't want to do that. It would feel like a huge failure and the last thing I want to do is ask my family for help. My only solution was to make sure the shop stays open as much as possible."

What she said rang true, and I knew that asking family for help was never an easy thing. I felt satisfied with the conversation and it felt like the right time to make my exit. "I think I better go," I said, rising from the couch. "I don't want to take up any more of your time. Just please know that I'm here for you."

Rina rose from the couch to walk me out, and I gave Brandi a nod before heading toward the door.

"Your boyfriend is an amazing person, by the way," she said as we stood in the entryway.

I laughed. "Well, this I know, but why do you say so?"

"You have to promise not to tell him what I'm about to say."

"Cross my heart."

Rina looked over her shoulder to see if Brandi was listening. She was preoccupied with something on her cell phone, and so Rina continued, lowering her voice as she spoke. "He took me back to the crime scene to do an experiment. I had to wear those plastic booties and everything."

I lifted an eyebrow. "What kind of experiment?"

"He wanted me to stand in the bathroom while he ran the tub and turned on some music. He was trying to recreate the evening, I guess."

"And?"

"Well, I stood in the bathroom like he said. He went out into the lobby to ring the buzzer. He wanted to know if I heard anything."

"Did you?"

"I did. It was very faint, but I heard it and it sorta made the wall vibrate. It's hard to explain. Well, at least when the door is released anyway. He had some other cop there to let him back in."

"Probably Higgins," I threw in.

"Well, then I guess Adam knocked on the door, once using the knocker and once not. I didn't hear it either time."

"I see." From what Rina was telling me, I gathered that Adam was testing to see what could be heard from the bathroom shower the night of the murder. "Sounds like Adam was trying to prove whether or not you're telling the truth."

"Well, yes," Rina replied. "But he also was playing with another theory. He had a thought that the murderer was already in the building."

CHAPTER 30

"I'm telling you, I think Kimmy is on to something." I was pacing my living room as I went into full rant mode with Megan, circling the coffee table and speculating on high speed. "After talking to Rina, I think Pamela sent us on a wild-goose chase to take the attention off of her."

Megan held up a hand. "Before you go any further. How the heck was it sitting with Brandi? That had to really be something."

I flared my nostrils. "Infuriating. She seems to have a soft spot for Rina, and if I didn't already think badly of her, I might say it's genuine. But I still don't trust her. There's something that doesn't sit right with me when it comes to her. I'm just not sure what anymore. I'm telling you, Pamela has to be the key to this whole thing."

Megan drummed her fingers on the kitchen table. "That can't be it. Kimmy said it herself, that girl couldn't knock over a wet-floor sign. How would she topple a man that's like seven inches taller than her?"

Kikko was following me around the coffee table, confused

by my actions. "Think about it. The girl can't sleep, she gets fed up and goes to confront him. He gets an attitude, he's drunk, maybe he calls her some foul names. She goes bonkers and *bam!*" I smacked my fist into my other hand. "Then she panics, shuts the door, slips back downstairs, and pretends like nothing happened."

"Lana, that sounds absurd."

"Don't underestimate a sleep-deprived woman. You of all people should understand that trauma."

"Fair point."

"Ugh, I'm so stupid. I fell for it, hook, line, and sinker. She has us running around chasing false leads. She's clever, this one." I shook my head as I continued to pace.

"You're jumping to conclusions. We still don't know that to be true."

"Adam must think it too. Otherwise why would he entertain the idea that the person was already in the building?"

Megan stood from the table. "Stop pacing, you're making me nervous. As far as Adam goes, it's possible he's thinking about someone else that you and I haven't even considered."

I paused, standing still for a few moments. My thoughts were moving faster than I could make sense of them. "We've wasted too much time putting our proverbial eggs in one basket. We should have been digging more into his other neighbors. What problems he might have had at home, et cetera."

"It's not too late," Megan replied. "We can go back and take the names off the mailboxes, and search them on the computer. It's a long shot, but maybe we can find out who we're dealing with."

"Okay, I'll drive. Grab your coat," I said, heading for the door. "Let's get this started."

"I'm ready, I just have to run to the bathroom before we leave."

Megan went to the bathroom, and I went to get Kikko's leash. She seemed to sense that something was up, so she peed right away and we headed back for the apartment door. When I got back inside, Megan was putting her coat on.

"I'm ready," she said.

I turned the doorknob and was about to tell Megan we'd have to be careful we weren't seen by Pamela. But before I could say anything, I realized that Adam was standing in front of me, his hand held in mid-knock.

I gasped. "Adam!"

"Surprise!" His eyes ping-ponged between me and Megan. "Did I interrupt something?"

"I thought I wasn't going to see you until tomorrow night," I said.

"Gee, you sure know how to make a guy feel loved."

I clucked my tongue. "That's not what I meant. I'm surprised, is all."

"Are you going to let me in?"

"Right, sorry." I moved out of the way. "Come in."

Megan gave Adam a tight-lipped smile. "We were about to head to the grocery store."

Adam began to remove his peacoat. "Do you guys want me to come? I can carry the bags."

"That's okay," I said, kissing him on the cheek. "It's nice of you to offer, but Megan can go. We didn't need that much stuff. It was more an excuse to get out of the house. Right, Megan?"

"Yeah, I can go alone. . . . I have the list," she said to me. "So, I'll be back. With food."

"Right. Bye then." I started to take my coat off. "Hope you don't run into anybody we know. Because . . . you don't have makeup on."

"Yeah . . . that is something I would like to avoid."

I led Adam into the living room and gestured for him to have a seat. Then I returned to the entryway to lock the door behind Megan. "Don't forget to get everything on the list." With my back turned to Adam, I widened my eyes as I said it. "We don't want to have to go back."

"I won't. I'm good at getting everything on the list." She scowled at me as she turned to leave.

Shutting the door behind her, I said a silent prayer that she didn't run into Pamela while she was jotting down the addresses.

"So that was weird," Adam commented.

"What do you mean?"

"I feel like I just watched an episode of *Laverne and Shirley*. What are you guys up to?"

"Nothing, I swear."

"Uh-huh. Maybe it's good that I stopped by. I've potentially saved you from getting into trouble. Although, I don't know what Megan's outcome is going to be. We need to find her a nice guy who can keep her occupied. Higgins' brother is single. Want me to make a call?"

"Don't you dare," I said, joining him on the couch. "If I set Megan up on a blind date, she'd have my head on a platter."

He wrapped an arm around my shoulder and pulled me close, kissing my forehead. "Well, we don't want that. I kinda like your head."

* * *

About an hour later, Megan returned from her information-gathering task. To my dismay, she was empty-handed. And even further to my dismay, Adam noticed before I did.

"Where are the bags?" Adam asked as Megan shut the door. "Did you leave them in the car?"

The blank expression on her face reminded me of a kid asked to produce their homework. Homework they clearly didn't do.

"Yeah, Megan," I chimed in. "Where are the groceries?"

"Oh, uh, they didn't have what we wanted."

Adam's eyebrows crunched together. "They didn't have *anything* on your list?"

"No, isn't that the darnedest thing?" A burst of laughter escaped as she hung her keys by the door. "I don't know what the world has come to these days. I mean, stock a shelf, am I right?"

If Adam wasn't eyeballing the both of us, then I probably would have smacked myself in the forehead. But I tried to remain calm. "Megan, can I speak to you in the kitchen, please?"

"Uh-huh."

I gave Adam's arm a pat before getting up and making my way into the kitchen.

Megan busied herself with the coffee maker.

"What are you thinking?" I hissed at her, trying to keep my voice down so Adam wouldn't overhear. "You couldn't go get a bag of groceries to make it more convincing?"

Out the side of her mouth, she said, "I wasn't thinking about it, okay? All I had in my head was to get all the names, and get home. I forgot about the whole grocery bit."

"Well, this is great. We look like idiots."

Megan poured water into the coffee maker's reservoir. "Do you want me to leave again? I mean, geez, Lana."

"No, that makes no sense now. Did you at least get all the names?"

"Yeah, I took a picture with my phone."

"Good, you'll have to research them while I keep him entertained."

"A 'thank you' would be nice." Megan closed the lid of the coffeepot, then pressed brew.

"Thank you, Megan," I replied, emphasizing sarcasm.

"Don't mention it." She spun on her heel and went out into the living room.

I listened to the coffee begin to drip into the carafe that was directly behind me. My objective tonight had changed. Instead of sifting through the names that Megan had collected, I had to put on my "girlfriend hat" and pretend like I wasn't up to anything. And since it was Adam's case, I had to be even more careful about getting caught poking my nose where it wasn't supposed to be. I had confidence that my own boyfriend wouldn't arrest me, but it could potentially harm our relationship. And frankly, I had enough problems already.

CHAPTER 31

Adam ended up spending the night, so there was no true opportunity for me to do any research with Megan. After the three of us had sat around sipping coffee and making small talk for about half an hour, Megan had excused herself to her bedroom, claiming she had a headache. But I knew what she was really going to do.

Adam and I watched some type of action movie that he'd spotted while scrolling through Netflix. I absentmindedly ate popcorn and ran scenarios in my head while pretending to be enthralled in what was on the screen.

I couldn't sleep that night, tossing and turning every few minutes, trying to get comfortable. More than anything, I wanted to ask the person who would know best if I was totally off track with my thoughts. But that person was Adam, and I couldn't go there with him.

Monday morning came as it always did—too soon. I felt exhausted and ready for a nap before I'd even combed my hair.

Going through the motions, I served the Mahjong Matrons, smiling at the appropriate intervals. Helen asked me how things were going with my sister, and they were upset to find out that we weren't speaking to each other. Pearl promised they would find a way to fix the mess I'd gotten myself into, but I begged each of them to stop talking about it. Whether they would follow through with my request was anybody's guess.

Nothing of relevance happened until about one o'clock when a delivery man showed up at the hostess counter holding a bundle of red roses in a vase. The vase was secured by a cardboard box that hugged the tinted glass. The roses were a beautiful spray of vibrant crimson accented with the usual baby's breath.

As I accepted the flowers, I began to wonder whether Adam had remembered our one-year anniversary after all. But I'd been so busy with everything else that I wasn't even sure of the dates. Maybe *I'd* completely dropped the ball.

I lifted the envelope from the plastic spear sticking out the center of the bouquet and pulled out the enclosed card. The smile on my face disappeared as I read the poem that was typed inside.

Roses are red,
Violets are blue,
Mind your own business,
This doesn't concern you.

My first reaction was an indignant snort. Who would send such a ridiculous message? But the more I thought about it, the more it began to unnerve me. Someone spent the time and the money to send flowers to me, at my place of employment, that hinted they knew what I was up to. There was no direct threat, but in a way, I felt that was worse. It was open-ended, left for interpretation.

Nancy came up from behind me and let out a delighted gasp. "Oh, how beautiful. These are from your boyfriend, yes? How kind of him."

I didn't say anything in return. It was easier to let her think that Adam sent them instead of explaining the sender was an unknown party.

"Can you watch the front for a minute?" I asked. "I want to call him and say thank you."

"Of course." She shooed me away from the hostess booth. "Take your time."

I grabbed the flowers and carried them into the back. As I passed Peter in the kitchen, he had his back to me and I could see his earbuds firmly tucked into each ear. I slinked by unnoticed so I wouldn't have to engage in conversation about the bouquet. Peter knew me better than his mother did, and he would know I was lying about them being from Adam.

In my office, I set the vase down on the edge of my desk and took a step back, staring at them as if they were going to do something.

I'd interacted with plenty of potential suspects in the past week, but there was only one person who knew for sure I was up to something. And that person was Pamela.

I entertained the thought that perhaps this was Brandi's inconspicuous way of telling me to mind my own business behind Rina's back. I considered that maybe Dan the drummer, having seen Rina in passing, maybe would have seen me in passing at the plaza as well. After all, he had been at Asia Village the night of the speed dating event— unbeknownst to me at the time. So, maybe he knew us before we'd ever said a word to him at the Grog Shop.

Reaching for my cell phone, I did a quick search for the flower delivery service. It was local. I used the call option on the flower shop's website and waited for someone to answer.

"Blossoming Concepts, this is Darlene, how can I help you?"

"Hi, I received a bouquet of flowers, but the card has no name on it. I was wondering if you could tell me who they're from."

"I'm sorry, we're not allowed to give out customer information."

"Are you able to tell me anything? Like if it was a man or a woman?"

"No, I'm sorry, dear. That isn't possible either. Sounds to me like you have a secret admirer."

"Yeah . . . thanks. Have a good day."

I dropped the phone onto my desk, rested both hands on the edge, and stared at the bouquet. It seemed silly to me after I began searching the flowers, but it crossed my mind that maybe there was a bug planted among the roses. Once I finished rifling through the petals, I laughed at myself. This was the result of watching too many spy movies.

Calming myself down, I called Megan.

She picked up almost immediately. "What's up?"

I told her about the flowers.

"That's a little unsettling."

"My sentiments exactly."

"Well, I'm sad to say that I didn't find anything useful through the name search. Two of the names I typed in didn't pull up anything. Other than that, I got some information from voter registration websites. There is only one single man that lives in that building aside from Gavin. He's in his sixties, and in case you're curious, he's a Democrat. The other people that pulled up results are likely families. I kind of had to dig around for that, and I won't bore you with the details, but I assume based on what I've seen that's accurate."

"So we're back where we started then?"

"I think so. I mean, no telling what an angry father might do to someone making a ton of noise and interrupting their kids' sleep. But I'd think a lot of these people would be of the cop-calling variety. Not to get involved and all that. The only other thing I can think of is we go knock on people's doors and see if anything strikes a nerve with someone."

I rubbed the back of my neck. "I think I need to put a little heat on Pamela. If she is the one that sent me the flowers, she wants me to get the message."

"What are you thinking?" Megan asked. I could hear the hesitation in her voice. "You don't sound like yourself, and you're beginning to worry me."

"I don't know what I'm thinking yet."

"Promise me you won't do anything until we sit down and have a conversation. We'll get out your trusty notebook and go over everything one more time. Maybe there's something we're missing and it's plain as day."

"Yeah, maybe."

"Promise me, Lana."

"I have to go," I said. "Peter's yelling for me." I disconnected before anything further could be said.

Though I often accused Kimmy of having a hot running temper, she wasn't the only one guilty of that trait. I have been known from time to time to lose my cool. And now was starting to seem like one of those times.

I felt pushed to my edge and backed into a corner at the same time. I was sick of my sister and her ridiculous drama, and the fact that my mother nagged me endlessly about the things she thinks I should be doing. Or that my own best friend doubted my train of thought as if I had completely lost my marbles.

And maybe I had. But I was tired and angry now. I wanted a resolution. This whole thing needed to be put to rest. As they say, if you want something done right, you have to do it yourself.

That's when I knew that I had the answer. I had to take matters into my own hands.

Pulling up to Pamela and Gavin's apartment building, I turned my phone on mute. Megan had tried calling me a few times when she knew I'd be off work. But I didn't answer. I had to do this my way. And I had to do it now.

But I was no dummy. I wasn't going to walk into a situation completely unarmed. Petite girl or not, Pamela might still try to harm me somehow. On the way over to her apartment, I'd stopped at a Discount Drug Mart and picked up a canister of pepper spray. I'd never used something like it before, but it seemed pretty straightforward.

And if that weren't enough protection, I had prepared a timed text to be sent to Megan if I wasn't out of there in thirty minutes. I'd downloaded the app a couple of months ago, but had yet to use it. Looked like tonight would involve some "firsts" for me.

I parked the car on the side of the building and hurried down the sidewalk that led to the entrance. It was almost dark outside and the front stoop light had turned on, but the lobby itself was dark. Fumbling over the buttons on the intercom, I typed in Pamela's number and waited for her to answer. There was no way to know if she was home, and I crossed my fingers behind my back.

Without saying anything over the intercom, she buzzed me in, and I mulled over the idea that she was expecting someone. Dismissing it quickly, I headed down the stairs in the direction of her apartment.

The little black dog barked from the commotion, and I heard Pamela disengage the dead bolt as I neared her door. When she poked her head out, she gasped. "Lana, what are you doing here?"

"I think we need to have a little chat, Pamela. Don't you?"

"Ohmigod, you need to get in here now. Before he sees you. God, he probably already saw you in the parking lot."

"What are you talking about?"

Instead of answering me, she grabbed my wrist and pulled me into her apartment.

As I was yanked into the confines of her home, I couldn't help but question what I had gotten myself into.

CHAPTER 32

Once I'd gained my composure and Pamela had let go of my arm, I watched her nervously check out her peephole. Then she scurried to her patio sliding doors and poked her head through the vertical blinds. "Okay, maybe he wasn't paying attention. Maybe he didn't see you coming here. God, Lana, what were you thinking?"

The black dog was sniffing my leg and wagging its tail. I surmised that it either smelled food from the restaurant or Kikko's scent. I bent down to pat its head.

"What the heck are you going on about?" I stood up from my bent position and glared at her. But she had yet to face me. "I know what you're up to, Pamela."

"Oh okay, because you're so smart." She readjusted the blinds, closing them tighter than before. "Just shut up."

My mouth dropped. "Excuse me?"

She ran her fingers through her hair, tugging on her roots. "Sorry, sorry. I can't take this anymore. I'm snapping."

"Calm down and tell me what's going on."

She began to pace, much as I had done the day before. "Would you believe me if I told you that I was dragged into covering up Gavin's murder?"

I felt a lump in my throat. "I'm listening."

"He came to my window." Pamela began to rub her hands together. "He tapped on the glass and scared me and Skittles half to death. He asked me to let him in. I didn't know why he was asking me. I mean, we know each other casually, but it still threw me for a loop. If only I'd fallen asleep that night or hadn't answered. But I was wide awake and didn't know what to do. I guess I wasn't thinking clearly and just reacted."

From what I gathered, I concluded that Skittles must be the black dog. But I didn't understand who "he" was. She didn't give me the chance to ask.

"He said that he had to talk to Gavin and that Gavin wasn't answering any of his calls. He said he was fed up with his antics. 'What antics,' I asked. But he wouldn't say. He . . . well he was drunk. I could smell the alcohol on his breath. But he said he needed me. He needed me to go up to Gavin's apartment and knock on the door. That was it. Just knock. Because he knew Gavin would look out the peephole. And if he saw me, he would answer. But if *he* went up there and did it, then he'd never get in, and he had to get in. I knew something was off, but I wasn't thinking . . . and . . . and . . ."

Pamela was beginning to hyperventilate.

I was still standing in the entryway and took a few steps in her direction. I held out my hands slowly and then squeezed her shoulders, nudging her over to the couch. "Sit down and take a breath. It's okay."

Tears welled in her eyes. "It's not okay, Lana. It's really not okay."

Glancing around the room, I tried to find a box of tissues lying around but there were none. I patted her arm and rushed into the kitchen. I saw some bottles of water on the counter, and a roll of paper towels and brought them over.

"Maybe take a few sips of water."

She tore off a paper towel and wiped her eyes, smearing black eyeliner all over her face in the process. "Thank you. I . . . I haven't told anybody this yet."

"Who is this 'he' you keep mentioning?"

"Dan," she said before bursting into tears again.

Alarm bells went off in my head. "I've met him."

"Oh, I know. He told me all about it. He saw you talking to me that night at Punch Bowl Social. That's when he started threatening me."

"You've been keeping this secret for him?"

"Yes." She blew her nose into the paper towel. "He told me I was an accessory and that I'd go to jail. I don't know if that's true or not. I helped him get to Gavin. That's all I know. It sounds stupid. Who would believe me?"

"What actually happened that night? Start from the beginning."

"Gavin was making a ton of noise like he always does. I couldn't sleep. I heard laughing and music . . . stomping. It sounded like he was having a party up there. Instead of even bothering with sleep, I decided it was better to watch a movie. So I camped out in the living room and tried to turn up the TV loud enough to drown out some of the noise."

"And that's when Dan showed up?"

She nodded. "About thirty minutes after I had gotten into the movie, there was a tapping sound at my window." She pointed to the patio sliding doors. "I thought I was imagining it at first, but there was a pattern to it, so I realized it had to be real. I should have called the cops right away, but my one neighbor, Phillip, has been known to lock himself out of the apartment when he goes to walk his dog. I thought maybe it was him." She paused, and I imagined her replaying the night's events in her mind.

"Go on, then what happened?"

"I went to check out the window and there he was . . . he asked me to let him in. At first, I just stood there staring at him. I didn't understand why he was at my window."

"You told me before that he's asked you to come see their band play, right? Same guy?"

A tear escaped her left eye and dangled from her chin. "Yeah, same guy. I figured okay, I know he's friends with Gavin so I'd let him in, plus it's not like we were strangers. I started to leave my apartment to open the door for him, but he tapped real loud on my window and I could hear a muffled 'no,' so I went back to the window. He told me to let him in that way."

I felt a chill go up and down my arms. Dan knew that the noise would be heard out in the hallway and that if anyone was awake, they could report that someone had entered the building . . . or potentially run into him on his way.

"He's been nice enough to me, you know. We've run into each other out at a couple of bars. He's bought me drinks and we've done the whole flirty thing a time or two. So after the initial shock of him being at my window, I didn't think too much of it. When I let him in, he started ranting about

Gavin and how terrible he was. That Gavin couldn't even face Dan like a real man should. He told me that he needed my help. All I had to do was what I told you already. Knock on the door. So I did."

"And then what happened?"

"They started yelling at each other. I don't know how anyone didn't hear to be honest with you. The music coming from the apartment was pretty loud already. Gavin tried to slam the door shut in Dan's face, but Dan rammed his shoulder into it and Gavin tripped on something and flew backward. I heard the crack when his head hit the table. It's made out of marble, I think.

"Before I knew what was happening, Dan was shutting the door and dragging me back to my apartment. He hid out here. We heard the cops come and investigate. Your boyfriend came to my door and asked me some questions. Dan hid in my bedroom closet until he left."

"Hold on, how did you know the detective was my boyfriend?"

"I didn't know right away. It wasn't until Dan started to figure out that you were snooping in his business. He dug into you, searched you online like some kind of crazy person. Then he sent me articles where you're in the newspaper. There was mention of you dating Detective Trudeau."

"Dammit!" I slammed my fist on my knee. My reputation was always getting in the way of my investigations. What did it take for a person to sneak around this city undetected?

My yell caused Pamela to jump.

"Sorry," I said, holding out an apologetic hand. "Then what?"

"Nothing, I told your boyfriend I hadn't heard much of

anything except the music and that was the end of that. Dan stayed here until the coast was clear and then made me promise that I'd never tell anyone what really happened. He said he'd drag me down with him."

"But wait, you told me about Dan the first time I met you. Why would you do that if you were trying to protect yourself?"

"I didn't know who you were, but I could tell that you and your friend were lying. It didn't sound like you knew Gavin at all. I slipped you that information because I was hoping it would make you check into it. I thought maybe you were undercover reporters working on an exposé story. I held out hope that was the case because then you couldn't give away my identity if you found any evidence, since you hadn't said anything about being on the record."

"Sorry to disappoint." My shoulders drooped. Not only had I failed to deliver on finding the true culprit, I had potentially put this woman in danger. Here I was thinking she was the guilty party. I couldn't have been more wrong. I flopped back on the couch. "I can't believe this. The signs were pointing to him, I just couldn't figure out how no one had heard a big man like that come in. I didn't see it for what it was."

The door buzzer sounded, causing both of us to jump.

Fear passed through Pamela's eyes. "Oh god, it's him. It has to be."

I sprang from the couch. "How do you know?" My eyes flitted around the room.

Skittles barked and circled the door.

"Because he's been coming here every night to check on me. To remind me that he hasn't forgotten me. That's why I was at Punch Bowl that night. I didn't want to come home.

But then he had to go and be there too. I can't get away."
She nearly pushed me out of the way to reach the buzzer.

"Wait! Don't let him in."

"I have to. You don't understand how he can be. You have to hide."

I started darting around the apartment unsure of where to go. "Call the police."

"If I call the police they won't get here fast enough . . . they never get here fast enough."

There was a moment where I felt time had frozen and I was an outsider looking in. All I saw was chaos. The dog barked incessantly, Pamela whined with fear, and I was ping-ponging through the apartment.

There was a loud banging on the window and I let out a scream.

"Shhhh!" Pamela hissed. "Get in the closet." She pointed to two bifold doors next to the entrance. "I'll try to get rid of him."

There was no time. I rushed over to the closet and stepped in, shooing Pamela's dog away. I shut the doors and clutched my purse to my chest, holding my breath.

I could hear Pamela opening the slider and mumbling an apology.

"Geez, woman, what the hell took you so long?"

"Sorry, I was napping."

There was a pause of silence. Then I heard Dan say, "Napping? More like crying. Your makeup is all screwed up."

The tone of his voice was unsettling. He sounded as calm as he had the night that Kimmy flirted with him. As if this were any other day and he hadn't murdered one of his best friends in the recent past.

"It's nothing," I heard Pamela say. "I kind of want to be alone, do you mind coming back another time?"

I heard the couch creak under Dan's weight. "Come on, you can't be alone all the time. I've told you before that isn't good for you."

As quietly as possible, I readjusted my purse and unzipped the closure, making a mental note to buy purses that had easier access from here on out. My hand grazed over the contents of my purse until I felt cold metal. I pulled out my phone, cupping the screen with my other hand so I could shield some of the light from the screen. Thankfully my phone had already been on mute.

Tapping my thumb on the screen, I dialed 911. It was the easiest thing to do. I would have to stuff the phone in my purse and let the call run, hoping they'd get a trace. My heart was pounding so hard I worried it could be heard from outside the closet.

The dispatcher answered. "Nine-one-one, what is your emergency?"

I thrust my hand into my purse, making sure not to end the call in the process. My hand grazed the canister of pepper spray, and I pulled it out slowly so it wouldn't brush up against the zipper. I aimed it at the door, hoping that I didn't have to use it.

All I could do was wait. Pamela might be afraid to take action against Dan, but I wasn't. Once the police showed up, I would make Pamela confess that Dan was behind Gavin's murder. She'd probably get an obstruction charge, but that wasn't my problem. Gavin's murderer would go to prison, and that person wasn't Rina.

Spurts of sniffing could be heard coming from the other

side of the closet door. I closed my eyes and willed the dog to go away.

I knew it was too late when I heard Dan say, "What's up with your dog? Did you close up one of her toys in the closet?"

Pamela protested and called Skittles over to her, but I still heard the sniffing sound. Enough time had passed and I hoped that the dispatcher was sending someone to our location.

"Don't worry," Dan said. "I'll get it. Geez, Pam, you really gotta get your act together. Your poor dog is suffering over here."

Suddenly, the darkened closet was filled with light, and I saw Dan's eyes lock onto mine.

CHAPTER 33

Dan had stared at me for what felt like ten minutes, though it was probably more accurate to assume ten seconds had passed. I was frozen in place, aiming the pepper spray upward, but my trigger finger was not cooperating. He reached down with his massive hand and grabbed ahold of my elbow, causing me to drop the tiny canister. I watched it tumble in slow motion to the ground and settle between a pair of shoes.

I tried to wriggle free, but there wasn't anywhere for me to go.

Skittles let out barks of disapproval, but Dan ignored the dog and threw me onto the couch where I smacked into Pamela. The contents of my purse spilled out between us, my phone bouncing on the cushion and landing on the floor.

"Well, what do we have here," Dan said with a sneer. "I guess you're not as lonely as I thought you were, Pam."

"Please," Pamela begged. "This doesn't have anything to do with her. Let her go. It's my fault."

"Sorry, no can do, Pam. I know you told her about me.

She wouldn't be here if you hadn't said something you weren't supposed to."

Pamela's eyes shifted to mine. I felt an apology through her gaze. I nodded and squeezed her hand.

"Did you like the flowers I sent?" Dan asked. "I was hoping you'd take the hint, but I guess not."

I lifted my chin. "For someone who's into music, I would have thought you could come up with better lyrics."

"Oh, we have a smart-ass on our hands, do we?" He reached his hand behind his back, lifted his shirt, and pulled out a long-barreled revolver. If I didn't know better, I would have thought it was a toy. "Well, maybe this will keep you in line." He didn't point it at me, but rather displayed it as if I'd won a prize.

I gritted my teeth. Eighty percent of me was frozen in fear, but the other twenty percent was outraged. How many times could I let someone pull a weapon on me? If I got out of this one, I would make sure that Adam trained me on how to use a firearm. "Bad place to carry a gun."

"Did you learn that from your cop boyfriend?" he spat back. "I know all about you, sweetness. And don't you worry about me, I know what I'm doing." He waved the gun nonchalantly in his hand.

In the back of my mind, I heard a distant voice saying, *"Bite your tongue, Lana."*

Pamela sobbed next to me, her body shaking the couch. Dan stood defiant on the other side of the coffee table, watching us squirm with a smug grin. Skittles had settled down—perhaps from exhaustion—and lay whimpering at Pamela's feet.

My cell phone was faceup on the floor to the left of the

coffee table. It had caught my attention because the screen lit up with an incoming call. Nine-one-one was calling me back.

Dan's eyes followed mine, and he regarded my phone with amusement. "Did you make a call while you were being a coward in the closet?"

"The cops are going to be here before you know it," I said. "It's best you leave now. You gain nothing by hurting us."

"Speak for yourself, I've got me two hostages," he replied. "Answer the phone and tell them you called on accident."

"*You* answer the phone," I shot back.

Dan pointed the gun at me. "You have a death wish, little girl? Answer the damn phone."

His question rang through my body and I began to wonder what had come over me. Where was this new rebelliousness stemming from? I bent forward to pick up the phone. "Hello," I said in a calm tone.

"Hello, miss, this is nine-one-one dispatch," the woman recited. "I'm calling to check on your situation. We have a cruiser headed out your way. Are you in immediate danger?"

"Yes," I said plainly. "I called by accident."

The dispatcher hesitated. "Are you being instructed to say that?"

"Yes, that's right. I called on accident. So sorry."

I heard the woman typing on a keyboard. "I understand, miss. The cruiser will be there shortly. Is the perpetrator armed?"

"Yes, I know I should have stayed on the phone to cancel the call."

"Understood, miss. Try to hold on, someone will be there soon."

She disconnected the call and I could feel Dan's eyes boring a hole into me. "That seems awfully long of a call to tell them you dialed wrong."

"That's what happens," I said, setting my phone down next to me. "They have to make sure you're not being coerced."

"So no one's coming then."

I did my best to make eye contact. "No one is coming."

"Good, then I have some time to think." He sat down on the matching chair across from us, the gun dangling carelessly in his hands. "I'd rather not kill anyone else. You know? It's not good for the band. And we're on our way up now that Gavin is gone. Don't want to mess that up for the guys."

"Is that why you killed Gavin?" I asked. "Because he was ruining your band?"

Dan glanced up. "No, I didn't kill him on purpose. I'm not that much of a jerk. But he had it coming. The guy was no good. He treated women like garbage, he treated his coworkers like garbage—especially his band. We were supposed to be best friends. But no, he just wanted to take, take, take.

"Well, I came here to tell him his days of being a glory hound were over. Brandi was going to be mine, and we were going to kick him out of the band. That's the end of it, man. People say you can't have your cake and eat it too. Well that's a bunch of bull. I'll eat the damn cake, you understand me?"

My attention skipped between his rant and the objects around the room. I had to gather my strength against someone his size, but I felt the determination in my veins. I hoped to spot a blunt object to give Dan a taste of his own medicine, but there was nothing in sight.

But eyeing the coffee table gave me an idea.

A moment later, a bright light flashed through the window. Almost as if we were under a spotlight. It blinked once and I had a feeling that the police had arrived. When my phone screen lit up again, my thoughts were confirmed. The number read as "unknown caller."

Dan lost his casual temperament, his eyes darting from the window to my cell phone. He aimed his gun at me again. "Pick that thing up and I'll shoot you, you get me?"

I held up my hands in defense.

He bolted up from the chair and used the barrel of the gun to slide a blind over. "Dammit, you lied to me. The cops *are* here. Looks like they brought the National Guard with 'em too."

"It probably wasn't your best move to hold a detective's girlfriend hostage." It seemed I couldn't resist taunting him.

He whipped around to glare at me, then stormed over to the couch and pushed me farther into the cushion. It knocked the wind out of me, and I struggled for a breath.

Pamela screeched. Skittles let out a whine, ran underneath the coffee table, and disappeared down the hallway.

He held the gun near my face, letting the barrel graze my cheek. The metal was cold and I could smell hints of gun powder. It told me that he'd used it before. I tried not to let my mind wander as to on what. "I'll take care of that smart mouth if you don't learn to keep it shut. I said I didn't want to kill anybody. Doesn't mean I won't."

My eyes began to water at the pressure he was using on my throat. I forced a nod of acceptance and he pushed me a final time before righting himself and returning to the window.

"They're probably calling to negotiate something with me. I bet you. That's how it goes in those cop movies. I gotta be smart about this." He tapped his leg with the side of the revolver. "Think, Dan, think. . . . What do you ask for? I can't have them following me out of here. It's not going to work. If I take you with me, then I have to listen to your crap. I doubt you can shut up for long."

I massaged my neck where his hands had been.

"Then again, I could always tape your mouth shut." He said with amusement. "Hey Pammy, you got some duct tape in this apartment?"

Barely above a whisper, Pamela said, "No."

"Packing tape? Freakin' scotch tape? Come on, woman, work with me here."

She shook her head from side to side so fast I thought it would rattle her brain.

"Never mind, you're both useless." He turned his back to us and peered out the window.

I prayed there was a sniper out there ready to take a headshot. I was pretty sure that wouldn't be the case, but I held out hope.

My phone screen lit up again. Dan didn't notice and I didn't say anything. I contemplated answering it, but I didn't know what that would do, and I'd already pushed the envelope far enough. I had to take a different type of action.

We could sit around and wait for either the cops or Dan to make a move, or I could convince Pamela to make a run for it with me. My eyes fell back onto the coffee table, a symbol of what started this whole mess to begin with.

I nudged Pamela's arm with my own.

A megaphone interrupted my plan. A voice that sounded refreshingly familiar spoke. "This is the Fairview Park Police Department. We are armed and you are surrounded. We can do this the easy way or the hard way."

My phone screen lit up a third time.

This time, Dan turned around. "Gimme the phone." He held out his free hand.

I passed it to him, and he accepted the call. "Yeah, what do you want?"

Dan listened for a moment as the other person talked. The voice was deep and gravelly, and in my heart I knew it was Adam. He was out there. Tears built up in my eyes.

"Forget it, I'm not letting them go first. Either they're coming with me, or you have to promise to let me get away. I didn't do anything to anybody."

He paused again, smirked, and then hung up the phone. "That guy can forget it. I'm not coming out there to talk to them. What does he think? I'm a total dumbass?" Throwing my phone on the floor, he went back to the window. "I bet they think I'm coming out the front. I could probably sneak out the back and those morons wouldn't know it."

While he ranted about his plan of escape, I tried nudging Pamela again. Defeat had taken over, and she barely had the energy to lift her head. Her face was red and swollen, her eyes bloodshot and lacking hope.

I gestured with my hands to direct her attention to our feet. Without causing too much of a stir, I lifted my foot, suggesting we kick the coffee table at Dan. It wasn't the best idea I'd ever had, but I hoped it was enough time to get us out of the apartment.

She shook her head no, and I nodded yes. We were doing this whether she liked the idea or not. I turned my head toward the door to check to see if it was locked. It didn't appear so.

I held up three fingers in between the two of us and jerked my head at the table.

Silently, I counted, *One . . . two . . . three!*

With all the force I had in my body, I flipped up the table and kicked it at Dan. It caught him off guard and his hand dropped as the table slammed into the backs of his knees, causing him to lose control on the grip of his gun.

I grabbed Pamela's arm and pulled her along as I reached for the doorknob. I flung it open so hard, it slammed against the wall, and started to close again. I took the hit on my right shoulder as I pushed her in front of me. "Go on!" I said, taking a good glance behind my back to check on Dan's status.

My hesitation was a mistake. There was no room for error or to pause. Dan had gathered himself pretty quickly and his red face was filled with anger. He lurched toward me, and I jumped, grabbing onto the stair railing.

Pamela was ahead of me by a few steps, and I urged her forward.

Dan grabbed me around my waist, and I yelled out.

Pamela turned around to see what had happened and screamed out my name. It felt distant as the sound of blood pumping filled my ears.

"Keep going!" I think I shouted at her. I couldn't be sure because my body had fallen so far into flight-or-fight mode. Pamela was frozen in place. And I was kicking my legs and beating at Dan's arm to let me go. A flash of metal passed through my peripheral.

Within a moment, I saw Pamela regain awareness, and she spun so fast, taking the rest of the stairs two at a time. As she opened the door to the vestibule, I saw black-and-white clothing run into her. A few seconds later, it registered that it was Adam. He pushed Pamela to the side and directed his gun at Dan.

Dan didn't loosen his grip on me one bit.

Adam took one cautious step toward the staircase. "You want to let her go. Put her down and place your weapon on the ground. We can all walk away from this."

I struggled to loosen Dan's grasp around my waist. His arm was slimy with sweat, and I was having trouble getting a solid grip. I was shaking so hard it felt like my eyes themselves were vibrating.

Adam took another step. His right foot landing on the first step. "Let her go."

"No way, man. I know what happens here. I let her go and then you shoot me."

Adam ventured another foot forward. "I'm not going to shoot you. Unless you do something to make me. Let her go. Now."

Dan shuffled back a little bit and my heart beat even faster. I knew he'd thought about disappearing through the back. If he got me out that door with him, no telling what would happen.

Adam had somehow made his way down the steps. "Put the weapon down."

I could feel Dan's heart beating into my back. I feared something would happen soon, but today wasn't the day I wanted to die. Not like this. No. I wasn't going out like this. I tried to call on my powers of reason and remembered it was helpful when you were being held captive to make your body go limp. I'd get heavy and he'd struggle holding on to me.

I tried to make my body go slack. Dan let out a string of profanities in my ear, and then shouted. "Fine, you want her so bad, you take her!" And he thrust me in Adam's direction as he bolted for the back door.

Adam and I toppled to the ground, his gun releasing a bullet that went sailing across the hallway as his index finger caught on the trigger.

CHAPTER 34

The bullet had missed Dan by at least a foot, and I regarded the hole in the wall next to the back door with an untamed panic. Adam lifted me off of him and pulled his radio from the holster on his belt. "We have a runner. I repeat, we have a runner. He headed out the north exit of the building. Requesting backup. He is armed and dangerous."

He turned to me, his eyes wilder than I'd ever seen them. "I have to go, are you okay?"

I nodded, tears spilling down my cheeks. "I think I hurt my ankle."

"EMTs are outside. I have to go. I love you." He took off out the back door.

I stood in the empty hallway crying and shivering. I wondered about what the people behind the closed doors thought. It was a miracle that no one had come out to see what the raucous was all about.

My ankle felt out of place and swollen. I held onto the railing and hoisted myself up the stairs, one step at a time. When I reached the doors, I saw a commotion taking place as two cruisers sped away. I heard cops shouting as they ran on foot to catch our captor.

I spotted Pamela sitting on the back of a paramedic truck. I hobbled over in her direction.

As I was reaching her, I heard metal hitting metal, then a gunshot, then shouting.

I yelled out, my eyes searching the darkness for answers, terrified that Adam had been hurt.

A uniformed officer noticed me approaching the vehicle and rushed over to me, putting my arm around his shoulders and maneuvering me toward the paramedics.

The radio on his shoulder crackled. "We got the SOB. We got him," a voice said with bitter victory.

I felt faint and nearly collapsed against the officer carrying me, but he gave me a jolt. "Stay with me here. We have to make sure you don't have a concussion."

My eyes struggled to stay open. "I need to take a little rest."

A beam of light flashed in my face. A gloved hand was keeping my left eye open. "Follow the light," a man's voice instructed.

"Okay, okay, I see you," I said. Then everything went quiet and became very still. Finally, they were letting me rest.

CHAPTER 35

I woke up feeling as if cotton had been packed into my mouth. I turned my head to the side and felt an ache in my neck that traveled well into my back. The custard-colored wallpaper that stared back at me told me I was in the hospital. Again.

I heard a metal chair screech against the linoleum. Then Adam's voice: "Lana, are you awake?"

I lifted a hand to touch my forehead. It felt larger than life. "How long have I been out?"

"We got here about an hour ago. You fainted, and they just wanted to check you out. I'm going to go get the doctor."

With blurry vision, I tried to investigate my current situation. My ankle seemed stiff, and when I checked it, I noticed that it had been wrapped. A clear bag of fluids was attached to my arm, and I concluded it must be saline. As far I could tell, nothing was wrong with me except the overzealous orchestra playing in my head and whatever had happened to my ankle.

A few moments later, Adam returned with the doctor. "Your parents and Megan are in the waiting room. I'll tell them you're awake."

He disappeared through the door, and I was left with a middle-aged woman with salt-and-pepper hair, a bright white lab coat, and a stethoscope wrapped around her neck. She smiled down at me, exuding compassion and a certain sense of tranquility. "Well, good news is, you're going to live to tell the tale. Bad news is, you're going to have to take it easy on that ankle for a few weeks. Your boyfriend there tells me you like to get into trouble. I don't recommend it for the next three to four weeks. You're lucky you didn't break your foot."

"Oh, trust me, I don't plan to get in any more trouble in the near future. I've retired from the business."

Adam had walked in with my parents and Megan as I was assuring the doctor there was nothing to worry about. "Don't let her fool you, Doc; she's a hard one to tame."

The doctor returned a devilish smile and said, "My dear, all the best ones are." She gave me a wink and patted my shoulder. "I'll leave you to your visitors."

My mother shuffled up to the side of the hospital bed and looked me over, her eyes landing on my wrapped ankle. She let out a tsk. "Ai-ya, Lana, you are making me older. I am always so worried about you. Now look, you are hurt. You need to be more careful. This week stay home from work and take it easy. Then no more trouble."

I was going to make a quip about getting hurt more often just to get some time off from work, but it felt like a tough crowd, and I didn't want to push it.

My father nodded. "Your mother is right, Goober. I hope

you've finally gotten this Nancy Drew out of your system. See these gray hairs?" he smirked. "At least forty percent of these are from you and your sister."

I didn't know if it was the painkillers they'd given me, but everything seemed extra funny at the moment. A giggle slipped out as I stared back at their faces.

Megan had been standing off to the side, behind my family and Adam, her chin cupped in her hand. The perturbed expression on her face sobered up the laughing fit that was threatening to unleash. I could read the emotion in her eyes, and I knew that she was struggling with seeing me in a hospital bed yet again.

"I'm okay," I said, ignoring everyone else.

She took a step forward. "I could really strangle you right now, Lana Lee. Do not do that to me again, you hear me? We do this stuff together or we don't do it at all."

Adam snorted. "How about you don't it at all? It would save both me and Mr. Lee from graying hair."

Megan ignored Adam's joke. "I'm serious, Lana."

My eyes began to well up. "I know. I promise. My days of confronting murder suspects is over."

Adam chuckled good-naturedly. "I think this time, Miss Lee, I'll need you to put that in writing."

EPILOGUE

I found out the next day, after I had been discharged from the hospital and felt the comfort of sleep in my own bed, that Dan had taken a bullet in the leg. I am not too proud a person to admit I felt he had it coming. Especially when I scoped out my neck in the mirror and noticed the fingerprints bruised into my skin.

Dan had tried for a speedy getaway in his car, but you don't mess with a Fairview Park police cruiser outfitted with a nudge bar. Adam had chased him on foot and had almost caught up to him before he slipped into his vehicle. Adam took aim and shot Dan in the leg before the door shut. For good measure, Adam had also expelled a bullet into one of the tires as the drummer attempted to drive away. He didn't get far on three wheels, especially when that cop car came blazing in his direction, shoving the car into a maintenance shed.

Brandi had been brought in for questioning that night as well. It was first thought that she had instructed Dan to kill

Gavin for her as a means of revenge for breaking her heart. Dan wasn't talking and had been quick to suit up with a lawyer. In the end, Brandi admitted to egging Dan on by feeding him lies. She'd convinced Dan that Gavin had confided in her about his plans to steal Dan's business clients from under his nose. She said it was her way of isolating Gavin from everyone and everything that meant anything to him. In her eyes, she felt he cared more about his career and his band than he ever did about her. But she crossed her heart and hoped to die that she'd never said anything to Dan about killing her former boyfriend.

As for Pamela, she was hit with an obstruction-of-justice charge, but she bartered some leniency for her testimony. It was her word against Dan's now.

And since I had been held against my will by Dan, there was a one hundred percent chance that I would be called to the stand. It made me nervous to face him again, but I knew that it had to be done.

My parents and Adam were, of course, still a little ticked at me, but the mood was beginning to lighten. I knew that their feelings stemmed from concern, and I couldn't fault them for that.

Megan had softened as well, and she even had a dozen of my favorite doughnuts waiting for me when I got home. That's not to say she wasn't holding it over me that I had declined her help, but I knew with time, that would fade.

Everybody—including me—was still a bit raw from the recent events that took place.

The only two people who didn't seem to have any conflict with me were Kimmy and Rina. Rina had been grateful for the lengths I went to prove her innocence, and

Kimmy racked it up as part of the job. But Rina did make me promise not to do anything so dangerous again.

I said the words, but we both knew I didn't mean them.

Anna May had contacted me the evening I came home from the hospital and apologized for her lack of presence. She informed me that while I was being admitted to the hospital, she and Henry were in the middle of breaking things off. She confided that things had gotten ugly, but her tone had been void of emotion as she said it. I was worried about how she was truly handling the breakup along with all the rumors. Before hanging up, she let me know that she wasn't happy about my new edition to her pending rumor, but she was willing to let it go after concluding that I wasn't in my right mind at the time. I apologized and promised that I would never get involved again.

Those words I meant.

I had the next week off of work while the majority of my injury healed. After a little R&R, the doctor said it was acceptable for me to return to work as long as I promised to stay off my feet for long periods of time. She got no arguments from me.

While home, I'd received a call from Border and Main Financial telling me that I'd gotten the job as their new receptionist. I politely declined.

At the present moment, I was propped up on my couch with my leg resting on a pillow to elevate my foot while my dog burrowed herself in my armpit. The house was silent except for Kikko's snoring, and I focused in on the ceiling, my eyes traveling over the repetitive popcorn pattern that covered it.

Life can be tough. *You* have to be tougher.

My thoughts lingered on those moments when I feared for my safety. The concept that time is fleeting is trite, but it's true. You never know what can happen at any given moment. Whether it be by some ill-gotten mistake, wavering health, or just plain bad luck, you have to take the moments you get and savor them for what they are.

I wasn't the best at being positive, and I thought about Cindy's words that seemed like a lifetime ago. I had to slow down and appreciate life, and find my damn inner chi or whatever she'd said. It could be hard advice to follow, but they were true words of wisdom.

I let my eyes close, focused on my breathing, and felt gratitude. I was still here. And I wasn't going anywhere. No one was getting rid of Lana Lee that easy.